George P. Pelecanos is the author of *A Firing Offense, Nick's Trip,* and *Down By the River Where the Dead Men Go,* a trilogy featuring PI Nick Stefanos, and *King Suckerman,* shortlisted for the 1998 Crime Writers' Association Golden Dagger Award. Pelecanos has been hailed as "the coolest writer in America" (*GQ*) and "a literary Tarantino with added heart" (*Mail on Sunday*) who "makes Jim Thompson look like Barbara Cartland" (*Mirabella*). These titles, along with his latest work, *The Sweet Forever,* are published by Serpent's Tail.

Pelecanos lives in Washington, where he "has carved out a territory – the seedier suburbs of Washington, D.C. – and a language of danger and sadness all his own" (*Chicago Tribune*).

GEORGE P.
PELECANOS

A FIRING
OFFENSE

Library of Congress Catalog Card Number: 96–072051

A complete catalogue record for this book can be obtained from the British Library on request

First published in 1992 by St Martin's Press, New York

First published in Great Britain in 1997 by Serpent's Tail, 4 Blackstock Mews, London N4 2BT
Website: www.serpentstail.com

This five-star edition first published in 1999

Printed in Great Britain by Mackays of Chatham

10 9 8 7 6 5 4 3

For Emily Hawk

A FIRING OFFENSE

ONE

Torn lottery tickets and hot dog wrappers—the remnants of Georgia Avenue Day—blew across the strip. At the district line a snaggle-toothed row of winos sat on the ledge of a coffee shop. A poster of the mayor, a smiling portrait in debauchery, was taped to the window behind them. The coke sweat had been dutifully airbrushed from the mayor's forehead; only a contaminated grin remained. My Dart plodded south under a low gray cover of clouds.

I steered my car into a space a couple of blocks down and killed the engine. Several strip joints had closed on this part of the avenue in the past year, ostensibly a reaction to pressure from local citizens' groups. The reality was that frequent, serious ass-beatings and one biker murder had closed down the clubs by way of revoked liquor licenses. Now the street was irreparably lifeless, a sodden butt drowning in the rot of a shot glass. A bathhouse and the Good Times Lunch had survived.

In the Good Times Lunch an industrial upright fan stood in the rear, blowing warm air towards the door. Malt liquor posters hung on the walls, showing busty, light-skinned women held by mustachioed black movie stars. Of the eight stools at the counter, three were occupied by graying men drinking beer from cans, and a fourth by a route salesman in a cheap suit.

Behind the counter were a sandwich block, grill, four baskets hung in a large deep-fryer, and a stocky little Korean named Kim, who walked with his feet wide apart and had forearms that appeared to be made out of brick. I took a seat at one of the remaining stools.

Kim acknowledged me with a slight tilt of his head. I ordered a fish sandwich, fries, and a can of beer. He brought the beer, and I tossed a quarter of it down as I watched him dump the frozen fish and potatoes into the same fryer basket. For the next five minutes I took long sips of beer and occasionally glanced out the window at the mounting northbound rush-hour traffic on Georgia Avenue.

The only sounds in the carryout were that of the fan and the barely intelligible music coming from Kim's radio, the dial of which was set on WOL. I thought of work, my reprimand, and my indifference to the subject. No one spoke to me.

I guess that was the day everything began to come apart. The day of my reprimand. The day the old man phoned me about the boy.

A rock gets pushed at the top of a hill, and it begins to roll, and then it doesn't matter who did the pushing. What matters is that nothing can stop it. What matters is the damage done. So how it started, I suppose, is insignificant. Because what sticks now is how it ended: with the sudden blast and smoke of automatic weapons, and the low manic moan of those who were about to die.

Earlier in the day, the name "Ric Brandon" had printed out across the screen of my desk phone, indicating an interoffice call. I had sipped my coffee and let the phone ring several times until the process reversed itself. His name disappeared letter by letter, from right to left. The call was then forwarded up to Marsha, our receptionist. Presently my phone rang again. It was Marsha.

"Nicky?" she said.

"Yes?"

"Ric Brandon's looking for you," she said tiredly. "He'd like to see you in his office as soon as you have a minute." Her words hung in the receiver apologetically.

"Thanks, Marsha." I picked up my coffee and headed for the john. The sound of printers, typewriters, and distaff voices swirled around me as I stepped down the hall. Passing Marsha's desk, I smiled and tapped the "Elvis Country" plaque that she had proudly set next to the switch-board.

I pushed open the door to the men's room and moved to the sink to wash up. In the mirror I saw the scuffed-up heel boxes on a pair of wing tips beneath the stall door. They belonged to Seaton, the control-ler. His trousers were around his ankles as he stood urinating into the toilet. I splashed some water on my face and looked in the mirror: I was thirty years old, and had drunk several beers backed with bourbon the night before.

I had figured out, incorrectly as it turned out, the reason for Bran-don's summons. One day earlier he and I and an executive from one of the local factory wholesalers had gotten together for lunch. The executive was one of those corn-fed, brighteyed men who seem to be hired by corporate giants like General Electric specifically for their slack-jawed lack of intellectual curiosity.

Our lunch began to deteriorate when the dapper little fellow had bragged about his company's impending contract on, as he put it, "that Star Wars thing." Despite a deadly stare and a nudge in the ribs from the equally vacuous Brandon, I plunged head on into a political discus-sion on the subject, though my enthusiasm was admittedly rooted more in my disgust for the man across the table than in my limited knowledge of the somewhat ridiculous, juvenile image of War in Space. At any rate, the executive's smile, that of a game-show host, faded, as he nervously touched the knot of his yellow tie. Our business lunch had gone immediately to hell.

Now I was about to receive what business people call, without irony, a "slap on the wrist."

On my way to Brandon's office I chewed a Lifesaver and passed by the switchboard once again. Over Marsha's desk was a huge, colorful bar graph titled "Nutty Nathan's Sales Leaders!" I noted with pleasure that Johnny McGinnes' bar was far above the pack.

Ric Brandon's office was rather spartan, with only a calendar hung on the bare walls around his metal desk. The bookshelves behind him housed software and two slim volumes, *A Passion for Excellence* and *See You at the Top*. On the computer table next to his desk was a keyboard, printer, and amber screen displaying the previous day's sales report sorted by store location, salesman, model number, sell price, unit cost, and profit margin.

Brandon smiled his toothy, equine grin as I entered. He was a big-boned Swede from Minnesota, a former high-school athlete who, at twenty-five, had already become soft and fleshy. He wore his navy suits and Johnston and Murphys proudly, and always had an unread copy of the *Wall Street Journal* on his desk. (Once, on a business trip, I had watched him stare glassy-eyed at the front page of the *Journal* for the duration of the flight.) Like many ambitious, recently graduated business majors on their first professional job in the D.C. area, he had a little boy's notion of how a businessman should look and act.

"Close the door and have a seat, Nick," he said.

I did both. Though he was already taller and broader than me, he had raised his chair higher than the others in his office to gain the psychological advantage, undoubtedly a tip he had eagerly extracted from one of his ladder-climbing guidebooks. He pulled out the bottom drawer of his desk, parked the soles of his wing tips on the edge of it, and leaned back.

"I've got an ad deadline for this afternoon," I offered, hoping to get it over with quickly.

"This won't take long," he said, segueing into a dramatic pause. I could hear the ventilator blowing and the murmur of the all-news radio station he listened to in his office. "As the sales manager of this company, I have to do certain things I really don't enjoy doing, but that are necessary in order to establish a continuity of discipline. One of those things is terminating those who consistently and deliberately fail to follow company policy."

I nodded that I understood, and he continued.

"Yesterday I told you that George Adgerson in our Marlow Heights store was getting to be a real problem—blowing customers out the door, smoking on the floor, not wearing his nametag, things like that— and I gave him several warnings. First thing this morning I walk into his store to let him go, he says to me, 'If you plan on firing me, Brandon, you should know that I've spoken to my lawyer, who advised me that if you *do* fire me, you had better be firing all the Caucasian salesmen who break your rules as well.' "

4

"What'd you do?" I asked, forcing down a smirk as I thought of Adgerson, up in Brandon's face.

"Oh, I fired him," he said casually, with an obligatory and false trace of regret. "Personnel can deal with his attorney, if he has one. The point is, Nick, he was ready for me. And you tipped him off."

I stared at my shoes for a while in what I thought would be a fairly reasonable display of humility, then looked up to see Brandon's facial muscles twitching as he awaited my admission. "Adgerson was a good man," I said slowly, "and he wrote a lot of business over the years for Nathan's. When we worked the floor together over on Connecticut Avenue, he had a huge customer following. To let go of a valuable employee just like that, because, I don't know, he blew smoke in somebody's face, or whatever—I just thought the guy deserved to know what was coming down."

"It's not your job to think of anything when it comes to salesmen and managers. I'll do the thinking in that department, understand?" I nodded, his features softened, and he continued. "If I didn't like you, Nick, I'd start looking for a new advertising director. I've discussed this with Rosen. He feels that your actions are a serious infraction. I've convinced him, however, that you're salvageable."

He hadn't, of course, spoken to Jerry Rosen, the company's general manager. He was merely trying to throw a scare into me while at the same time taking credit for being a regular Joe.

"Nick," he said, "all I want for you to do is get with the program." His thumb and forefinger met to form an "O" as he talked, a peculiarly delicate gesture for such a large man. "This is a very tough year for us. Margins have eroded to the point where we're working on ten dollar bills. Overhead is way up. And the power retailers are coming to town to put independents like us out of business. What I'm saying is, I need your experience on the team. I'm putting the ball in your court, Nick. What do you think?"

"I think you're overheating the sports metaphors," I said. Then I shrugged sheepishly and grinned like Stan Laurel.

"I'm serious," he said. "I really believe in this company. I want us all to move forward, and I want you to be a part of it."

Coming from a sales background, I had a natural distrust for managers. I didn't really dislike Brandon; I guess it was something closer to pity. I wanted to tell him to loosen up his windsor knot, sleep with some strange women, and generally act in an irresponsible manner for the next five years. But like many men my age, I was only mourning the passing of my twenties.

"I'll make the effort," I said. He showed me some teeth, put his hand in the shape of a pistol, pointed it in my direction, and squeezed off an imaginary round. I smiled back weakly and left his office.

I picked up a stack of messages from the front desk, where Marsha had fanned them out in a decorative pattern. On the way back to my own desk I passed a girl from our service department who had an unusually tight and beautifully formed ass. We looked each other over, and I got a smile. As she slid past, I smelled dime-store perfume laced with nicotine.

I looked over the messages at my desk. Two were from radio reps and a third was from a salesman from one of the local papers. My rep at the *Post*, Patti Dawson, had called. I threw all of these messages away but made a mental note to return Patti's call. The last message was from a Mr. Pence, a name I didn't recognize. I slipped that piece of paper beneath my phone.

For the remainder of the afternoon I traded retail clichés ("Katie, Bar the Door," "Passin' Them Out Like Popcorn") with Fisher, the company merch manager, and finished laying out my weekend ad for the *Post*.

A breathy intern answered the phone when I called the *Post* looking for Patti Dawson. She said that Patti was on the road and that I should try her car phone.

After four tapping sounds and two rings, Patti answered. There was some sort of light pop in the background, Luther Vandross or one of his imitators. Patti kept her car stereo cemented on WHUR.

"What's your schedule like today?" she asked, her voice sounding remote on the speakerphone but characteristically musical.

"I've just finished my Ninth Symphony," I said. "Later I'm performing brain surgery on the President."

"You got any time in your busy day to give me an ad?"

"It's done. I'm gonna cut out early. I'll leave the ad on my desk. You can just drop Saturday's proof here and I'll correct it tomorrow."

"I'll also drop our new rate card by."

"Courtesy of those philanthropists at the *Washington Post?*"

"You got it," she said, her voice beginning to break apart. I said I'd talk to her later, and she said something I couldn't make out, though somewhere in there she used the word *lover*.

I switched off the crane-necked lamp over my drawing table, considered calling Mr. Pence, but decided to take his number with me and leave before any more assignments came my way. En route to the stairwell I passed the glass-enclosed office of Nathan Plavin. He was sitting in a high-backed swivel chair with his chin resting on his chest, watching his fingers drum the bare surface of his oak desktop. Over him stood his top man, Jerry Rosen, who was pointing his finger very close to Plavin's chest. Nathan Plavin, the owner of a thirty-million-a-year retail operation, looked very much at that moment like a little boy being scolded.

I looked away, oddly embarrassed for him, and passed by Marsha's desk. Reaching the stairwell, I hollered back to her that I was gone for the day. Marsha yelled to me that Karen had called, but I continued down the steps.

A nearly lifesize cutout caricature of Nathan Plavin dangled from the ceiling at the bottom of the stairwell. I had designed it two years earlier and since then used it in the head of all our print ads and mailers. The caricature depicted Nathan with an enlarged head topped by a crooked crown, overflowing with stereos, televisions, and VCRs. There were dollar bills in his clenched fists, and a wide smile across his fat face. One of his teeth was golden.

Kim brought my food and set it down. The fish had no taste and the fries tasted faintly of fish. I quickly finished my early dinner and brooded some more over another beer. Kim took my money and nodded as I headed out the door.

My apartment was the bottom floor of a colonial in the Shepherd Park area of Northwest. I walked around to the side entrance, where my black cat hurried out from behind some bushes and tapped me on the back of my calf with her nose. I turned the key and entered.

She followed me in, jumped up on the radiator, and let out an abbreviated meow. I scratched the top of her head and tickled the scar tissue on the socket that had once housed her right eye. She shut her left eye and pushed her head into my hand as I did this.

In my bedroom I undid my tie as I pushed the power button on my receiver. The tuner was set on WHFS, and I moved the antenna around on the back of the set to better the reception. Weasel was ending his show, predictably, with some NRBQ from the *Yankee Stadium* LP. I switched over to phono and laid Martha and the Muffin's "This Is the Ice Age" on the platter.

I walked through my tiny living room to the kitchen. Behind me I heard the four paws of my cat hit the hardwood floor simultaneously with a mild thud. She followed me into the kitchen, jumped up on the chair that held her dish, and sat down. I found a foil-covered can of salmon in the refrigerator, mixed a bit of it into some dry food, and put it in her dish. She went at it after the obligatory bored look and a slow blink of her left eye.

The phone rang. I walked back into the living room and picked up the receiver.

"Hello."

"Is Nick Stefanos in?"

"Speaking."

"My name is James Pence," an old voice said on the other end of the line. I fished his message from my shirt pocket. "I'm sorry to bother you at home."

"I received your message at work," I said. "Forgive me for not returning your call—I get a load of people calling me all day, trying to sell me advertising space or services. If I called them all back, I'd never get anything done."

"I'm not selling anything," he said, though there was a hurried, desperate edge to his voice.

"What can I do for you then?"

8

"I'm Jimmy Broda's grandfather."

After some initial confusion I brought Broda up in my mind. He was a kid, late teens, who had worked briefly in the warehouse of Nutty Nathan's. We had struck up a mild sort of friendship after discovering that we had similar interests in music, though his tastes ran towards speed metal and mine to the more melodic. I had chalked that up to the difference in our ages. Broda had apparently quit a couple of weeks earlier. I had not heard from him, assuming he had joined the ranks of other young, low-level employees who tended to drift from one meaningless job to the next.

"How is Jimmy?" I asked.

"Your personnel girl called a couple of weeks ago and said he had not reported to work for two days straight. Asked me if I knew where he was. Of course I didn't know. It wasn't unusual for him not to come home for stretches at a time—the crowd he ran around with and all that."

I had no idea what he was talking about or what he wanted. I had the urge to excuse myself and hang up the phone right then.

"Two days later," he continued, "personnel calls again. She says to inform Jimmy, when I see him, that he's been terminated. Job abandonment, I think she called it."

"Listen, Mr. Pence. I'm sorry Jimmy lost his job—"

"He liked you, Mr. Stefanos. He mentioned you at home more than once."

"I liked him too. But Jimmy probably had a bigger idea of what I am than what's reality. Those guys in the warehouse, they think anybody who works upstairs and wears a tie has a piece of the action. I'm just a guy who lays out ads and buys time on the airwaves. I don't even talk to the people who make hiring and firing decisions. What I'm saying is, I don't have the influence to get Jimmy his job back."

"I don't need you to get his job back, Mr. Stefanos," he said. "I need you to help me find him."

A long silence followed. He made a swallowing sound, then cleared his throat.

"Why are you calling *me?*" I asked.

"I bought a TV years ago from John McGinnes in your store on

Connecticut Avenue. This year I bought a toaster oven from him. He's my man there," he said with that peculiarly elderly notion of salesman ownership. "I talked with him yesterday morning. Said he didn't know anything but you might. Said you're pretty good at finding people when you put your mind to it." I made a mental note to slam McGinnes for that.

"Mr. Pence, if you're worried about your grandson you should call the police," I said with what I hoped was an air of finality.

"Please. Please come see me, only for a few minutes. I have something to give you, anyway. A cassette tape you made for Jimmy." I remembered it, the usual soft punk and hard pop. Though it was no big deal, the Broda kid had seemed mildly touched when I gave it to him.

"I have somewhere to go tonight," I said, "But maybe I could stop by for a minute. I mean, if it's on my way. Where do you live?"

"I'm on Connecticut, the first apartment building northeast of Albemarle. Apartment ten-ten. Do you know it?"

"Yes." It was right up from the store.

"I'll meet you in the lobby then," he said excitedly.

"Right. Twenty minutes."

TWO

My gym bag was in the trunk as I headed down Thirteenth Street. Bob "Here" was the DJ on HFS and spinning some post-patchuli oil nonsense. I pushed a Long Ryders tape into the deck. The first song, "Sweet Mental Revenge," had a guitar break reminiscent of the Eagles, the difference being that the Ryders had testicles. I turned up the volume.

I made a right on Military Road, passed under Sixteenth, and neared the Oregon Avenue intersection where I hung a left into a severely sloped, winding entrance to Rock Creek Park. As kids we had as a rule driven this stretch of the park with our headlights off, navigating by the moonlight that cut a path through the treeline above. God or the dumb luck of youth had always brought us safely through; tonight, even with my hi-beams on, the darkness seemed to envelop me.

At the bottom of the hill I crossed a small bridge and turned left onto Beach Drive. Soon after that I made a right on Brandywine and cut over to Albemarle, cruising by million dollar Tudor houses with dark German and British automobiles parked, like hearses, in their driveways.

At Connecticut and Albemarle I looked across the street to the left. Though there was no foot traffic at this hour, Nutty Nathan's was open. I decided against dropping in on McGinnes. By this time of day the effects of malt liquor and marijuana would have rendered him incoherent.

I parked on Connecticut, an after–rush-hour privilege, and walked across a brownish lawn to a tall, tan-brick building. As a salesman at Nathan's on the Avenue, I had often delivered and installed air conditioners here for the elderly residents of these rent-controlled apartments.

When I entered the first set of glass doors, a guy in the lobby who looked to be on the green side of seventy caught my eye. He motioned to a bored-looking young woman behind the switchboard and a buzzer sounded. I pulled on the second set of doors and entered the lobby.

The old man strode towards me quickly and with deliberate posture, though he looked as if it pained him some to do so. His handshake was firm.

"I'm Nick Stefanos."

"I knew when I saw you," he said in a self-congratulatory manner, then looked me over. Either Pence liked what he saw or felt he had little choice; he pointed a slim hand towards the elevators.

We passed an obese young security guard with a seventies Afro who was talking to the woman at the switchboard and ignoring us and all the old people sitting around the bland lobby. The lobby had the still, medicinal smell of a nursing home.

Pence took me to a metal door that led to the elevators and attempted to pull it open. A look of mild panic appeared on his face as the weight of the door knocked him off balance. The security guard said something behind us about the old man forgetting to take his Geritol.

We heard the laughter of the guard and the woman at the switchboard as we entered an elevator.

The old man was silent as we rode to the tenth floor, though his lips were moving and there was a slight scowl across his face. He was wearing workpants pulled high above his waist, a white cotton T-shirt, and oxford Hush Puppies that he wore laceless like loafers. The thick leather belt drawn tightly around his abdomen looked water-damaged and was permanently bent in several spots. Time had eaten him like a patient scavenger.

The elevator bounced to a stop, causing Pence to grab the handrail with reluctance. The doors opened, he bolted out and I followed. He stopped at 1010 and with no trouble at all this time negotiated the lock and door.

We entered as he flipped on a master light. The apartment, with its florid, cushiony sofa and armchairs and a curio cabinet filled with delicate porcelain figures, had obviously been decorated by a woman. But a glass caked with milk on the table and the general disarray of the place told me that his wife or companion was gone.

"Have a seat," he said. I chose one, noticing as I sat that its cushion contained a rogue spring. I remained seated, as none of the other chairs showed better promise. Though it was rather cool, I had the desire to crack a window. His apartment had the smell of outdated dairy products.

"Goddamn security guard," he muttered, unable to forget the fat rent-a-cop in the lobby. He quit pacing and lit on a seat next to an end table, on which sat a crystal lamp, a TV directory, an ashtray, and a pack of smokes. Pence shook one from the deck directly to his mouth, looked up at me, and said, "You mind?"

"Not at all." He lit it with a Zippo and let out a long stream of smoke that continued to pour out erratically as he began to talk.

"You always have to ask now, before you smoke. It seems like every time I light up, in the Hot Shoppes cafeteria, or wherever, some young guy in a suit tells me the smoke's bothering him. I've got to laugh at your generation sometimes. You guys spend all your time in health clubs in front of mirrors, you're repelled by smokers, you drink light this and light that—and with all your health and muscles you're basically a bunch of powderpuffs. Forty years ago I could have kicked your collective asses—with a cigarette hanging out the side of my mouth."

I looked at my watch and said, "I don't mean to be rude."

"Of course. I apologize. I bring you up here and then I ramble like some bitter old man."

"Don't worry about it. What's on your mind?"

Pence's veined hands clutched the arms of his chair. Some ash from his cigarette fell to his lap. He glanced down to make sure it wasn't live, then looked back at me, making no effort to brush the ash away.

"I don't know how much you really know about Jimmy," he said. "His parents were killed when he was eleven, in a wreck on the Beltway, near what they used to call the Cabin John Bridge. He was their only child, and my only grandson." He stopped to stub out the butt of his smoke.

"Is your wife still alive, Mr. Pence?"

He shook his head. "Janey died a year after we took Jimmy in. I guess you can imagine how hard it was. A man gets set to retire with his woman, all of a sudden he loses her and has to raise a son." I had a quick, painful image of my own grandfather, a fisherman's cap resting on his huge pinkish ears.

"How did it go for the two of you?"

"Fairly well, from my side of things. Jimmy was an easy boy to raise, easier than my own daughter."

"Has he ever gone away before without telling you?"

"He's nineteen years old," he said by way of an affirmative.

"So what makes you think this is any different?"

"I'm not naïve, Mr. Stefanos. The kid goes out with his friends, has a few beers, they wind up down at the shore, or Atlantic City maybe, if one of 'em has a few bucks in his pockets. But he always called me the next day, let me know where he was."

I shifted in my seat. "I'm not a detective, Mr. Pence. What Johnny McGinnes was talking about, we did some process serving together a couple of summers ago, for extra cash. It was for kicks mainly, we made a game of it. But I'm not licensed for anything like this. And I told you before that I thought this was a cop job. Unless there's something you're not telling, some reason you can't or won't go to the police."

He lowered his eyes and lit another smoke. The sound of the Zippo slamming shut echoed in the room. He was squinting through the smoke when he looked back up at me.

"Jimmy has been hanging out with some tough customers," he said. "The last couple of months, the guys who came to pick him up, they weren't just kids out to get a little drunk and have a good time. They were different somehow."

"How so?"

"I don't know exactly. They wore a lot of leather. None of them ever smiled. And the music he started listening to in his room since he met those guys—it was, you know, more violent than what he used to listen to."

"Go on." So far, nothing he had described was all that disturbing, and the music probably wasn't much different from the music I used to listen to in the clubs downtown almost ten years earlier.

"He's been staying out all night, listening to music in bars supposedly. The way he looks when he walks in, I don't know. I've done some drinking in my day. He just doesn't look like he's been on a bender. So I can only guess, maybe the boy is mixed up with drugs."

"Do you know the names of any of his friends?"

"No, I'm sorry. They looked alike to me. All of these guys had crewcuts, shaved even closer than the kids wore them in the fifties."

If they were skinheads, they either hung out at the Snake Pit on F Street or at the Corps, which was near National Place. I figured the old man had the kid pegged on his drug use, though there was no way to tell how far he was gone.

"I don't mean to make light of Jimmy's situation, Mr. Pence. But I frequented the same clubs and listened to the same kind of music myself. I still do, occasionally. As for drugs, I've used plenty and I came out of it more or less intact." His eyes seemed to widen, but only for a moment. He was obviously more interested in finding his grandson than in my lapses of morality.

"You *are* making light of this situation. You most certainly are. Because you don't want to take any responsibility here. I *know* this boy. Even if he were on drugs, he would have called. He's in some sort of trouble. If you don't want to get involved, then fine. But don't tell me there's nothing wrong."

"I admit there could be some problem," I said. "And I see your angle for going private. If he's just underground because of drugs, a private cop could get him home and to some help without a possession or intent to distribute rap on his record. But I'm not that person. I paste down pictures of television sets for a living."

"You *are* the person." He was on his feet now and close to me. I could smell cigarettes on him and, for the first time, a trace of whiskey. "Why do you think Jimmy talked to you so much at work?"

"What do you mean?"

"Your background and Jimmy's background—they were very similar. Jimmy told me that you were born overseas. Your parents sent you to the States to live with your grandfather when you were very young, until they could afford to join you. For some reason or another they never made it, and you were raised by your grandfather. Is this correct?"

"Roughly," I said.

"Jimmy was at that age—he needed someone to relate to. I think he found that a little bit in you."

"My grandfather died last April," I said, though I was no longer talking to Pence. The moment his life ended I was doing lines off the bar in an after-hours club on upper Wisconsin Avenue.

I rose from the chair and walked to the window. The traffic had thinned out on Connecticut, the northbound headlights approaching at a relaxed pace.

"I don't know if I'm up for it," I said. He was silent behind me and I turned to face him. "I'll ask around downtown. Maybe somebody knows where he is. But that's all, understand?"

"Thank you," he said, moving towards me and gripping my hand. "I'll make it worth your while."

I backed away. "We don't need to discuss that now. I have some-where to go. I'll phone you tomorrow."

I walked out quickly. He was shouting his phone number as I closed the door behind me.

* * *

I let the cat in as I stepped into my apartment. I put some dry food in her dish and drank some ice water from a bottle in the refrigerator. Then I took two cold cans of beer with me into the shower.

After leaving Pence, I had driven to a junior-high gym in Northwest to meet Rodney White, a friend of mine who had the curious distinction of being both a physician and a black belt. Though I knew next to nothing about tae kwon do, I had done a fair amount of Boys Club boxing, and enjoyed hooking up with White every couple of weeks to spar, provided he showed me some mercy.

We warmed up with some stretching and light movement. Gradually we began making contact and our sparring intensified. After punishing me for a while with hand and foot combinations, he motioned me to stop. We tapped gloves and removed our mouthguards.

"What were you just doing?" he asked. "You let me back you all the way across this gym. You accepted all of my forward energy."

"I was letting you kick yourself out. Anyway, I tagged you pretty good at the end."

He shook his head. "You had already lost. You start backing up, you're defeated, believe me."

"I thought I'd use a little strategy."

"Don't get too wrapped up in strategy. Technicians lose in the street. The winner in a fight is usually determined before the first punch is thrown."

"Too mystical for me" I said, adding, "I'll stick to boxing."

"Stick to whatever you want, Homeboy. But step on over here and let me show you a little something."

In the shower I drank the first beer while washing. A bruise had formed on my bicep from a Rodney White side kick, and there was a scratch on my cheek from the nylon tie of his footgear.

After rinsing, I popped the second beer and leaned against the tile wall, shutting the cold spigot off completely. I drank deeply of the icy beer and closed my eyes, as the burning hot water rolled down my back.

THREE

The next morning I called the office at nine A.M. from a payphone located in the side parking lot of the Connecticut Avenue store. Ric Brandon picked up his extension.

"Hello, Ric?"

"Yes."

"Nick Stefanos here."

"Where are you?" In his typically tight-assed manner he was asking why I was late for work.

"I'm on my way to Connecticut Avenue," I lied, not wanting to get the boys in trouble. None of them had arrived yet to open the store.

"What for?"

"Listen, Ric. All of last night I thought about our discussion yesterday in your office. I think one of the reasons I don't have that team spirit is that I've lost touch with what's going on out in the stores, out on the firing line." I stopped speaking so as not to make myself sick.

"I understand." Since he had never been on the "firing line," that imaginary, danger-filled zone that lowly salesmen are so keen on referring to, he could not have understood. But I had counted on that.

"What I figure is, I'll get back on the floor for a few weeks, see what's going on again, talk to some customers and find out what they do and don't respond to in our ads."

"What about your regular duties?"

"What I can't do here, I'll finish up at night. I have a key to the office, and my *Post* contacts can do pickups here at the store. As for any important meetings or appointments, you call me here, I can be back in the office in fifteen minutes."

"I can see the merit in this," he said, adding, "if you apply yourself. Understand that I'd like you to report to Gary Fisher every day as to the merchandising and advertising plans."

"Sure, Ric. Transfer me over to Fisher then, will you?"

The phone rang several times, then Fisher picked up. In contrast to the dead calm of Brandon's office, I could hear people laughing, typewriters clacking, and unanswered phones ringing in the background. I imagined a cigarette lodged above Fisher's ear.

"Fish, it's Nick."

"Where the fuck are you?"

"The Avenue. I'm going to be working out of here for a while. I had to get away from the office, man. You know what I mean?"

"Not really. You worked your way up from stockboy to sales to management, now you want to go backwards. Besides, I need you here."

"I'll still do my job, only I'll do it from the store."

"You see Electro-World's ad today?" he asked, changing the subject as if to ignore it.

"I haven't seen the paper yet."

"They ran a TP400 for two ninety-nine, the lousy giveaway artists. Tell the fellas not to match that price, hear? If we have to take a bath, we can wait till Black Friday."

"You're going to wait till the Friday after Thanksgiving to run a piece that everyone's in the paper with now?"

"I'm not worried," he said. "There's gonna be a shortage of low-end goods this Christmas. The Japs and the Koreans are holding back, trying to drive up the costs to the distributors. My guess is, the longer we hold back on the bait, we'll be the only ones in town with the plunder come D-Day. We bring 'em through the door, pass a few out, lose our asses—we'll make it up on add-ons and service policies."

Fisher was a typical merch manager, a sloppy, chain-smoking, audiophilic pot-smoking salesman who had grudgingly been promoted to management. He was built low to the ground, had an unfashionably long Prince Valiant haircut, and motored around the office pitched forward, his fists clenched like some driven cartoon villain. He would never advance beyond his current position—the image wasn't there, and neither was the will—but he was unequaled at Nathan's in his knowledge of retail.

"What else?"

"That bitch Fein called again from Montgomery County Consumer Affairs," he said. "Said we've got to stop using the word *sale* in the head of our ads if we're not lowering our everyday prices."

"So I'll call this next ad a *blowout*."

"Perfect."

"Do me one favor, Fish. Keep Brandon away from me as much as you can, will you?"

"Yeah, sure. But, Nick, why does the guy spell his name R-i-c?"

"I guess R-o-c-k was already taken."

"Talk to you later." He hung up.

I walked around the building to the front of the store and looked in the plate-glass display window. Louie Bates, the store manager, had arrived. He ambled along the left wall, switching on television sets.

I pushed on the door and entered. The layout of the floor had changed very little. Up front was a glass case that surrounded a desk and register and contained small electronics and accessories. This was also the cashiers' station and the area where the salesman closed, TO'd to the manager, and wrote deals.

The left half of the store contained televisions of all varieties, portable to widescreen. An aisle in the middle of the store was wide enough to handtruck merchandise from the stockroom to the front door. The right half of the store contained low-end rack stereos, boom boxes, clock radios, auto sound, microwave ovens, small appliances, and other low-commission goods. The entire rear of the showroom housed high-end audio, a "room" that was simply a thinly carpeted part of the store where the lights had been dimmed. A banner hung across its entrance, grandly announcing this area as "The Sound Explosion."

Gold and red, Nutty Nathan's official colors, dominated in the form of signage, tags, and "accent striping." Salesmen were at one time required to wear gold sportcoats with a red coat-of-arms sewn across the breast pocket, consisting of a triumvirate depicting a television, stereo, and microwave oven. Salesforce rebellion in the form of filthy jackets forced management to end this dress code. The day this requirement was lifted McGinnes and I had poured lighter fluid on ours and burned them ceremoniously in the parking lot.

The outright tackiness and near-vulgar ambience of Nathan Plavin's stores were intentional. Plavin had picked the colors, as well as the jackets. On slow Saturdays he'd call managers and instruct them to scatter empty cartons in the aisles, to make it appear as if the salesmen were too busy writing up bargains to bother with keeping the place clean. But that had been in the past, when Nathan was more on top of the day-to-day operations of his company.

Louie was surprised to see me in his store. He was a short, barrel-chested guy in his fifties with a wide, flat nose that appeared to have been smashed in by a shovel. As he walked towards me, I noticed that his gut had swelled, his neck had all but disappeared, and there was much more gray salted into his hair. He looked somewhat like a cinder-block with legs.

"You lost, Youngblood?" he asked.

"Could be," I said, shaking his hand. "I'll be working here for a couple of weeks. Management wants me to get back in touch with the business."

"You wouldn't be spying on your old boss, would you, buddy?"

I didn't answer that but said, "I'll stay out of your way, Louie."

"Whatever." He threw up his arms in a gesture of surrender. "Listen, your boys are late as usual, and I got to get this place open. I'll talk to you later, hear?"

Louie returned to the television section. As the manager of the highest volume store, he knew what his priorities were: to put out fires and to protect his salesmen from the main office. In turn, he was covered by his employees during his daily afternoon visits to his girl-friend across the street in the Van Ness apartments, and on those mornings when his hangovers kept him paralyzed with his head on the desk in the "employee lounge" at the rear of the store.

A small bell sounded as the front door opened, and I turned to see Andre Malone flowing towards me. He was tall, reedy, and elegant in his no-vent sportcoat, silk shirt and tie, reverse pleated trousers, and Italian loafers. Though he'd come out of one of the most hopelessly dangerous sections of the city, there was something of the aristocrat in his bearing and in the way he held his head. He saw me and widened his eyes in mock amazement.

"What's goin' on, Country?" he said. I touched the sharp crease on his trousers and pulled my hand away quickly as if I had been cut.

"You may be the prettiest person I've ever known."

He smiled and revealed a perfect row of teeth below his Wyatt Earp mustache. "I see you're doin' all right yourself. Finally wearin' some cotton. Used to be I was afraid to light a match around your polyester ass."

"I'm on the fast track, Andre. I *had* to upgrade."

"What you doin' here, man?" His forehead wrinkled as he found a Newport in his breast pocket and lit it in one fluid movement.

"I'll be working here for a while," I said vaguely. "Whatever deals I write, I'll throw to you or Johnny. I might need you to protect me every so often from the office, in case I'm not here."

"Uh-huh," he said suspiciously, then jerked his head towards the door as the small bell rang. "Here comes your boy now."

Johnny McGinnes blew through the front door and goose-stepped towards the back. There was neither surprise nor delight on his face when he saw me. In acknowledgment he pulled two sixteen-ounce cans of Colt 45 from each of his stretched-out pockets and wiggled his eyebrows in my direction, then continued by.

A young woman entered just behind him and hurried around the glass case, stowing her books and purse somewhere below the counter. I caught her eye and she straightened her posture.

Malone was walking alongside Louie now, pleading with him to call an irate customer and iron things out. Louie would eventually do it, but at the moment was torturing Malone with silence. I made my way across the worn gold-and-red carpet squares of the Sound Explosion and entered the back room.

I walked through a short hallway that contained Louie's desk. The hallway led to the "radio room," the toilet, and the entrance to the stockroom in the basement. I stepped into the radio room. McGinnes was finishing a swallow of malt liquor and hiding the can behind some stock.

He was not especially tall, though his perfect posture gave the illusion of presence. His clothing was invariably a polyester blend and always clean. He had lost more of his straight black hair since I had last seen him and had begun combing it forward, out and across his forehead in an almost Hitleresque fashion. His tiny nose was set on his flat Mick face like a blemish.

I looked at the top of the Colt can showing from behind a clock radio box. "It's a little early, isn't it, Johnny?"

"Early as hell. But if they get too warm, I can't drink 'em." He frowned. "Fuck are you, my mother?"

"Let's go downstairs, man. I need to talk to you."

I followed him down the noisy wooden steps to the stockroom. The musty odor of damp cardboard met me as I descended the stairs. Naked bulbs dimly lit erratic rows of cartons. We walked to the far corner of the basement. McGinnes pulled a film canister and a small brass pipe out of his pocket and shook some pot out of the vial.

As a stockboy, I'd spent a good portion of my first two years at Nathan's in this room getting high with McGinnes. I was skinny but cockstrong then, usually wearing some kind of rock-and-roll T-shirt, tight Levi's cuffed cigarette style, Sears workboots on my feet. My stance was straight up, cigarette between the first two fingers with the occasional thumb flick on the filter and a shake of my shoulder-length hair for punctuation. McGinnes had slightly longer hair in those days, and mutton-chop sideburns pointing in towards a Fu Manchu that he wore proudly. As we were always stoned, I considered his every word in that basement to be prophetic, and he played the role of sales sage to the hilt.

Somewhere along the line I became a salesman, worked on commission as I put myself through college, cut my hair, was promoted into management, got married and divorced, and generally lost the notion that life was a series of adventures and opportunities waiting to happen. One day a stockboy in one of the stores called me "sir," and I was alarmed by that panicky, universal moment when we realize that aging is real and for all of us, not just for watery-eyed relatives and quiet old men on the bus.

"So," he said, folding his arms and cocking his hip, "you're back."

"I'm on a sabbatical."

"You're no professor. And you sure as hell ain't no priest, Jim." McGinnes' speech patterns were peppered with his idea of black slang, which he picked up not from "the street" but from the pimp sidekick characters on seventies cop shows. Though I had lived in D.C. all my life, I had never once heard a black person use the expression "jive turkey." Yet McGinnes used it all the time.

"You remember a guy named Pence?" I asked.

McGinnes smiled nervously. "Yeah, I know the old cocker. Lives across the Avenue, in those apartments. I sold him a TV set a long time ago, something else this year."

"Toaster oven."

"That's right. He came over the other day, wanted to bullshit about his grandson or something."

"You gave him my name?"

"Yeah, I figured it couldn't hurt. You worked with the kid, maybe you knew something."

"It's not like you to help somebody out for nothing."

"He's a good customer, that's all." McGinnes shrugged, pulled a plastic tube of eyedrops from his pocket, and tilted his head back for a double shot. When he brought his head back down, a tear of eyewash was rolling down his cheek. "So what are you gonna do, look for the kid?"

I nodded. "I only told him I'd ask around a little. The old man's afraid the kid's in with the wrong crowd. Drugs, who knows what else. If the cops find him first, he may end up busted. A mistake like that can blow your life before you get out of the gate. Maybe I find him, talk him back home, whatever."

"So what do *you* get out of this?"

"I knew the kid and the old man's desperate. I can't just blow it off."

McGinnes glanced over his shoulder at the stairs, tapped another hit into his pipe, fired it up, and tapped out the ashes into his palm. This one he blew towards my face. "Well, it will be a helluva lot easier to work on that out of here than in the office. You know Louie won't bother you. Besides, you'll be back on the sales floor, which is where you belong."

"I might have to remind you how it's done."

"You'd just be reminding me of what I taught you in the first place, son."

23

"Remember that day I sold a sandbox to an Arab?"

McGinnes said, "That ain't shit. What about the time I sold a blind man tickets to a silent movie?"

Louie called down that there were customers on the floor. We approached the stairs, and McGinnes elbowed me in the chest and moved ahead, gunning up two steps at a time. He was giggling like a schoolgirl as he hit the landing.

FOUR

McGinnes chewed on a mint and checked out the floor as we walked down the showroom's center aisle. Malone stood in the Sound Explosion talking to a light-skinned woman in a leather jacket. He had a Frankie Beverly ballad playing through the stereo, and was close up in her face as he made a slow and awkward attempt at moving to the music.

A guy in a hundred dollar suit with disheveled graying hair stood with his hands in his pockets, blinking absently at the confusingly long line of TV screens lit against the wall. He unfolded my *Post* ad from his jacket, stared at it, then returned his gaze to the wall.

"Malone's back there talking himself out of another deal," McGinnes said. "I'll take that *yom* over there by the TVs."

McGinnes walked over to the customer, staying loose but erect. "How are you today?" he said, extending his hand. The customer shook it limply, without looking McGinnes in the eye.

"Fine. Thank you."

"Something special for you today?"

"Yes." The customer jabbed a finger at a spot on my ad. "I'm interested in the nineteen-inch Zenith for one ninety-nine. Do you have it to look at?"

"Oh yes, it's right over here," McGinnes said, pointing at the far left section of the wall and gesturing for the man to step ahead of him.

McGinnes turned his head back to me, crossed his eyes and hung his tongue out of the side of his mouth. Following the customer, he dragged one leg like a cripple, recovering his posture just as the customer turned to face him.

"What can you tell me about this set?"

"It's a fine set," McGinnes said, "and a good value." The picture on the set was lousy. McGinnes had attached the faulty antenna lead, the one he switched each week to the advertised piece, onto the Zenith.

By comparison the nineteen-inch Hitachi, which sat next to the Zenith, had a beautiful picture. The customer became distracted by this, his head moving back and forth between the two sets.

"Why does that set have a better picture than the Zenith?"

"Oh, they have a high-contrast tube in the Hitachi," McGinnes said offhandedly.

"What is that?"

"Here, I'll show you." In his shirt pocket McGinnes had clipped two pens, a jeweler's screwdriver, and a small folding magnifying glass, which he pulled out. He placed it over the tube of the Zenith. The color dots were dull against a pale gray background. McGinnes looked back at the customer for effect, then switched the glass to the tube of the Hitachi. The dots were brilliantly illuminated against a black field.

"Interesting," the customer said. "How much is the Hitachi?"

"Two forty-nine."

The customer frowned, then pushed his glasses up over the bridge of his nose. "That's more than I wanted to spend."

"Well, if you think about it, you'd actually be *saving* money by buying this set."

"How's that?"

"Electronic tuner. The Hitachi's got an electronic tuner, no moving parts in the tuner whatsoever. The Zenith, which is a fine set, don't get me wrong, has an old-style click tuner, the first part to go bad on any TV set." McGinnes spun the dial on the Zenith harshly. "You do that every day, it's going to wear out. And when it wears out, it's going to cost you more than the extra fifty bucks you're going to spend initially on the Hitachi. Not to mention, of course, the Hitachi's got a much better picture, which you can see for yourself. With a TV set, when you get it home you're not going to remember what you paid for it. You're only going to know whether you like the picture or not."

"Well. . . ."

"Plus the fact that we're an authorized Hitachi service center for this area. In-home service. And for a small charge, which most customers recognize the value in, you can have a maintenance agreement with Nutty Nathan's to extend that in-home service."

"I don't think I'd be interested in that. Besides, if the set's as good as you say it is, I won't be needing any service." The customer smiled smugly.

"Oh, it's a gamble, I know," McGinnes said quickly. "And chances are pretty good you'll never need the service. But you know what they're charging now just to walk through your front door? Fifty bucks! Just to step in your house, before they even touch the set! I can give you the names of ten people who've called to thank me personally for suggesting a maintenance agreement. Anyway, I'm not trying to belabor the point. You *do* want the Hitachi, though, don't you?" McGinnes was nodding his head rapidly, a trick he used to make the customer do the same.

"Yes, I'm pretty sure I do." Though McGinnes had closed, the customer's fists were balled defensively in his pockets.

"Where are you from?" McGinnes asked, and smiled.

"From up around Lancaster, P-A."

"No kidding. I'm from the Allentown area." The customer seemed to relax as he unhunched his shoulders. McGinnes, an army brat, was from many places, but Pennsylvania wasn't one of them. "This city's fine, but I tell you, there's a lot to be said for my hometown. I miss the slower life, don't you?"

"Yes, I do."

"Let's just step up to the counter and get you written up." They walked to the front of the store, McGinnes' hand gently on the customer's arm.

The young woman who had walked in earlier carrying her books tapped me on the shoulder and I turned. She was half a foot shorter than me and had a brown speck in one of her very green eyes.

"Hi," she said cheerfully and smiled. Her front tooth was chipped, just a little. She had on short, black, buckled boots, black patterned stockings, and a jean skirt. Her white oxford was open four buttons down, revealing the beginnings of strong, smallish breasts.

"Hi," I said.

"You working here now?"

"Yeah. For a little while, anyway. My name's Nick."

"I'm Lee. I work the register and sell add-ons up front. Can you take a sales call?"

I looked around. Malone was still in the Sound Explosion and appeared to be chewing his customer's ear off, literally. McGinnes was up front, writing the deal.

"Where's Louie?" I asked.

"Out making a deposit."

"I thought he made his 'deposit' in the afternoon."

Lee chuckled. "This one's monetary, not seminal."

"What line?"

"Pick it up on two," she said, jerking her thumb behind her towards the small appliance wall. "Over there."

I found the phone and punched in the extension. "How can I help you?"

"To whom am I speaking?" said an effeminate voice, lowered purposely to affect masculinity.

"Nick Stefanos."

"And your title?"

"I'm in management," I said emptily.

"Well, then, maybe you can help me. I have a complaint."

"What can I do for you?"

"My name is Evan Walters. Last summer your company ran a promotion where you gave away an ice bucket with any major purchase. I came in and purchased a VCR, which I'm very happy with, incidentally. The clerk explained at the time that they were out of ice buckets. Frankly, I was warned by friends beforehand that Nutty Nathan's never lived up to their advertised promises, but I was willing to give you people a try."

"Who was your salesman, Mr. Walters?"

"A Mr. McGinnes. He promised me he'd get me my ice bucket. At first when I called he repeatedly said the ice bucket was on its way. Then he stopped returning my calls altogether. I know it's a small matter, but I want what was promised me. And I resent the rather cavalier attitude of your salesman. I don't want to take this any further. I *am* a lawyer," he growled.

Of course. Announcing one's profession unsolicited was one of the more irritating affectations of eighties Washington.

"I apologize for the delay," I said. "Mr. McGinnes may have run into some red tape in getting your ice bucket. I happen to know that they *are* in now. I'll call the warehouse manager and have him put one on the transfer truck. You can pick it up tonight."

"Thank you," he said curtly, and hung up.

I dialed the main office and punched in the extension of Joe Dane, the warehouse manager. I asked him to find an ice bucket and throw it on the truck that day to the Avenue.

I walked over to the cashier's station where Lee was wiping off the shelves with glass cleaner. McGinnes was handing the customer his receipts.

"Here is a copy of your paid invoice," he said, "and this is a copy of your extended maintenance agreement. I've stapled my card to your receipt in case you need anything. You're really going to love your set. It's got the highest IS rating of any set we sell."

"What *is* the IS rating on this set?" I interrupted. IS stood for "internal spiff," a Nutty Nathan's incentive to step off the advertised product onto profit pieces.

"This one's rated at twenty," McGinnes said coolly, then turned back to the customer. "If you'd drive around to the back door, I'll load you up."

Lee touched my arm lightly to move me out of the way. I caught a whiff of her as she slipped by. Malone walked his customer to the front door, his arm around her waist, his hand just brushing her jeans above her crotch. They talked softly for a few minutes, then he held the door open for her, giving her his model's grin.

McGinnes, knocking the dirt off his shirtsleeves, moved quickly up the aisle towards the cashier's station. Malone arrived at the same time. McGinnes folded his arms and stood straight.

"Yeah," he said. "Twenty dollar spiff. Another ten bucks commission at four percent. And a fifteen dollar pop for the service policy. Forty-five bucks for fifteen minutes' work." He paused to rock back on his heels. "I love this business."

"I'd love it too," Malone said, "if I could get an up."

"You had an up," McGinnes said.

"That wasn't no up," Malone said. "That was just a freak."

McGinnes said, "If you hadn't been dickdancing around with her in the back, you could have had my customer up front."

"That's all right. I got a date with that redbone tonight. And I'm *still* gonna smoke your ass this month, Mick."

"Listen, you guys," I said, "this is fascinating. But I've got to run across the street for about an hour. Tell Louie when you see him, hear?"

The old man's apartment was in the same disarray as the night before. Sunlight came through the window in a block, spotting the layer of dust that had settled on the cherrywood furniture.

Pence was wearing what appeared to be his only outfit. His hair was slicked down, and he had begun a part on the left side of his head but apparently had given up on the idea halfway through. He smelled of whiskey and Old Spice.

"You want some coffee?" he asked. "I reheated it when you buzzed me from downstairs."

"Black, thanks." He marched into the kitchen with short, quick steps.

I avoided my old chair and found another seat. Near the dining room table, on a two-tiered stand, was the color set McGinnes had sold the old man, a middle-of-the-line profit model. Below it was a videocassette recorder that I didn't recognize. I got up and walked over to the unit to examine it more closely. The nameplate read "Kotekna," which I gathered to be a Korean brand. Stamped across a metal plate on the back were the model and serial numbers, the model number being KV100. Following industry logic, "KV" stood for "Kotekna Video" and the "100" series indicated that this particular unit resided in the lower end of the line. The recorder was not hooked up to the television.

"Professional curiosity?" Pence asked, returning with two mugs of coffee and setting one down on the small table next to my chair. I got off my knees, crossed the room, and took a seat. Pence sat in his chair, lit a smoke and leaned forward.

"A bad habit of mine, from being in the business too long. My hosts always catch me inspecting their equipment."

"My grandson bought that recorder for me," he offered. "Some kind of employee purchase deal he worked out with your company."

"That's a new brand for us, then. I didn't even know we sold Kotekna."

"You sell it, son. It came from your warehouse. Still have the box." He dragged on his cigarette.

"When's the last time you saw Jimmy, Mr. Pence?"

The old man waved some smoke away from his face to get a better look at me. I sipped from the mug of coffee. "It was the last Monday in September. He left for work at the usual time, near eight."

"And you haven't heard from him since?"

"No. Your personnel lady called two days later, on a Wednesday."

"And you made no effort to contact anyone about this until you reached me, two weeks later?"

"That's right."

"You must have been worried."

"You're damn right I was worried," he said, agitated. He butted his cigarette. "Let's go on."

"When he said goodbye to you that morning, was there anything unusual about the way he acted, something that may have made you suspicious in any way?"

"I've thought about that a lot since he's been gone, as you can imagine. Jimmy wasn't one to show his affection. But on that last morning he kissed me good-bye and squeezed my hand."

"Like he knew he wouldn't be seeing you for a while?"

"That maybe. Or he was in trouble and asking for help."

"Was he carrying anything with him that morning? A suitcase?"

Pence laughed sharply. "I'm old, Mr. Stefanos, not senile. He only had a small knapsack, and he carried that with him every day. Kept a radio in it with earphones."

"Is his suitcase gone?"

"No."

"Mind if I have a look in his room?"

"Of course not."

I followed him down a short hallway. We passed Pence's room on the way. The shades were drawn and the air was stale with cigarette smoke. Pictures of his dead wife and daughter sat on his nightstand, facing an unmade bed. I walked on.

Jimmy's room was brighter than the old man's. The single bed had been made up neatly and clean underwear had been folded and placed upon it. Posters of postpunk bands like the Minutemen and Husker Du were crookedly tacked to the wall. A bulletin board hung over his dresser, on which were tacked ticket stubs from concerts. Many of the stubs were from larger halls, like Lisner and DAR. A few were from the Warner. But the majority of them were small red tickets with black stenciled lettering, reading "The Snake Pit."

"You see anything?" Pence asked.

I shook my head and admitted, "I don't know what I'm looking for. I'll head downtown tonight and ask around. I could use a photograph of Jimmy if you have one."

"I thought you might," he said and produced two folded pictures from his back pocket. "One of him's his graduation picture from Wilson High last year. The other one I found in his drawer. Looks like him at a party or something."

I took them both. The graduation picture was typically waxen and told me little about the boy, though there was a small skull and cross-bones pinned to his lapel which suggested a touch of insolence, not unusual for someone his age. I thought his eyes drooped rather sadly at the corners.

The second photo said more about the boy. He stood erect, facing the camera, while his companions danced around him. He was un-smiling, had a cigarette cupped in his hand, and wore black motorcycle boots, jeans, and a T-shirt. A shock of hair hung down over his left eye.

I felt a faintly painful blade of recognition slide into my stomach. Though the T-shirt had changed from Led Zeppelin to Minor Threat, this was me, over a dozen years ago.

"This is how he looks now?" I asked.

"Everything but the hair. He shaved it off a couple of days before he disappeared."

I put the photos in my jacket as we left the room and walked towards the front door of the apartment. The old man grabbed my arm to slow me down.

"I took the liberty of calling some private detective agencies this morning," he said. "The average going rate seems to be two hundred a day plus expenses. That will be my offer to you."

"I'm not a private detective," I said. "And anyway, I could run into him tonight. We'll settle later."

"Yes, of course," he said halfheartedly. He looked small standing in front of me. My sight lit again on the VCR wires lying unconnected on the floor.

"You want me to hook up that recorder for you before I go?"

"No, thank you," he said. "Jimmy brought that to me, and he can hook it up, Mr. Stefanos. When you bring him home."

The old man's eyes were still on me as I closed the door and stepped out into the hall.

FIVE

Malone said, "Where you been, Country? I done closed two deals while you were gone."

"I had to see a friend."

McGinnes was nearby, waiting on a compact stereo customer. He turned to me, cupped his hand around his tie, and began stroking it feverishly, his eyes closed and face contorted.

Louie was moving slowly down the center aisle, his short arms propelling him forward as they swung across his barrel chest. I could hear his labored breathing as he approached.

"Call your girl from the *Post*," he said.

"You mean Patti?"

"Yeah. She sound nice. She look good too?"

"Too young for you, Louie. You'd stroke out."

"Never too old to gyrate," he said, and demonstrated briefly with his hips. "Matter of fact, I'll be headin' over to Van Ness in a little while to take care of business. Might take the evening off."

"Fine with me. Who's on the schedule tonight?"

"Lloyd just came in. He's on till six. Malone's on till six too. Lee takes afternoon classes, but she'll be back to work on through. That means you, her, and McGinnes will close tonight. That okay?"

"Yeah."

"Hey, Nick," Malone said. "Check out our boy Void today. He lookin' good."

Lloyd was absently bumping into displays as he attempted to light his pipe while making his way to the front of the store. The pipe was a Holmesian prop, an Anglophilic symbol that he believed suggested intelligence, but Lloyd was a pale, painfully thin man with a frighteningly deathlike grin, whose appearance more accurately reflected the high school outcast who hears voices from beyond as he clutches his hall locker. Today his woodgrain crucifix hung on a rawhide string over a lime green polyester shirt, hooked up with forest green bellbottoms.

The boys used Lloyd to run errands and as the butt of their practical jokes, while Louie kept him around to fill in odd hours on the schedule. As a stockboy I had been continually demeaned by him in the presence of customers, when he wasn't critiquing my heathen lifestyle or trying to convince me of his close personal relationship with Jesus. His full name was Lloyd Danker, though all of us, Louie included, called him Void Wanker.

Lloyd looked me over in that way of his that always expressed superiority. The corners of his mouth spread into a sickly smile, and he yanked his pipe out to reveal a cockeyed row of yellow teeth.

"I see management's been good to you, Nick. You've come a long way."

McGinnes' customer, who was walking, reached the front door, turned his head back, and said, "Thanks." McGinnes, waving to the customer, said, "Thank *you.*" And then, still waving and in a quickly lowered voice, added, "You piece of shit."

33

The customer smiled, waved back, and disappeared down the Avenue.

"Good close, Johnny," Louie said.

McGinnes shook his head and said, *"Putz."*

McGinnes, Malone, Louie, Lloyd, and I were standing in a circle near the counter. McGinnes had his arms folded. Louie leaned against a "stack and sell" microwave oven display with his hands in his pockets. Malone had just lit a Newport and was blowing the first heavy drag towards Lloyd, who stood awkwardly in forced casualness with his hip cocked, the pipe hanging from the side of his mouth like some comic-strip hillbilly.

"Yeah," Malone said slowly, "looks like I might be top dog around here this month." He gave McGinnes a sidelong glance and held it there rather theatrically.

McGinnes said, "The month ain't over yet, Jim."

Lloyd jumped in with, "I'm having a pretty good month myself."

"Yeah," McGinnes said, "for a guy who couldn't sell a lifeboat on the *Titanic,* you're having a good month."

Lloyd blinked hard and pulled the crucifix out and away from his chest, holding it gently as if Christ himself were still upon it. "I wouldn't really expect you guys to understand, but there's more to life than closing deals and spasmating your genitals."

Malone ran an open hand across his own crotch and said, "Maybe so, but I plan on spasmatin' these motherfuckers tonight, Jack." He and McGinnes gave each other skin and chuckled. Louie snorted but didn't look up.

Lloyd smiled hopelessly and shook his head. "Anyone want coffee?"

"Yeah, get me some java while you're out," Malone said, then fanned away Lloyd's outstretched hand. "I'll get you tomorrow, hear?" Lloyd left the store, looking something like a human scarecrow.

"Thank you, Jeeesus," McGinnes said.

"Now that Numbnuts is gone," Louie said, "maybe we can talk a little business. You girls don't mind, do you?"

McGinnes looked my way and smiled impishly. His eyes were slightly glazed, undoubtedly the result of several more trips to the stockroom.

"I got a call from the office today," Louie continued. "The Boy

Wonder's been looking at his computer again. 'Profit margins have eroded, competition's fierce,' blah, blah, blah. Bottom line is, we've got to start selling more service policies, and I mean now. Anything you guys have to do to get the job done, you do it. If a customer refuses the policy, reduce the product price on our copy of the ticket, then add the service policy back into it to bring the total up to its original amount—*after* they've left the store, understand?"

"What if the customer finds out later they 'bought' a policy they didn't want?" McGinnes said.

"I'll handle the complaints," Louie said with a hard stare at McGinnes, "like I always do." He glanced out the window. "Now you all have a nice day, and write some business. In case the office calls, I'm out for the rest of the day, shopping the competition." Then he was gone, out onto the sidewalk and heading south with his short-man's swagger.

McGinnes and Malone split up, Malone heading back to the relative darkness of the Sound Explosion. McGinnes had picked up a sales call and was gesturing with his hands as he talked into the phone. I went around the counter and dialed Patti Dawson's number on another line.

"Pat Dawson's desk," her assistant said.

"Is Patti in?"

"She's away from her desk."

"When you see her, tell her Nick Stefanos called."

A pause, then, "She's back at her desk now. Hold please."

I held for at least a minute and listened to New Age whale music. Finally Patti picked up.

"Where you at, lover?" she said.

"In hell."

"Back on the Avenue, huh? What's going on?"

"Some free-lance work I couldn't get away with in the main office. I figure I can get the job done from here, with your help."

"What do you need?"

"You got a pen?"

"Shoot."

"The ad I mocked up for the weekend," I said. "Have ad services run the proofs over to me here at the store. For next weekend I want to pick up an old ad."

"Which one?"

"Take the ad I did the second week of September, I think the head was 'September Savings.' Change the head to 'October Values.'"

"How do you keep coming up with these zingers?" she asked.

"It's pretty scary, isn't it?"

"Yes."

"Have you got any camera-ready art down there of a horn-of-plenty?"

"I'm sure we do," she said.

"Good. Put that in the head too, and paste down some art of televisions and radios spilling out of the horn. Got all that?"

"Yeah. It's absolutely brilliant, Nicky. I'm sure it will create a feeding frenzy. Anything else you want, while I'm doing your job for you?"

"That ought to do it."

"They know in the office that you're just picking up old ads?"

"Patti, Nathan Plavin comes to work every day to be taken out to lunch. I doubt he's even cognizant of the advertising. The GM, Jerry Rosen, he spends more time out of the office than in. I can't even tell you what it is he does. Ric Brandon's just a boy in a suit. Only Gary Fisher keeps an eye on those things, and I'm tight enough with him."

"Just want to make sure you know what you're doing, lover."

"Thanks, Patti. Talk to you later." We hung up.

Lloyd was waiting on a small appliance customer from whom the others had hidden when she walked in. McGinnes was going down the row of televisions, writing something on the tags. I dialed the office, got Marsha, and asked for Gary Fisher.

"Fisher," he said, catching his breath.

"Fish, it's Nick."

"Nick! What's happening?"

"Nothing much. Just wanted to keep you apprised of the ad situation."

"Apprise me," he said. "And trim the fat."

"We're running the 'blowout' ad this weekend. Next week we're doing an 'October Values' ad very similar to the 'September Savings' promotion we ran last month."

"So you're rerunning the same ad with a different head, right?"

"That's right."

"As long as it pulls, I don't give a shit what you call it. Sometimes I think the public doesn't read the ads anyway. They see something's going on, they come in and spend money." He said this almost sadly.

"Well, if you want to make any changes, let me know. By the way, when did we start buying Korean goods?"

"You talking about that Kotekna *dreck?*"

"Yeah."

"Rosen saw those at the CES show in Vegas and brought in a hundred. One of those 'show specials.' Every time I'm in the barn, I see them sitting there, I get a pain in my fucking gut."

"They're not going to turn if they're not out on the floors. They don't even have one on display here in the store."

"Whatever. It's Rosen's problem. Later, Nick." He hung up.

Lloyd was still with his customer, an older woman who seemed to be edging away from him in fear. I walked over to McGinnes, who was scribbling seemingly unrelated letters and numbers onto the sales tags.

"You remember the system?" he asked, continuing his markings.

"Refresh my memory."

"The first two letters in the row are meaningless. The next set of numbers is the commission amount, written backwards. The final letter is the spiff code, if there is a spiff. *A* is five, *B* is ten, *C* is fifteen and so on. So, for example, the figure on this tag, *XP5732B* means twenty-three seventy-five commission with a ten dollar spiff. That way, you're pitching the bait that doesn't pay dick, you look right beside it on the next model, you see what you get if you make the step, in black and white." He stepped back to admire his handiwork.

"Just in case one of these customers asks, so we keep our stories straight, what do we tell *them* the numbers mean?"

"Inventory control codes," he said with a shrug.

"By the way, Johnny. I talked to a buddy of yours today, an Evan Walters. Something about an ice bucket."

He shook his head and chuckled. "Yeah, I know him. A flaming asshole. I could have had that fifty-nine cent ice bucket over here months ago, but I thought I'd let his droopy ass stew about it for a while."

"I've got it coming over on the truck today. He'll be in tonight to get it."

"Thanks, Nick. You always did like to pick up those loose ends around me."

"There's an awful lot of them," I said.

He pinched my cheek, looked at his watch, and smiled. "Time for my medicine," he said. Then he turned and headed for the back room.

That afternoon we waited on customers and put out some fires. I closed two deals, though one of them was a write-up, an advertised piece that I was unable to get off of. The boys informed me that the next time I sold the plunder, I would follow it out the door.

On one occasion I TO'd to McGinnes, introducing him as my manager. He held the line by throwing in a TV cart, which retailed for thirty bucks but cost Nathan's nothing.

For another tough customer I excused myself to call the main office for permission to drop a price. I dialed the weather report, listened to the recording, and nodded my head repeatedly, the oldest ruse in a very old book. I returned to the customer with "permission" to cut the price only ten dollars, and wrote the deal.

I observed the other salesmen and noticed that Lloyd was still awful. The boys were obviously feeding him just enough sales to keep his job for him and thereby keep another hotshot off their floor.

Malone's specialty was audio. His technical knowledge was extensive, though that was also his biggest weakness. He often talked himself out of deals, talked much further than the point at which the customer was giving off buying signals. But his rap was strong and especially impressive to the white clientele. To them he was the ice-cool jazz enthusiast, on a mission to turn the average Joe on to the music via fine audio equipment.

McGinnes, however, worked the floor with the care of an craftsman. He could pick up two or three customers at once, sometimes keeping their attention in groups. All of the tricks were there, and the lies, though these were vague enough to be open-ended in a confrontation. With McGinnes, the customers rarely left the store with what they had intended to buy, but they were satisfied they had made the right decision.

By four o'clock, traffic had heavied up northbound on the Avenue. Most potential customers would be focusing now on maneuvering home through the rush hour. I found the store's Polaroid up front beneath the register. I took it into the back room, had a seat at Louie's desk, and opened his junk drawer. In it I located an Exacto knife and glue.

I brought out the party picture of Jimmy Broda and laid it on Louie's white blotter. Then I swung his desk lamp over the picure and switched on the light.

Carefully, I cut the hair off Broda's head with the Exacto. After that I etched around his body, as I would cut out clip art, and pulled him out of the picture. I shot a Polaroid of the naked wall behind the desk. When it developed, I pasted the bald cutout of Jimmy Broda onto that. It looked a bit as if he were floating in a pale room.

McGinnes walked out of the radio room, belched, and bent over the desk. He popped the top on a tall Colt 45 and placed the can in front of me.

"You need to start drinking," he said. I had a pull. It was cold and had some bite.

"You just get these?"

"I've got a twelve-pack chilling in a compact in the back. I use it when I close without Louie. You here for the duration?"

"Yeah."

"Good." He bent further over the desk and squinted. "Who's that?"

"Pence's grandson, Jimmy Broda. Or my version of him, the way I think he looks now."

"Skinny little fucker. Where you gonna start?"

"I'm heading down to the Corps after work. You come along?"

"Sure, why not? But it's a long time before we close this place up."

"So?"

"So, shit," he said, pulling the pipe and film canister from his pocket. "Let's get our heads up."

SIX

Lee returned to the store somewhere around five and parked her books beneath the counter. When she had straightened up, she waved to me briefly and smiled, then turned her head away in mock embarrassment. Her hair was uncombed, and I imagined it matted and spread out upon a pillow. My blood pressure jumped a bit, and I kept my stare on her until she felt it enough to look once more in my direction.

When the transfer truck pulled around back, the sales crew typically scattered. McGinnes bolted for the back room, and Lloyd gathered up his things and left for the evening.

As I went to the back door, I noticed Malone and a younger guy talking in the Sound Explosion. The man was wearing a velvet maroon jogging suit and a thick, braided gold chain around his neck. They shook hands for an artificially long time, then Malone buried his fist and its contents into his pocket.

I unloaded the truck with the help of a driver I recognized from the warehouse, a wiry, hard-looking young man who wore his Nathan's cap backwards and had a cigarette lodged above his ear. We worked without speaking until he departed with a tough nod.

I managed the merchandise onto the conveyer belt, which ran parallel to the stairs leading down to the stockroom. I walked alongside the crated goods until they hit a flat, rollered surface at the foot of the stairs, then pulled the power lever back from "forward" to the "off" position.

I heard the crush of an empty can and looked up to see McGinnes stepping out of the shadows of the stockroom's far corner. A fresh malt liquor filled one hand, his brass pipe the other. He handed me the can while he filled the pipe.

I drank deeply from the can. He lit the pipe thoroughly and then we traded. The pot was smooth passing my throat but singed my lungs. I made it through half an exhale before coughing out the rest and reaching back for the malt liquor. McGinnes pulled another can out from the inside of his sportjacket, popped the tab, and tapped my can with his. We tipped our heads back and drank.

We stood in a fairly thick blanket of smoke. McGinnes knocked the ash from the pipe onto his palm and filled another bowl. He lit it evenly with a circular motion of the disposable lighter flame he held above it. We smoked that while downing our Colts. I thought of how good a cigarette would taste, then thought of something else. I looked at McGinnes' face and laughed. He thought that was funny, and both of us laughed.

"Evan Walters' bucket came in," I said. "You want it?"

"Yeah," he said, and a wedge of black hair fell across his forehead. "Give it to me."

I found it on the conveyer belt, a green cylinder wrapped in plastic and secured with a twist tie. I took a four-point stance, centered the bucket to myself, stepped back, and passed it to him with a surprising spiral. He caught and ran with it halfway across the stockroom, were he stopped and did some weird end-zone strut.

Walking back my way, he let out a short, mean burst of laughter. His jaws were tight and his eyes looked directionless, and I realized, in a sudden rush of alcohol and marijuana, that the way I felt just then was the way *he* felt all the time.

"Evan Walters," he said, "deserves a little extra something for all the trouble he's been through." Mimicking Walters, he lowered his voice to an effete growl, and said, "I've been calling you for months, Mr. McGinnes, and frankly I don't appreciate . . ."

He continued the speech as he unraveled the plastic, removed the top, lowered the bucket beneath his crotch, and unzipped his fly. He looked at me glumly, shut his eyes, found his pecker, and let fly a hard piss-stream into the mouth of the bucket.

"Come on, man. . . ."

"I'm a lawyer," he whined, "and I want my ice bucket!" McGinnes washed the urine around with a circular motion, then flung it out and across the room where it crackled as some of it hit a hot, naked bulb. He reaffixed the plastic and secured it onto the bucket using the tie.

McGinnes handed me a mint, popped one in his own mouth, and

raced up the stairs. I followed him up and out into the showroom. He seemed to be skipping down the aisle, swinging the bucket at his side as if it were a picnic basket. At the front counter he handed the bucket to Lee, who gave us both a disapproving look.

"Give this to a Mr. Walters when he comes in tonight," he deadpanned, then walked away.

I had accumulated some dirt on my sleeves while unloading the transfer truck. Lee knocked it off, then brushed a hand across my chest to finish the job. I noticed that brown speck again in her eye.

"What have you boys been up to?" she asked, her smile twisting to one side.

"Science experiment in the basement."

"Who's closing tonight?"

"You, me, and Johnny." She laughed, rather evilly I thought, and walked back behind the counter.

Malone stopped to tuck a silk scarf into his jacket before leaving. He patted his breast pocket, felt the deck of Newports, and showed a look of relief.

"All right, darling," he said to Lee by way of goodnight, then turned to me. "All right, Country."

"What about tonight, Andre? You meet us down at the Corps?"

He shook his head and pursed his lips in an exaggerated manner. "Uh-uh. I got that redbone freak, uh, young lady, coming over to my joint tonight for dinner, some cognac, you know what I'm saying?"

"Yeah."

McGinnes yelled from across the floor, "You gonna get your face wet tonight, Jim?"

Malone said, "I don't eat nuthin' you can't buy at Safeway." He looked at Lee and said, *"Pardon* me, darling." Then he turned and left the store.

The evening progressed with McGinnes and me hammering malt liquors one for one in the back room at an alarming rate. I was through smoking pot for the night, though the damage had been done during our earlier basement sessions. I lost count of our alcohol consumption, but I remember McGinnes racing next door to Mr. Liquor (in my opinion, *the* classic name for a spirit shoppe) and coming back with a tall brown bag in his arms, his eyebrows wiggling excitedly like the kid with the fake ID returning to the party.

Lee was reading a textbook up front and pretending to ignore us, though I caught her looking up often. By seven she had cracked a Colt and had begun nursing it in the back.

We had some traffic that night and initially handled it well. The early customers seemed oblivious to the fact that I was on a tear. I went through a good bit of eyewash and quite a few breathmints.

McGinnes, as was his fashion, became more aggressive and quicker with customers as his sobriety deteriorated, though this did not affect his closing rate. If anything, the alcohol made his rebuttals more certain, less open for debate.

I luckily hit upon several open, friendly customers who were intelligent enough to have an idea of what they wanted when they came through the door and not afraid to spend some money on it if it was offered at a fair price. Consequently, the pressure to perform impossible switches in front of McGinnes was taken off me. The confidence gained after my first sale of the evening spilled over into my rap with subsequent customers, and I was suddenly on a roll.

McGinnes became troubled by my momentum. At one point, when I moved to take an up, he stepped in front of me and threw an elbow into my stomach, keeping a wide smile plastered on his face as he greeted the customers. They turned out to be bait-snatchers who demanded to be sold the plunder, which only served to shake him further.

After he had written them up, he signaled me to the back. I followed him into the radio room, where he cracked two Colts. He handed me one and we both had long pulls.

"What's on your mind?" I asked.

"Nothing," he said defensively, and reached into his pocket. He unraveled his fist to reveal two orange hexagonal pills, then jabbed that hand in my direction. "Eat one of these."

"What is it?"

"Like a 'lude, only not as heavy." He became impatient. "It's just a painkiller."

"Huh?"

"Eat it, you pussy."

I took the pill and washed it down with a healthy dose of malt liquor. He popped his dry with the flat of his palm.

"So," I said, wiping something wet off my chin, "what else did you bring me back here for?"

He finished another swallow. "I just wanted to tell you that you looked good out there tonight. You haven't lost it, man, you *belong* on a sales floor. That guy in the red jacket, I saw you step him into that Mitsubishi, that was *clean.*"

"He stepped himself."

"That's the point. You saw where he was going, you kept your mouth shut and let him roll right into it." He paused. "Most of the good ones are dead or selling mattresses, Nick. There aren't many left like you or me." He winked and tapped my can with his.

"Is this 'The Closing of the Sales Frontier' speech?" I asked.

"I'm just telling you that you need to be back on the floor."

"I don't think that's what I need."

"You'll be back," he said smugly. I could only hope that for once the silly bastard would be wrong.

Our small evening rush came and went without major incident. We did walk most of our customers, however, as our pitches and counter-objections increasingly consisted of alcohol logic.

At one point McGinnes nudged me and walked up to the backs of a man and, judging from her magnificent, showcase ass, his extremely attractive companion.

"Fuck your wife for you today, sir?" McGinnes asked cheerfully, running the words together rapidly as if they were one.

"No thanks," the man said, turning and smiling. "We're just looking around."

I had hoped that McGinnes would someday be caught in the act of this, his oldest and stupidest trick. It was his contention that people never listened to the salesman's opening line, so anything could be said, so long as it had the proper speed and inflection. Often he'd pinch the cheek of a toddler and say to his proud parents, "Cute little cock-sucker!" or wipe his brow on a summer day and to sympathetic customers tiredly proclaim, "Sure is cock today." And always get away with it.

By eight o'clock the down had kicked in and brought to the forefront all the alcohol that had preceded it. McGinnes, who had begun bumping into displays and cackling at me from across the showroom, had fallen off what was for him a very wide ledge. It was plain now that both of us were on a violently twisted binge.

When it became obvious that a Japanese-American woman who had wandered in was not going to buy, McGinnes began substituting the *r*'s in his words with *l*'s, and the outraged woman, who probably had more class in her pinky finger than he had in his entirely moronic body, walked out in disbelief. We'd get a letter on that one in the office, and she'd get an apology, most likely from Louie.

A little later, an elderly woman came in and asked for McGinnes. I broke away from Lee up front and found him in the basement. He was walking down a row of stock, jamming his forefinger through the cardboard cartons with a scream, before stepping up to the next box and repeating the act. There was blood on the tip of his finger.

I left him in the basement and returned to the floor to help the woman. The false confidence gained from eyedrops and mints had equalized me, and I was doing quite well with her, explaining the features and benefits of a blender as if they were earth-shattering.

I *was* doing well, until I looked over her shoulder. Sporting an utterly absurd smile, McGinnes stood casually behind her, one arm leaning on the display rack, one foot crossed over the other like some cologne cowboy against a split-rail fence. His freckled dick drooped lazily out of his unzipped fly.

In the course of a few seconds, as she turned around to see what I was smirking at, the zipped-up McGinnes stepped forward to greet her. She walked out ten minutes later, receipt and blender in hand.

McGinnes followed me to the Sound Explosion and tried to slap me five. I pulled my hand away.

"There's no way I'm going back on that floor with you tonight."

"Easy, Jim," he said and pointed to the front door. A skinny man in an L.L. Bean costume and his very plain, pregnant wife entered the store and approached the counter. He said something to Lee, she handed him the ice bucket, he nodded curtly, and he and his wife exited the store.

Evan Walters ran across Connecticut Avenue to beat the onrushing traffic and left his pregnant wife stranded on the median strip. From the east side of the street he impatiently waved her across.

"Piss-bucket," McGinnes mumbled.

In the last hour of work few customers came in. Those who did left quickly, undoubtedly recognizing the smell of marijuana that McGinnes was now smoking openly on the sales floor. More letters, apologies, denials.

Just before closing time, McGinnes, who had been ranting about management for the last fifteen minutes ("Fuck Brandon. . . . Fuck him!"), emerged from the back room with a Crossman pellet gun that would have exactly replicated a Magnum if not for the CO_2 thumbscrew beneath the grip.

"This is for you, Nutty," he yelled, and began firing into the card-board caricature of Nathan Plavin that hung suspended from the ceiling in the middle of the store. McGinnes, who had spent a few troublesome years in the army but had escaped combat duty, was a fair shot, and the pellets tore right through Plavin's ample middle and below to his vitals.

Lee immediately shut down the showroom lights and locked the front door. I took the gun away from McGinnes and instructed him to wait for me up front. Lee walked by with the paperwork, said she'd be a minute, and disappeared into the back room. I followed her back.

She was finishing her Colt and stashing it in a plastic trashbag filled with empties when I walked in. I stood and watched her file the papers. She looked at me and at the gun, which I held at my side.

"What are you going to do with that?" she asked. "BB me to death?"

"Thought I might bring home a bag of sparrows. For my cat."

"Sounds yummy. But why don't you put that thing away. He keeps it in the radio room, where he keeps his beer."

I entered the small room, had trouble finding the light switch, and groped along the wall for the spot of boxes where he usually stashed his paraphernalia. I looked to my left and saw that Lee was behind me, silhouetted against the low-wattage bulb of the office. I clumsily stashed the gun behind the nearest box.

"Where are we going?" she asked. She was near me, and her hand touched mine.

"The Corps," I said.

"I like that place."

"Good." I moved closer and felt her warm breath near my face. "Thanks for helping tonight. Things got a little out of hand towards the end."

"You're welcome," she said.

I cupped the back of her head and kissed her. Her tongue slid over my teeth and along the roof of my mouth. She pulled her mouth away and arched her back. I moved my hand inside the top of her shirt, reached into her loose bra, and lightly skimmed her swollen nipple. She kissed me harder this time and made a guttural sound. I reached down with my right hand and tugged on the back of her upper thigh below her buttocks, pulling her lower body up as she ground it into mine. We broke apart, and she pushed some hair away from her face.

"Well, then," she said, and exhaled. "Let's get going."

SEVEN

The three of us were in the front seat of my Dodge and heading downtown. McGinnes had slithered into Mr. Liquor and had emerged, mercifully, with only a six of domestic that we were now trying to kill before we reached the club.

"Drink up," McGinnes explained, as Lee elbowed my ribs. "The way the prices are in these places now, you've got to catch a buzz *before* you go in."

I started to push a tape into the deck, but Tom T. was on HFS and launching into a propulsive set that was kicked off by Camper Van Beethoven's reggae-fueled "One of These Days." I let that ride.

We cut down Cathedral into the park, then took Pennsylvania Avenue across town. As we passed the White House, McGinnes reached across Lee and blasted the horn on the steering wheel, raising his beer to toast the protesters squatting in Lafayette Park.

In the area of the National Theater I hung a left and drove around the block a couple of times looking for a space. Between the revitalized Willard and the Shops there was plenty of nighttime congestion in this area now. I ignored McGinnes' repeated shouts, over the wailing sax solo in the Cure's "A Night Like This," to park illegally, and eventually found a spot.

Lee and I crossed the street and looked back to see McGinnes standing in the middle of the road, his head fully tilted back, his small belly protruding, as he shotgunned the remainder of his beer. A carload of kids honked as they drove by, and McGinnes held out his empty so that they could see the label, then met us on the sidewalk.

There was no midweek line on the polished stone steps of the Corps. A pumped-up guy in a muscle shirt with a blond mass of hair that had been plastered up to resemble a slab of cake opened the door and blocked our way. The thud of heavy bass came out with him.

"Five dollars," he said coldly, with a fashionably down-under accent. I had loosened my tie and was wearing black pleated trousers with a blue oxford. Lee, of course, looked fine, but when the doorman got a look at McGinnes, polyestered to the nines and swaying on the steps with unfocused eyes, he seemed to regret asking us in.

"We're with the band, mate," McGinnes said.

"There is no band, *mate*. Five dollars."

We paid the cover and entered. I noticed the doorman signal another muscleboy next to the bar, pointing in particular to McGinnes, who was already pushing through the crowd to get to one of the several bars around the dance floor. The DJ was blasting some anonymous House music, and the air was very warm and damp.

Little had been done to the club since it had been converted from an old bank, a stately blend of marble and brass. As a child, I had come here with my grandfather, stepping on the shiny floor with deliberate force to produce a cavernous echo that would raise the heads of the elderly, wool-suited tellers. Now it was one of those trendy "new wave" clubs that had sprouted up in this part of town, and in Adams Morgan and around Dupont Circle, but was in fact less new wave than seventies disco.

We had seen this coming in the early eighties, when Devo had a Top Forty novelty hit with "Whip It," when major labels began scrambling to sign any groups wearing skinny ties and funny haircuts. About this time the Angry Young Men, originals like Costello and Graham Parker, were eclipsed by no-talent fops like Duran Duran and Frankie Goes To Hollywood. We began to realize that those early years, of the punk and new wave emergence, of rediscovering ska and dance music, of separation and alienation from all the youth movements that came before us, were over.

The result was clubs like the Corps (an utterly false play on the term *hardcore*), where Reagan youth, wealthy AU and GW students, and gold-chained, coke-carrying sons of diplomats came to party. These "struggling" students got their forty dollar "punk" haircuts, paid the seven dollar cover, drank five dollar, sugar-filled, lime-necked beers, and danced to the new wave beat.

I looked at them on the dance floor, enshrouded by the smoke of dry ice, while New Order pumped through the speakers. They were perfectly coiffed, with their predominately black with-a-touch-of-white uniforms, fashionably bored looks on their blankly androgynous faces. I turned to the bar for a beer.

When I caught her eye, a woman stepped into a light that was spotted up, which accentuated her thick, white makeup and black hair. She had a tight cocaine smile and lifeless eyes. It seemed a struggle for her to unglue her lips.

"What can I get you?" she asked, wiping in front of me with a bar rag.

"I'll take a Bud."

She produced one and uncapped it with an opener that was attached to the cooler with fishing line. She reached for a glass but replaced it as I waved it away. I grabbed the beer by the neck, had a long pull, and bent over the bar. She leaned her ear in towards my mouth.

"Joe Martinson still work here?" I asked.

"He's working the upstairs bar," she said, too loudly.

"How much for the beer?"

She held up three fingers. I tossed four on the bar and made my way around the dance floor to the regally wide marble staircase leading to a balcony that surrounded the entire club. Young coeds with loose coat-of-arms sweaters passed me as I walked up, descending the stairs slowly and unemotionally like drugged debutantes.

I found Martinson behind a barely lit bar in the corner, doing what was probably a placebo shooter with three cute college-age girls. They laid down a ten and walked away. I stepped up to the bar.

I'd got to know Joe Martinson when he was a bartender at a wild, short-lived, tiny dance bar near Chinatown aptly called the Crawlspace. At the time his trademark was cotton oxford shirts, the sleeves of which he tore off and fashioned as headbands. The bar was always sweat-soaked and to capacity with drunks, and opened at about the time that slam-dancing had a brief run of popularity in D.C. The slamming eventually closed it down, when some Potomac preppies came in for "the experience," walked out with bloody noses, and sued the owners. But for one hot, lunatic summer, that had been the place to go.

"Nick," he said, and shook my hand. He was wearing black pants with a tuxedo shirt and a black bow tie. Though working out had heavied him up in the chest and shoulder department, he looked less tough than in his earlier, wiry incarnation. "What are *you* doing here?"

"I should be asking you that, Joe."

"A bar is a bar," he said, "and anyway, that scene is over with. I wouldn't fit in if it *were* happening."

"Yeah, but *this* place?"

"If I remember right, you were some kind of art major in college, Nick. I've seen your ads in the *Post,* and let me tell you, you cut out pictures of television sets very artistically." We laughed uneasily.

"How about a shot," I said, "and pour one for yourself."

"Sure, Nick," he said, and looked at me as if I didn't need one. I looked over the railing to one of the bars near the dance floor. McGinnes was standing very close to a girl twenty years his junior, talking to her with his mouth very nearly on her ear. Her companion, a pretty young blond boy with a wedge haircut wearing a white mock turtleneck, was standing on the other side of her gripping a beer bottle, angry but timid nonetheless.

Joe Martinson pushed a shot glass towards me and picked up his own. I looked in my glass and then up at him.

"Bourbon," he said.

"Rail?"

He frowned an of-course-not and said, "Grand-Dad."

We did the shots, and I finished my beer before placing the glass back on the bar. A couple walked by me, whispered to each other, and chuckled. Martinson slid a fresh Bud in front of me and I took it by the neck.

They were playing some Pet Shop Boys now and the dance floor was packing up. Lee was with a group of friends at one corner of the floor, pointing up at me and smiling. I raised my beer to them, and one of them laughed and said something to Lee, who winked at me, then turned back to her friends.

I fished the photographs out of my jacket pocket and put the graduation picture on the bar, pushing it towards Joe Martinson.

"You recognize this guy?" I asked.

"No," he said without thought.

"How about this one?" I placed the doctored, bald-pated photo of Jimmy Broda on the bar. He looked it over and shook his head.

"I don't know him. What's his story?"

"A runaway I'm trying to locate. I think he's hanging with skinheads. Thought you might have seen him."

"Not in this place. They don't even let those guys through the door anymore, after they came in one night and pushed some gays around. That was one time I took the side of the bouncers here."

"Where would they hang out?"

"Depending on who's playing, either the Snake Pit or maybe the Knight's Work on Eleventh, in Southeast. But they've pretty much stopped going to the Knight's Work—the Marines down there were kicking the living shit out of those guys on a regular basis."

"You know any names, people I should be talking to?"

"Not a one, Nick."

I put the photos in my jacket and looked back over the railing at the floor below. I noticed some movement from the right side of the room. A bouncer was pushing through the crowd, heading for the main bar. The DJ had begun spinning the twelve-inch version of Big Audio Dynamite's "Hollywood Boulevard."

I looked to the center of the bar. McGinnes had his hands on the blond boy's chest, bunching up his turtleneck and breathing right up in the kid's face. Martinson yelled something to my back as I moved towards the steps.

The stairs were a blur. I was on the dance floor, the strobe light stylizing the rapidly scattering partners as it synchronized its patterns with the song's drum machine.

I was vaguely aware of large bodies converging from the left and right, and as the crowd parted, I saw the redfaced blond boy, unhurt and on his ass. McGinnes had turned back to the bar to resume his drinking.

A big guy with something like an ax handle in his upraised fist brushed by me and moved for McGinnes' back. I swept him with my right foot, and he went down to his knees, dropping the weapon as he fell.

I was grabbed almost immediately from behind in a bear hug. McGinnes had turned and realized what was happening, an apologetic look on his drunken face, accompanied by a slightly sad grin that told me what was inevitably going to go down next. Nevertheless, even as he sensed another bouncer approaching him from behind, McGinnes futilely lunged for the steroid boy whose arms were around me.

McGinnes was dropped with a kidney-shot before he could get near me. The one I had tripped was up and walking towards me, a tight sneer on his chiseled, Aryan face.

I thought, as he took a wide stance and drew back his fist, how easy it would have been to drop him with a front kick square in the balls. But in those few protracted seconds I had decided that there was no way out of the club that night without being pummeled, that I might as well take it, and that McGinnes and me, we had it coming.

The lousy prick went for my nose, but I turned my head and went with the punch, catching it high on the cheekbone. The sound of the blow must have sickened the man holding me, and I was released. Then I was pushed from behind with the momentum of a wave, pushed as if my feet were off the floor. McGinnes was being moved similarly, covering his sides and face with his arms from the potshots that the bouncers were taking as they pushed him forward. Many in the crowd were yelling and laughing, the first sign of spontaneous joy on their faces that I had seen all night.

McGinnes was shoved out the door first. He tripped down the steps and fell to one knee on the sidewalk. I kept my balance as someone gave me a final push, walked down the steps, and helped McGinnes up. He mumbled, "I'm sorry, man," and I could see that he really was, and that he was in some pain.

His pants were ripped at the knee, exposing a clean scrape beginning to redden with blood. I said calmly, "Let's just walk," and we did, crossing the street like two gentlemen to the occasional jeers of the spilled-out bar crowd behind us.

Lee was leaning against my car, fist up to her mouth and tears in her eyes as we approached her. "I can drive," I said, and indeed the events of the last few minutes and the cool night air had made me feel somewhere near sober. We slid into the front seat with Lee in the middle. I turned the ignition key and drove slowly down the block.

I headed east. McGinnes found a beer under the seat, cracked it, muttered "Jesus Christ," drank, and passed the can. Lee handed me the can after having some herself. We drove in silence for a few blocks. McGinnes, whose right ear appeared to be larger than his left, chuckled as he turned his head my way.

"Well," he said, "we showed 'em."

"That we did, Johnny."

"Yeah," Lee said, "you sonofabitches really showed them."

She was laughing through her tears and we joined her, a release that had McGinnes alternately coughing, spitting out the window, and laughing some more. He cried, "Irish bar!" as if there were no other choice.

Lee kissed him on the cheek and then me on my mouth. I continued driving east.

* * *

We parked on the corner of North Capitol and F, in front of Kildare's, McGinnes' favorite pub. He almost exclusively drank there now, though at one time his bar had been Matt Kane's on Thirteenth and Mass, until Kane died and McGinnes began complaining about the place being full of "wine drinkers and ghosts."

We entered and crossed a crowded room where a tenor was singing, passed the main bar, and arrived in the back room, where a few tables were empty. A waitress directed us to a four-top. We must have looked like accident victims, though no one here seemed to take notice.

The place was all muted greens and mahogany. A geezer with a long gray beard, his cane hung over the back of his chair, drank dark beer methodically, closing his eyes with each sip. A couple of young Scots sat near us, discussing rugby as they washed down their ham sandwiches with mugs of ale.

"Now *this* is a bar," McGinnes said, winking at Lee and smiling to expose some blood seeping from the top of his gums. He signaled a waitress who arrived with a bartray at her side.

"How you doin', Johnny?" she asked pleasantly with a shockingly thick Irish accent. She was plump with thick calves, but had a lovely, pale freckled face topped by thick, wavy black hair.

"Meg," he said, gesturing around the table, "I want you to meet my friends, Nick and Lee."

She pulled out a wet bar rag and lightly dabbed around my eye. "You boys had some fun tonight. Better wash that up in the WC."

"Thanks, Meg," I said.

"What will you be having, then?"

McGinnes said, "Is Carmelita in the kitchen tonight?"

"She's just got off. Getting changed now."

"Tell her I'm out here, Megan. And give us four Harps and four 'Jamies.' "

"Carmelita's already drinkin' a shift beer."

"Then send out three Harps," McGinnes said, "and four whiskeys."

I got up and made my way to the stairs that led to the toilets. At the sink I ran some cold water into my cupped hands. Someone in the stall behind me expelled unashamedly as I splashed water onto my face. In the mirror I saw that I had been slightly marked and was a little swollen, but it had all been relatively bloodless. My hair was wild and I dampened it, moving it around into some semblance of uniformity.

When I returned to the party, Carmelita, a girlfriend of McGinnes', with whom I had partied once before, was seated at the table. She smiled when I kissed her on the cheek.

Carmelita was wearing a plaid skirt, pumps, and a crisp white blouse, though she had worked in the kitchen all evening. Her hair, highlighted by a reddish rinse, was set off by her deep red lipstick. Like many other working immigrants in this city, she had an admirably fierce pride in how she looked when not on shift.

She and Lee were talking when McGinnes interrupted, and we raised our glasses without a toast, drinking down the smooth Jamison's whiskey. The amber lager was a fine complement, and we had another round of both.

We left Megan five on twenty and exited Kildare's. McGinnes told us to wait on the sidewalk, entered a smaller bar next door that had off-sale, and emerged with two sixes of longnecks under his arm. He smiled obtusely as he goose-stepped towards us and said, "Let's get going."

He and Carmelita climbed into the backseat of my car, cracked some beers, and handed one up to Lee, whose leg was against mine.

"Where we going?" I asked into the rearview.

"Head on up to Mount Pleasant," McGinnes slurred. "Carmelita lives that way. And we can drop in on Mr. Malone, see how his date's going."

"Come on, Johnny . . ."

"Do it, Jim," he ordered, "and put on some Irish."

I slid some Pogues into the deck, *Boys from County Hell,* and turned up the volume. McGinnes was trying to sing along to the group's wild, punked-up bastardization of Irish music, but mostly he and Carmelita were fitfully laughing and making out.

Lee passed me the bottle and told me what a great night she was having. I laughed at that but agreed and gave her a long kiss, mightily struggling to stay within the lines of my lane, as Shane McGowan shouted at an ear-numbing volume through my ravaged speakers.

* * *

We pulled up to Malone's rowhouse on Harvard Street, a darkish block dimly lit by old-style D.C. lampposts. This was a real neighborhood, a mix of Latins, blacks, and pioneer whites. There was just enough of a violent undercurrent here to keep the aspiring-to-hipness young professionals away and on the fringe of their beloved Adams Morgan, which had become an artificially eclectic mess of condos, "interesting" ethnic restaurants, Eurotrash discos, and parking lots.

When Malone opened the door of his basement apartment and saw the four of us on his steps, beers in hand with swollen faces and ripped clothing, like some escaped group of mentally ill Christmas carolers, a look of exasperation clouded his face. McGinnes put a shoulder to the door and a beer in Malone's hand, and we all stepped in.

In my Connecticut Avenue days I would often pick Malone up here on my way to work. We'd sit in his living room, trading bong hits and listening to Miles or Weather Report until it was time to go in. Though he'd upgraded his audio and video equipment since then, the apartment was still decorated primarily in variations of red.

Malone wore a silk kimono over pressed jeans and soft leather slippers. His date, who had changed her hairstyle since the afternoon, was standing by the kitchen door and staring in disbelief. McGinnes was already by the stereo, moving the dial off WDCU and undoubtedly searching for something more offensive.

"Just make yourself at home, Mick," Malone said sarcastically, and McGinnes thanked him.

Carmelita was trying to talk to Malone's date, who was answering in Spanish but not encouraging the conversation. Malone had a cognac in one hand and now a beer in the other. He shrugged, tapped my bottle with his, and drank.

"Thank you *so* much for dropping by tonight," he said. "Will you be staying long?"

"We weren't interrupting anything," I said, "were we?"

"Bitch has some big red titties," he whispered, then looked at me more closely. "Looks like you motherfuckers got into some *shit* tonight, boy."

I rolled my eyes, took a swig, and stumbled backwards. Lee stopped me with a hand on my shoulder. McGinnes had lost patience locating a radio station and was rifling through Carmelita's purse, finally finding a cassette and slipping it into Malone's deck.

Latin music blared out of the speakers. Carmelita broke away from Malone's date, excitedly crossing the room to McGinnes, who was dragging the center table away from the couch and moving it to a corner of the room. Malone mumbled something and followed his date, who now appeared to be spitting mad, into the kitchen.

The four of us began to dance. McGinnes was spinning and dipping Carmelita. Lee touched my cheek, and we kissed as we moved. Malone raised his voice in the kitchen. McGinnes cackled and turned up the volume.

Malone walked back into the room, moving to the beat, and started dancing with Lee and me, a fresh bottle of beer in his hand.

"Where's your friend?" I shouted.

"She says I 'did her dog' by lettin' you in," he said, and continued dancing.

Another song began that was harder, faster, and, courtesy of McGinnes, louder. This was one of those horn-driven salsa numbers that stop periodically on the beat for two seconds of silence, then begin again. The repetition was hypnotic.

Carmelita had one palm on her stomach, the other upraised, shaking her shoulders, sliding her feet four steps, then turning ninety degrees and repeating. We all followed, freezing when the music stopped, then yelling out and continuing our line dance as it began again.

Malone's tongue was out the side of his mouth, concentrating on getting the steps down, then smiling broadly when he had it, yelling, "No wonder you Latins are so happy. The music be so *festive* and shit!" Carmelita slapped him on the shoulder. Malone explained to McGinnes, "Carmelita be sayin', 'Right on time,' " and he rolled his *r* in imitation of her accent.

The music ended. McGinnes yanked the cassette from the deck, put it in his pocket, and said, "Let's go." We gathered our things and stood by the door.

Malone's date was staring contemptuously from the safety of the kitchen doorway. Malone, who looked genuinely disappointed, said, "Where you goin'? We just beginnin' to throw down!"

McGinnes and I walked over to Malone and poured the remainders of our beers over the top of his head. His date spun furiously and strode back into the kitchen.

I caught one last look at him before we booked. Beer streamed down the front of his face, falling onto his silk kimono. He still had a bottle in his hand, and he wasn't moving, just staring at us and trying to look hard. But he was fighting a smile, the deep dimples of his smooth face betraying him, threatening to implode. The four of us left him just like that, and fell like sailors out Malone's front door.

We dropped McGinnes and Carmelita a couple of blocks from Malone's, on Seventeenth Street. I watched them walk away beneath the light of a streetlamp, his arm around her shoulder, hers around his waist, until they faded into early morning fog.

That is the last I remember of being in my car. Lee drove us to her place, where she undressed me and got me into her shower, then followed me in.

She washed my back, then reached around and soaped beneath my balls. I took the bar from her and noticed with some relief that I was getting a strong hard-on. I began soaping her entire body, lingering on her hard breasts and the insides of her muscular little thighs. I slipped two, then three fingers inside her with ease. She bit my lip and sucked on my tongue with a deft roll of her own. We moved each other around the shower for several minutes, our bodies sliding together, until she put her hands on my shoulders, her back to the tiles, locked her legs around my waist, and pulled me in, arching her lower back to take it all.

When her breathing became more rapid, and her lips turned cold, I hooked a soapy finger into her asshole and she straightened against the wall, eyes toward the ceiling. She yelped, then shuddered, and buried her teeth into my shoulder, while I shot off with a spasm that traveled down my legs.

We held each other until the hot water began to expire. She put on her bathrobe and dried me with a large blue towel.

Sitting on the warm radiator, I watched her in the bathroom mirror as she carefully combed my wet hair. Then I was in a deep, dreamless sleep.

EIGHT

I wouldn't have minded dying but that would have taken too much energy. I had dry-mouth and my stomach had less stability than an African government. My hands smelled like a woman and my hair hurt. The part about the smell didn't bother me much.

Lee roused me, handed me a glass of Alka-Seltzer, dropped two aspirin in my hand, and said that breakfast and coffee awaited me in the kitchen. I sat up and washed down the pills with the seltzer.

She had folded my clothes for me, and I began to dress, pausing often to sigh and rub my forehead meaninglessly. She was not wearing my shirt, a morning-after ritual that I find neither cute nor practical, and I suddenly liked her even more for that.

I made it into the kitchen and sat with her at a small table. She looked fresh and was dressed for school in jeans and a gray sweatshirt. I took a sip of the black coffee.

"So," I said, "did you take advantage of me last night?"

"Repeatedly."

"And where am I?"

"Tenleytown," she said, and after watching my expression as I looked around the nicely appointed apartment, added, "Yes, Mommy and Daddy take care of the bills."

"You're from where? New York? Jersey?"

"Long Island. And I'm Jewish. And I go to AU. Do I fit the profile?"

"Yes," I said, gamely forking in a mouthful of runny eggs. "I usually don't go out with Jewish girls."

"Why's that?"

"Generally," I said, "they turn me down."

She chuckled and gave me the once-over. "I doubt that. Though I wouldn't try asking *anybody* out for a few days."

"My eye, you mean? Is it that bad?"

"It's not pretty. But it's not terrible." I got up to pour another cup of coffee, and she asked, "Anybody going to miss you from last night?"

"Only my cat."

"Johnny told me about your one-eyed cat."

"I guess he told you I've been married, too."

"Yes, he mentioned it. But I would have known anyway. By the way you held me last night when we were sleeping."

"Forget about the sleeping part," I said. "Was I a gentle lover?"

"Yes," she said. "Well, sort of. Like a gentle freight train."

"Sleeping with my wife—I mean, literally sleeping with her—was probably the best part of being married."

"You must miss it. Even the bad parts must seem pretty good now."

"Time heals all wounds? Bullshit. I miss some things. But I don't think I miss the bad parts."

I stewed about that for a while, and she let me. After she finished her coffee, she put on her jean jacket and hung her knapsack over her shoulder. "Your keys are on the counter and your car is on the street behind this building. I called Louie and told him you'd be late. Do me a favor and wash the dishes, and lock up on your way out."

"Sure, Lee."

"I had fun," she said, in a way that both explained and negated the entire evening. She kissed me on the side of my mouth and exited the apartment.

It was near noon by the time I finished my third cup of coffee, read the *Post,* and did Lee's dishes. I phoned Gary Fisher in the office.

"Fisher," he said, short of breath.

"Fisher, it's Nick."

"What's up?"

"I need a favor. How about we meet for lunch today, at Good Times, say a half hour from now?"

"Lunch is fine. What's the favor?"

"Before you leave, go into my desk, top drawer. Collect all the business cards from the media, I've got them all grouped in rubber bands. Bring them with you to lunch, okay?"

"Why can't you come in?"

"I was out last night, things got a little crazy. I got my eye dotted in a bar."

"Okay, Nick. Half hour."

A line at the bank machine made me late. When I walked into the Good Times Lunch, Gary Fisher was already seated at the counter, drinking coffee and hot-boxing a Marlboro. A couple of beer alkies sat near him and stared straight ahead.

I sat on Fisher's right. His hair was pulled back in a ponytail. He was wearing brown corduroys with a tan poly shirt and a brown knit tie squared off at the end. He checked his cigarette, determined there was some paper left over the filter, took a final drag, mashed it, exhaled, and patted the pack in his shirt pocket.

"What's going on, Nick?"

"Nothing much," I said, removing my sunglasses. He checked me over and shook his head.

Kim walked over with a green checkpad in his hand to take our order and gave me his usual blank nod. In the mirror above the register I noticed the poster of Billy Dee Williams, smiling over my shoulder. Public Enemy's "Black Steel in the Hour of Chaos" was blaring from the tinny speaker of the store radio. Fisher ordered a burger and fries. I asked for the fish and a bowl of soup.

"Mr. Personality," Fisher said as Kim walked away.

"He's the Korean Charles Bronson. It's a big responsibility."

"Here," he said, handing me a paper bag filled with business cards.

"Thanks." I placed the bag on the counter to my right. "So, what's happening in the world of electronics retailing?"

He shrugged. "The manufacturers are trying to soften the blow of price increases by policing 'minimum advertised prices' in the newspaper. In other words, they're trying to fix retails by controlling the giveaway artists. It's a good idea, but the FTC will stop that shit real fast once they get enough consumer complaints. If everybody's in the paper with the same price, all the business will go to the house with the biggest advertising budget, the power retailers. Let's face it, the days are numbered for the independents and the 'mom and pops.' "

Fisher had been predicting gloom and doom since I'd met him. For him it was just an excuse to work longer hours and smoke more cigarettes.

"How's our business been?"

"We're up from last October."

"What about our turns?"

"We're at about eight turns. But our 'open to buy' status shows us at a hundred grand in the hole. I'm telling you Nick, the barn is so full it's ready to burst."

We had our lunch. Fisher ate his quickly, as if it were a barrier standing in the way of his next cigarette. My fish was tasteless, as usual, but the soup was thick with beef stock and fresh vegetables, and I began to feel human.

"How's McGinnes?" he asked, pushing his plate away and lighting up.

"He's good."

"Best retail man I've ever seen," he said almost dreamily. "Sonofabitch could sell an icemaker to an Eskimo."

"They miss me at the office?"

"Nobody's throwing themselves out the window. Marsha asks about you."

"How's my desk look?"

"A ton of messages."

"Throw them all away when you get back, will you?"

"That's very professional of you."

"And one more thing."

"Another favor?"

"No, just a question. You remember that kid used to work in the warehouse, Jimmy Broda?"

"Yeah?"

"When I got back from vacation, he was gone. I borrowed a tape from him, I want to give it back. I heard he didn't show up for work a few days in a row, they let him go."

"I know who you're talking about," he said, "but that's not why they aced him."

"What do you mean?"

"He was a gonif. They caught him with his hand in the fuckin' cookie jar."

I thought that over. "What did he steal?"

"A third world briefcase, what else? Same thing you would have hooked if you were nineteen. He lost his job for a boogie box."

I turned the check over, which came to seven and change, and left ten bucks on the counter. Kim watched me pay up. There was a gleam in his eye as he stared at my shiner.

My cat, trying to act bored as I approached her on the stoop of my apartment, blinked her eye and looked away. I sat next to her on the stone step and scratched behind her ear. She lay on her side and stretched. It was a fine, warm October day.

I changed into sweatpants, throwing my dirty clothes into a mounting pile next to my dresser. I boiled some water, made coffee, took the mug along with a pen and pad of paper, and sat down next to the phone. In the white pages I found the numbers for the bureaus of licensing in Maryland and D.C.

I dialed the Maryland number and inquired about the requirements for a private investigator's license in that state. A cool, efficient voice explained that one must have had at least five years' experience as a police officer or served under a licensed investigator in an apprenticeship arrangement. I thanked her and hung up.

The woman who answered the phone at the D.C. bureau reluctantly ran down the requirements. "Basically," she said, "you come into our office and pick up a private detective agency package. There are several forms to fill out, and a blank application for a surety bond. You'll need four full-face wallet-sized photos of yourself when you come in. They can't be more than three months old. And you'll need to be fingerprinted down on Indiana Avenue. After that we do a background check as to any felonies or misdemeanors you might have. That takes at least a couple of weeks. If you check out, you get a license."

"What does the license give me? The right to carry a gun?"

"No, you *cannot* carry a weapon, by law. The license and certificate that comes with it merely legitimizes you."

"Where's your office and what's it going to cost me?"

"Two Thousand, Fourteenth Street. Third floor. The application fee is one hundred and fifty-eight dollars. Fingerprinting fee is sixteen-fifty."

I thanked her and replaced the receiver. Then I dialed Pence's number. The old man answered on the second ring.

"What's the dope, Mr. Stefanos?" he asked anxiously.

"I may have gotten a lead last night," I lied. "I'm going to follow it up this evening. Have you heard from Jimmy?"

"No."

"Mr. Pence, has Jimmy ever been in trouble with the law? Vandalism, shoplifting, anything minor like that?"

It took him a while to answer. "Not to my knowledge, Mr. Stefanos."

"Good. I'll call you tomorrow."

"Tomorrow, then," he said, and hung up.

I dumped the rest of my coffee and walked into my bedroom, the largest single area of my apartment. In my gym bag I located my rope.

I moved my rocking chair from the center of the room, put Tommy Keene's EP, "Places That Are Gone," on the turntable, cranked up the volume, and began to jump rope. After twenty minutes my T-shirt was soaked through.

I had a hot shower, shaved, put on clean jeans, a deep blue shirt, and a gray, light wool Robert Hall sportjacket I had picked up at the thrift shop for twenty bucks. On my way out I carried the cat in one hand and her dish in the other and placed both of them on the stoop. I climbed into my car and headed towards Connecticut Avenue.

The store was strangely quiet when I entered. Lee was behind the counter reading a textbook. Lloyd was sitting on a console watching the soaps. He turned his head, looked me over, and returned his gaze to the television.

Lee looked up from her book and smiled. I walked around the

counter and touched her arm, leaned into her and said, "Do you mind?"

"Not at all," she said. I kissed her. "You look better. Do you feel better?"

"Yes."

"What are you up to?"

"I came in to correct the proofs for the weekend. Then I've got an appointment downtown."

"The courier delivered this an hour ago," she said, handing me a thin white bag filled with tear sheets and proofs.

The art department at the *Washington Post* was a sweatshop, and showed it by the manner in which eighty percent of my proofs were returned to me. In this particular proof, several different type styles were inexplicably set, art was shot upside down, key words were misspelled, and most of the phone numbers for the stores were incorrect. For this and other services my company paid a major account "discount rate" somewhere over $120 per column inch.

I corrected the proof, using the standard editing symbols, then called ad services to tell them where to pick it up. McGinnes arrived at the counter as I hung up the phone. His eyes were watery and he was very pale. He took my jaw in his hand and turned my face to the right.

"Not too bad," he said.

"No. It will be gone in a couple of days."

"I wish I could say the same. The guy who dropped me *knew* what he was doing."

"You hurting?"

"Some," he said. "I pissed a little blood this morning."

"You should have a doctor check it out."

"I'm on medication right now."

"I know," I said. "I can smell it on you."

I shook his hand and said good-bye to Lee. Lloyd kept his eyes on the television, his mouth piped and jaw ajut, like an emaciated Douglas MacArthur.

I spent the remainder of the afternoon running between offices downtown, standing in lines, being fingerprinted, and filling out forms in triplicate. By the time I was finished my hangover was gone, and the previous night's activities had become a romantic memory. Which is to say that I was ready, once again, for a drink.

But first I had to make another stop, to see a guy McGinnes and I knew, a whale of a man who went by the alliterative name of Fat Fred.

NINE

Souvenir City was a small shop on Ninth between F and G run by Fat Fred, whose real name was the somehow even less appealing Fred Bort. Fat Fred had worked with McGinnes and me on the Avenue for a brief period in the late seventies, until the company got hip to the fact that he was fencing goods stolen from the store. He stayed in the fencing business, opening this store as a thinly veiled front. McGinnes called the place, which sold an indescribably garish inventory of useless trinkets, "Souvenir Shitty."

Fat Fred had been a fair retail salesman, though he lost more than a few deals due to his appearance and lack of hygiene. Besides hovering at an indelicate two eighty, quite a load for a man who stood five feet seven, he smelled like an ashtray and apparently showered only on a novelty basis.

Fat Fred was in the rear of the shop when I entered, a lit weed in his hand. He took a deep drag from it and blew a cloud my way as I walked up to greet him. He was still buying his clothes from the "Work 'n' Leisure" department at Sears, and his hair, which was plastered to his scalp in topographic sections, resembled black spinach.

"Nick," he said.

"Freddie. What's happening?"

"You're looking at it." He waved his club of a hand the width of the store. "Slow tourist season. Must be the murder rate thing."

"What about your other business?"

He grinned, then wheezed, "What can I do for you, Nick?"

"You still do licenses?"

"Sure. What did you have in mind?"

"I need a relatively authentic private investigator's license, D.C. style. Can you swing it?"

"Yeah, not a problem."

"How much?"

"Say, thirty."

"Say twenty, Freddie. And when you take my picture, take four extra for the real thing."

He shrugged and motioned me to the side of the shop, seating me in front of an old-fashioned box camera. "Turn your head to the left some," he said, looking down into the viewfinder. "You don't want that black eye showing up on your license. Good." He took the shots.

"How long will this take?"

"Not long. Spell the name and address you want to use on the card."

I did that on a piece of scrap paper and asked, "Will this thing pass?"

His jowls shook with his nod. "I wouldn't go flashing it in front of D.C.'s finest. But, yeah, it'll pass."

I walked around the shop. Sweatshirts and T-shirts seemed to be Freddie's big number, the cheap Indonesian variety that begin to fray before the tourists reach the Pennsylvania Turnpike. Likenesses of President Bush and his first lady were decaled on some of these, stars haloed around their heads. I noted with some pleasure that, even when it was the artist's job to make Mr. Bush seem strong, he still came off as the seventh-grade music teacher whose ass was kicked at least once a year by that particularly gene-deficient brand of student who always seemed to disappear or enter the Marines by high school.

In the center of the store were souvenir racks full of salt and paper shakers and paperweights, all in the shape of monuments. One of these racks held dinner plates and mugs, on which were enameled the "sights of Washington." I picked up a plastic sphere half-filled with water containing a tiny Washington Monument, and shook it. Snow fell over the Elipse.

Fat Fred emerged from the back room about fifteen minutes later with my card. It certainly looked official enough, though I had no basis for judgment. What in the hell did I think I was doing?

"I laminated it," he said proudly.

"You do good work," I said, and gave him the original thirty he had asked for.

"Why do you always gotta fuck with me, Nicky?

" 'Cause I like you, Freddie." I slapped his arm, which should have been on a meathook. "Thanks, buddy." I put the ID and extra photos in my wallet and left the store.

Two doors down was a combination lunch counter, bar, and arts house called the District Seen, where one could get a decent sandwich, listen to some music, and hear anything from readings by modernist beat poets to *a capella* new wave. Though the acts more often than not were sophomoric, there was that sad and noble quality in them of the intrepid amateur.

I picked up the latest copy of *City Paper* at the door and had a seat at the black and white tiled bar. At this early hour the bartender was the only employee in the front of the house, though there was the sound of prep work coming from the kitchen.

The bartender was a burly, balding, redheaded guy I had seen working in several clubs through the years. Gregory Isaacs, the "cool ruler" of reggae, was pouring through the Advents on either side of the bar.

I ordered a club, a cup of split pea soup, and coffee, and opened the tabloid to the arts section, skipping over the paper's customarily unfocused cover story. Joel E. Siegel, the most intelligent film critic in town, who made waste of the *Post*'s hapless duo (the gushing Hal Hinson and the unreadable Rita Kempley), had reviewed a couple of interesting documentaries. And Mark Jenkins, who on the plus side was a Smiths fetishist but on the minus side a Costello basher, had done an enthusiastic review of the neo-psychedelic Stone Roses.

After my dinner I ordered a dark beer and drank it as I finished reading the paper. I nursed a second as the place began to fill up and become noisier. When the bartender switched over to Pere Ubu on the stereo, I settled up and left.

It was dark now, between eight and nine o'clock. Working Washington was safe in the suburbs, leaving this part of the city virtually deserted. The storefronts, mostly shoe shops displaying the latest Bama-ish styles, were closed and secured with drawn iron gates. This section of town had its own smell in the early evening, of dried spit and alley dirt in the wedges of cracked concrete.

Pigeons fluttered as I turned right off of Ninth and moved down F. Some punks were hanging outside the entrance of the Snake Pit, smoking cigarettes and looking patently sullen. The all-black dress and hairstyles had changed very little in ten years.

I maneuvered around them and entered a long hallway postered with announcements of shows around town. As I neared the doorway, humid, smoky air rushed towards me, along with the sound of a chainsaw electric guitar.

I paid for a ticket through a box office window and handed it to the doorman, a slight kid in black jeans and an army green T-shirt, with a bleached blond brush cut on his pale head. He ripped the ticket in half and returned the stub with his soft hand.

The main room was half-filled with young people dressed in dark clothing, blending in against the black walls of the club. They were an odd mixture here of artsy college students, punks, black hipsters, geeks, and even a few rednecks who dug the music. An overweight computer-science major who haunted used record stores could fit in just as well at the Snake Pit as the latest trendy.

I moved past the main bar and stage and headed for the back bar, which was located at the end of another long hall. The DJ was blasting through a set of garage rock, segueing from early Slickee Boys to the Hoodoo Gurus. The volume lessened as I entered the back room.

I removed my jacket, hung it on a peg, and took a seat on the wall stool at the far end of the bar. Cocktail napkins were fanned out on the bar like white flowers blooming randomly from the dark wood.

Bartenders at the Snake Pit generally had the look of the undead. The one who placed a coaster in front of me had thin, druggy arms and was sloppily dressed in purple on black. Her face was bloodless and set off by eggplant-colored lipstick, though not entirely unpleasant.

"What can I get you?"

"A Bud bottle," I said, "and an Old Grand-Dad. Neat."

She hooked me up with a quick and professionally deft handling of the bottles. I thanked her and suggested she pour one for herself. She opted for Johnnie Walker Black in a rocks glass. I like scotch drinkers, when it's a woman doing the drinking. We tapped glasses and drank slowly.

"Who's playing tonight?" I asked.

"The Primitives," she said coolly. "Blondie via the Jesus and Mary Chain."

"A lot of feedback?"

"Yeah," she said. "Feedback and angst."

"Who's opening?"

"The Deaf Pedestrians. *Pedestrian* describes 'em."

"I'm looking for the little brother of a friend," I said, pulling out the shaven picture of Broda and sliding it in front of her. "I think he hangs out with some of the skins here."

"Fuckin' skinheads," she said viciously and looked at the photo. "I don't know him. But you might ask those assholes." She pointed out the entranceway towards the stairwell, where two head-shaven boys were leaning against the wall smoking cigarettes. "They're always here."

"Maybe later. How about another shot?"

She poured one for me and moved down the bar to take an order. The place was getting denser and smokier. I had a warm, even buzz.

The DJ was playing something hard and fast. The bartender sauntered in my direction and leaned in towards me, her forearms resting on the mahogany bar. There was color now on her cheeks.

"Anything else?"

"No, thanks. Cash me out." She pulled my tab from between two rum bottles on the call rack.

"Nine dollars," she said.

I put thirteen down on the bar. "See you later, hear?"

"Sure. I've seen you around."

I grabbed my jacket off the wall and walked out into the hallway. The two skins were heading down into the narrow stairwell that led to the john and cloakroom. They were of average size and both wearing black jeans and black, steel-toed workboots. One had on a flannel shirt, the other a black T-shirt. I followed them into the stairwell. The DJ had kicked in Sonic Youth's "Teenage Riot."

I said, "Hey," and they turned, four steps down, to face me.

They looked smaller and more vulnerable now. The one wearing the flannel shirt had eyelids at half-mast and his mouth hung open. The other had pale, girlishly veinless arms that hung like strings from the sleeves of his T-shirt. Both were trying to look tough, but I recognized them for what they were—pussies with crewcuts.

"You guys mind if I ask you a couple of questions?" I used the friendliest tone I could stomach.

"You a cop?" the one closest to me asked, but before I could answer his friend spoke up.

"He's no cop. Cops don't get black eyes." They both laughed drunkenly.

"I'm looking for my little brother," I said, pulling a twenty from my pocket along with the photo of Jimmy Broda. I kept the bill and handed them the picture. They stared at it rather stupidly for a long while.

"What's this dude's name?" flannel-shirt finally asked.

"Jimmy Broda."

"The picture's not too good," he said, quickly adding, "but I seen him around."

"Recently?" He looked at his friend, then at the jacket pocket where I had replaced the Jackson.

"All this talk is making me thirsty, big brother."

"You're covered on the twenty," I said. "Go ahead."

"I think I know who the dude is, if it's the one I'm thinking of. He runs with a guy they call Redman, you know, this redheaded motherfucker."

"Yeah?"

"And sometimes I seen him with this good lookin' older bitch. But it might be that she hangs out with Redman."

"This Redman got a real name, or the girl?"

"I don't know his name or hers," he said, disappointed but still hungry.

"When's the last time you saw him or his friends?"

"It's been awhile. I don't know, a few weeks maybe."

"Would they hang out anywhere else?"

"No, man," he said, "this is it now. This place is happenin', even though there's too many niggers come in here for my taste." His friend chuckled uneasily.

"Who else would know more?" I asked, revealing the twenty once again.

"We know *all* the skins, man," he said defensively. "You know that graffiti—you can see it on the Red Line near Fort Totten—says 'United Skinheads' over an American flag?" I nodded that I had seen it. "*I* did that."

"That's a nice piece of work. But there must be somebody else I can talk to who might know a little more."

He looked at his friend, then at me. "It will cost you another ten."

I pulled out the bill and slapped it together with the twenty.

"There's a rowhouse on Ninth and G, Southeast, got a red awning over the porch. The dude you want to talk to is John Heidel. But don't tell him we turned you on to the address." I handed him the thirty, and he eyed me suspiciously. "You sure you're no cop?"

I looked him over and said, "If I was, I would have called for backup by now."

"Damn straight," he said, missing the irony and walking, with his friend, down the stairs to hang out in the cloakroom.

I followed them down but veered off into the men's toilet. I stood at the urinal and drained, reading the names of bands and slogans etched into the black walls.

Below an anarchy symbol, two words were dug deep into the heart of the plaster: "No Future." I buttoned up my fly and flushed the head.

TEN

The red-awninged rowhouse stood in the middle of G between Ninth and Tenth, just as flannel-shirt had said. I parked in front of it the next morning somewhere around eleven o'clock.

Real estate salesmen pitched this area as Capitol Hill, and it was, though a far cry from the connotations that such a prestigious name would suggest. There were residential homes here, struggling group houses, neighborhood bars and shops, and a few marginally upscale businesses that quickly came and went.

I opened a chain-link gate and stepped along a concrete walkway split and overgrown with weeds and clover. A mongrel shepherd in the adjacent yard was on the end of its tether, up on its hind legs and growling viciously.

I stepped up onto a small porch with brown brick columns and knocked on a thin wooden door. A dirgelike bass insinuated itself through the walls of the house.

I knocked again. The door swung open and a girl stood before me. She was taller than me, even allowing for the fact that she was up a step. Her legs were long and her hips immaturely narrow. Through the sides of her green tank top I could see the curvature and bottom-fold of narrow, sausagelike breasts. Her tired eyes bore the mark of experience, though her childlike bone structure put her at around seventeen.

"I'm looking for John," I said. "Is he in?"

Leaning in the doorframe, she looked behind her, then back at me, and said, "Which one?"

"I'm sorry. I didn't know there was more than one. John Heidel."

"There's a lot of people live here, man, on and off. Johnny's in his room, upstairs and through the second door on the left."

I thanked her, but she was already walking away. The sound of several loud male voices came from the kitchen, where she was heading. From the mismatched, worn furniture in the living room to the requisite black and white television with foil antenna, the place resembled a student group house without the books.

I grabbed the loose wooden banister and took the steps slowly. At the top of the stairs I passed a room where a kid sat in the window box smoking. He didn't return my nod.

My knock on the second door was hard enough to open it halfway. A young man lay on his back on an unmade bed, reading a paperback. Smoke rose slowly from behind the book. An emotionless voice told me to "come on in."

He lowered the book and, squinting from the smoke of the cigarette that was planted in his mouth, cocked one eyebrow as he sized me up. He sat up on the edge of the bed and butted the weed in an overflowing ashtray set next to a radial alarm clock. From the looks of his wrinkled jeans, this would be the first time he had risen from the bed that day. His shirtless upper body was thick and naturally strong, without the artificial bulk obtained from weight machines, and there was a crescent scar half-framing his right eye.

"What is it?" he asked, slowly rubbing the top of his shaven head.

"John Heidel?"

"Yeah."

"I'm Kevin DeGarcey from the *Washington Times.*" I flashed him a card imprinted with the *Times* logo, not giving him time to read DeGarcey's title of advertising account executive. I extended my hand and received a grip weak with suspicion.

"What do you want?"

"The *Post* ran an article several weeks ago about the local skinhead movement that in my opinion was very negative. My editor feels they only captured, or chose to print, one side of the story."

"I would agree with *that.*"

"He's assigned me a different type of story on you guys. I've been working on it awhile now, doing interviews, talking to different people."

"Why did you want to talk to *me?*"

"I heard you knew most of your peers on the local level."

"From who?"

"Two younger guys I met at the Snake Pit last night. I didn't get their names. One of them wore a flannel shirt, the other one was a little guy. They looked like they could have been in your group, but I have to admit, they were very eager to sell information."

"They're 'wanna-bes,' not skins. I'll have to speak to those two about giving out my name."

"What are you reading?" He seemed to warm to the question as I pulled a wooden chair next to his bed and had a seat. I took a pad and pen from my jacket.

The Territorial Imperative," he said, "by Robert Ardrey." He spelled the author's name for me as I wrote.

"Any good?"

"Interesting ideas. The man doesn't judge violence. Violence just *is.*"

"What do you think about violence?"

"In what sense?" He smirked. He was probably smarter than the majority of his friends, but it was a relative intelligence. There was something stupid in his dead eyes and slack jaw.

"Skinhead violence, specifically," I said. "The *Post* said your group beats up gays, the occasional black who gets in your way. Is that true?"

"You and me, they call us human, but we're really animals, right? And even though we're animals, we're supposed to suppress our natural instincts to preserve and protect our turf." He paused to rub his head. "It just boggles my mind that there isn't *more* violence out there, that people aren't wasting each other wholesale in the street. I'm saying that since violence is a natural instinct, it's amazing that there's so little of it happening."

"Why gays, though? Why blacks? The *Post* article said that the recent P Street Beach beatings were done by the skinheads."

"Look," he said, leaning in, "here's the thing. We don't care what people do in their own homes. We really don't. But take that part of the park—P Street Beach—that's *my* park too. I should be able to walk through it without stumbling on some freak faggots. So they get stomped once or twice, maybe they'll take that shit back indoors where it belongs. As for the blacks, we send them a message every so often to remind them that we live here too. Fuckin' bootheads act like they own this town."

"Do you personally approve of these acts?"

"I'm not even saying we do the violence ourselves. But it *is* understandable. It's a matter of protecting your turf."

"I interviewed a guy they call Redman," I said abruptly.

"You mean Eddie Shultz?" Heidel looked surprised and a little sad.

"That's him." I wrote the name. "He made some interesting connections between the music you guys listen to and the violence. Any thoughts on that?"

"Yeah. My thought is that anything Eddie Shultz says is bullshit." He looked at me sourly and flipped open the top of his hardpack, put a smoke in his mouth and lit it, then absently threw the blown-out match onto the nightstand.

"I thought he was one of you guys."

"He ain't shit. Eddie was okay once, but he fucked up."

"How so?"

He looked at me warily. "You writing a story about Eddie or the skins?"

"The skins. But that's the point. If I find out why someone falls out of favor in your group, I find out more about the group itself. Maybe the article will be more sympathetic."

He dragged hard on his cigarette. "Eddie started hanging with the wrong kinds of people. I mean, we just don't get into the drug thing here, as an unwritten rule. We do consume some alcohol, though." He smiled for the first time, revealing chipped and dirty teeth.

"The times I interviewed him, he was with a younger boy and a good-looking woman."

His smile faded. "That's what I'm talking about, man. He started running with this kid, and they were using a shitload of coke, and flashing it around like there was quantity. Then the chick starts hanging out with the two of them, and Eddie falls for her. I told him that the bitch had no interest in him or his friend, she just wanted to be around the drugs. It was so obvious."

"What was her name again?"

"I have no clue, man. Never wanted to know."

"The boy?"

"Uh-uh."

I was losing him. "You don't know where I can reach any of them now, verify my facts?"

He snorted. "You ain't verifyin' nuthin' with Eddie. He left town with those two a couple of weeks ago. Headed south is what he said, whatever that means. I don't know where he is."

I didn't bother to try and shake his hand. Heidel was staring out the window as I left, smoking and squinting, as if straining to see his friend Redman walking down the street.

At the foot of the stairs I noticed the girl who had answered the door, sitting with her legs draped over the arm of a shredded easy chair. She was watching a game show on TV while listening to Joy Division on the stereo. I walked in and turned the amplifier's volume knob down. She looked over at me, only mildly bothered.

"Hi," I said.

"Hey."

"John said it was all right to ask you a couple of questions."

"Who are you?"

"I'm a reporter." An image of Jimmy Olsen came to mind.

"What do you want to know?"

"I need to talk to Eddie Shultz and the girl he was going around with."

"Eddie left town," she said, looking out the corner of her eye at the interchangeable horse-toothed host on the television screen.

"I know. You wouldn't happen to know where they went?"

"Uh-uh. He and Kimmy just split, with that Jimmy kid. A couple of weeks ago."

"Kimmy."

"Yeah. Kim Lazarus."

"She a local?"

"I don't know," she said, anxiously shifting her gaze to the screen. "Why don't you ask Redman's old lady. They live in Prince Georges County someplace. I was there with him once."

"You remember the address? The street?"

"Something 'wood.' Edgewood, Ledgewood, some shit like that."

"Thanks," I said. "Eddie and John were pretty tight, weren't they?"

"They were, until this Kimmy chick came around."

I readjusted the volume on the stereo, walked to the front door, and stepped out. I breathed cool, fresh air as the funereal bass trailed behind.

ELEVEN

Marsha picked up and responded in her usual cheerful manner when I phoned her from my apartment.

"Nutty Nathan's," she nearly sang.

"Hi, Marsha. It's Nick."

"Nicky! Where are you?"

"Home. Taking the day off."

"That's nice," she said.

"Marsha, I need a favor."

"Sure, Nicky."

"Go to service dispatch and borrow their *Hanes Directory,* you know, the 'crisscross.' "

"Okay."

"Now write down this name." I spelled *Shultz* for her. "In P.G. County, locate all the Shultzes for me who live on streets that end with the word *wood*, like Dogwood Terrace or Edgewood Road. Know what I mean?"

"Yeah?"

"That's it."

"Okay, Nicky. Want me to call you back?"

"Please. You've got my number?"

"Yup. I won't be long," she promised, and hung up.

I pulled the metro phone books from the hall closet and laid them out on my desk. There were about forty total listings for the last name of Lazarus, and I began calling.

It was early afternoon and many people weren't in, though I left messages on their machines. Those that were home generally muttered the "wrong number" response and hung up quickly; a couple of elderly folks were eager to talk, but these too were not the homes of Kim Lazarus.

Two hours later I dialed the final listing and received the same treatment. I called Marsha back.

"It's Nick, Marsha."

"I've been trying to get you for over an hour," she scolded.

"What have you got?"

"I found a Joseph Shultz on Briarwood Terrace in Oxen Hill," she said. "And there's a Thomas and Maureen Shultz on Inglewood in Riverdale."

"Give me both phone numbers and the addresses." She read me the information. "I owe you lunch, Marsha. Thanks a million."

When I dialed the second number and asked for Eddie, Maureen Shultz told me he wasn't in. I identified myself as DeGarcey from the *Washington Times* and explained the sympathetic portrait of Eddie and his friends that I was struggling to finish on deadline. Could I come over to the Shultz residence to get those last few details? Sure, she said.

I drove north over the district line into Maryland, then made a right on 410, which wound, primarily as East–West Highway, through Takoma Park, Chillum, Hyattsville, and Riverdale. Inglewood was on my detail map. It was a street of Cape Cods with large, treeless front lawns. A row of oaks ran down the government strip the length of the street.

Judging by the number of nonrecreational pickups parked in the driveways, this part of the neighborhood was largely blue-collar and middle-income at best. But the properties and houses had been functionally kept with that quiet pride peculiar to the working class.

I knocked on the door of the address Marsha had given me and a heavy-hipped woman answered. Her worn housedress and graying, closely cropped hair made her appear older than I would have guessed from her phone voice. She let me into a house that was visibly free of dirt but smelled of dogs. One of them, an old setter, moved his eyes and nothing else as I passed with his mistress into the kitchen.

I sat at a table that had a marbleized formica top. She made instant coffee while I looked around the room. The appliances were avocado green and the refrigerator had no kickplate.

Maureen Shultz was an outwardly pleasant woman with whom it was fairly comfortable to sit and share coffee and conversation. But she seemed to get more anxious as we talked. Soon it became clear that she was interviewing *me,* and had apparently agreed to my visit for that purpose. She was worried about her son.

"When was the last time *you* saw him?" she asked.

"About two weeks ago," I lied. "He was with an attractive woman and a younger boy."

"An attractive woman," she sniffed. "I suppose she was, on the outside." She took a sip of coffee, visibly embarrassed by her display of judgment or jealousy. "I'm sorry. I really didn't know much about her. It was just a feeling I had."

"I got the feeling they didn't belong together, if you don't mind my saying so."

"He brought her over here once. Eddie's friends were always welcome here. But you're right. She might not have come from money, but she had done some high living. Eddie hadn't, not yet."

"What gave you that impression?"

"Small things," she said, sipping her coffee. "She was older, for one, and the etiquette she used at dinner. She commented on my china, which isn't actually very good at all. But the point is, Eddie wouldn't know china from paper plates."

"What about her background?"

"She never said, exactly. Neither did Eddie. She had a slight Southern accent that became more pronounced as her guard began to drop, if you know what I mean."

"Yes."

"She mentioned that she had a little college and worked in stores and restaurants before she moved up here. She said that she liked to go to the seashore back home."

All of that information was meaningless. Kim Lazarus could have been from any coastal state south of the Mason–Dixon line.

"I talked to John Heidel today," I said, dropping a name that perked her up a bit. "I got the impression he might know more about the girl, but he wasn't eager to talk."

"He knew the girl too," she said vaguely, straightening her posture and wringing her hands.

"What do you think about the crowd Eddie and John were in, the group they call the skinheads?"

"Eddie and John went to high school together. Grades wise, they weren't the brightest boys. I know they drank beer, raced their cars a little too fast. But that's all a part of growing up. What they do now, that's a phase too."

"Mrs. Shultz, you must be aware of the allegations against their group. The violence against minorities."

"Yes," she said bitterly. "I've read the articles. And I'm not blind to the ways of my son. His father put that hatred into him. He's an insecure man, and it passes from the father to the son. But Eddie wouldn't beat up anybody if there wasn't a reason."

"I'd like to explore his side of things. But I need to talk to him again to do it."

"How can I help you?"

"You've known John Heidel for quite a long time. Give him a call and see if he has any idea where they were headed. I'll be at this number." I handed her the number to my answering machine that I had written on my pad.

She began walking me to the front door but stopped in the living room to take a framed photograph off the fireplace mantel. She faced it towards me.

"That's Eddie's high school picture. He looks an awful lot better with all that hair. It's funny," she chuckled. "At the time, I gave him hell about it being too long."

I could see why they called the boy Redman. His hair, long in the picture in some sort of shag, was bright orange, as were his eyebrows and the hopelessly weak mustache above his thin lips. Eddie's eyes were narrow and rather cruel, a trait I found completely absent in his mother.

"Talk to John and give me a call later," I said.

She nodded. I hurried to the door and turned to say good-bye. I watched her replace Eddie's picture on the mantel, feeling vaguely intrusive as I saw her lightly run her finger around the edge of the frame.

Sitting in my car in front of the Shultz residence, I found myself watching a young mother a few houses down who was watching her child crawl upon a white blanket that had been spread upon the lawn.

I studied them until the mother noticed me and appeared to become uncomfortable at my presence. I cranked the ignition, and the engine turned over with some reluctance. Then I pulled off Inglewood and headed west on the highway, towards the office headquarters of Nutty Nathan's.

TWELVE

The Nutty Nathan's warehouse was adjacent to the offices and occupied about eighteen thousand square feet of the entire building. Since the bruise below my eye was still healing, I avoided the office altogether and went in through the service entrance.

It was late Friday afternoon, and the women in service dispatch sat in a semicircle discussing the weekend. I walked by them quickly and with my head down, but not quickly enough to escape a whistle and then some laughter.

I took some concrete steps up to a locked door that opened onto the warehouse loft. Upon my promotion to upper-level management I had been given a skeleton key that fit all the locks in the building, necessitated by my frequent trips to the warehouse to check inventory while writing the copy ("Only 10 to Sell!") of the ads. I used the key in this lock as I turned the knob and stepped into the loft.

The warehousemen called this area "the zoo" because of the cages along its wall that contained the heistable goods: small appliances, boom boxes, tapes, accessories, and anything else that could be stashed underneath an employee's jacket. A large sign in red lettering hung on the wall near the first cage, and read, "Lock all cages. Don't tempt an honest man."

One could look down from the loft and survey the entire warehouse. It was arranged in five long parallel rows that ran the length of the building. Between each row was twelve feet of space, an allowance for the swing of forklifts that would then have a straight shot to the truck bays located directly beneath the loft.

There was a twenty-five foot drop to the warehouse floor. A three-tiered railing ran along the edge of the loft, broken only at one point to allow entrance to a caged lift that was used to move stock from one level to the next.

This time of year, as Fisher had overemphasized, the "barn" was full to capacity because of the annual fourth quarter load-in. Boxes rose from the floor and approached the legal limit, which was gauged by their proximity to the ceiling sprinklers. In several spots one could step off the loft directly onto the top of a row of stock.

I pulled open the metal gate, entered the lift, and hit the lower button on an electrical box hung over the railing. The crate lowered me in spasms.

I stepped out and walked past the bays where returning drivers were checking their manifests with the assistant warehouse managers. It was payday. Several of the drivers looked as if they had cashed their checks earlier at the liquor store. I could hear the deliberate farting of young warehousemen, and, after that, commentary and laughter as to the degree of looseness of their respective sphincters. By the time I reached Dane's office this had degenerated into a discussion of an activity called "jamming," which involved gerbils and then other progressively larger mammals.

The glass-enclosed office of Joe Dane, the warehouse manager, bordered the last bay. I looked in and saw the delivery manager talking on the phone. I rapped on the glass. She looked up, smiled, gave me a shrug and an exasperated look, and waved me in.

Their office smelled like cigarettes and fast food. Dane was an unashamed slob, but his female coworkers had tried to humanize the place with remnant carpeting, Redskins pennants, and stick-up Garfield cats, one of the strangest fads to come to D.C. since the Carl Lewis haircut.

Jerry Chase hung up the phone, mouthed the word *asshole,* slumped back in her chair, and dragged on her cigarette. The cherry from the last one was still smoking in the ashtray. I perched on the edge of her desk and butted it out.

"A good one?" I asked, looking at the phone.

"Oh, yeah," she said, the smoke breaking around her mouth as she talked. "We miss a delivery, and the customer starts about how he makes two hundred dollars an hour, he can't afford to sit another afternoon off and wait for a delivery. I wonder if he knows how many important people like him I talk to every day. I'm so tired of hearing that. If a guy really makes that kind of dough, then he wouldn't get hurt missing a couple hours of work. To top it off, these problems always come up Friday afternoon payday." She chin-nodded through the glass towards the drivers. "You think I can get any of these guys to go back out on a delivery now? They've been half in the bag since this morning."

"Well, the day's almost over," I said, hoping to slow her down, though admittedly she had the worst job in the company.

"And people want to know why I drink," she said, giving me a knowing look. "So what brings you down to the underworld?"

"I'm looking for Dane."

"He got wise and split early. The 'my baby's sick' routine."

"Yeah, well. Maybe his kid really is sick."

"Maybe," she said, tossing her cigarette in the ashtray. I crushed it for her.

"Why don't you ever put those things out?"

"That's the man's job," she said, and shook her hair in what she thought was a sexy manner. She had a P.G. County haircut that had gone out of style at about the time that "Charley's Angels" was entering its third season.

"Take care, Jerry." I walked out and closed the door behind me.

The warehouse had the same musty odor as the stockroom, though its rows were perfectly aligned, the floors relatively dirt-free. Except for the true summer months, it always seemed cold here, and the combination of naked steel girders, unfinished concrete, and bleak lighting heightened that chill. The young men in here worked a hard day every day, beneath insulated flannel shirts and gloves. Their occasional laughter almost always came at the expense of each other, and the turnover was tremendous.

I walked down the center aisle, dwarfed by the cardboard walls at my sides. A kid I knew gave me a short horn-blast of recognition as he motored by on his forklift.

The barn *was* loaded. I took note of what we were heavy on as I walked. I would have to start dumping some of these goods, or, more likely, advertise the bait that would lead into the overstocks.

At the end of the aisle I turned left to the far corner of the warehouse, the section entirely occupied by videocassette recorders. I noticed the Kotekna VCRs that Rosen had purchased at the electronics show. Virtually none of them had moved. I made a mental note to remind Fisher that these "dogs" would have to be shipped out to the floors.

Aware of someone behind me, I turned to face two warehousemen I had never met. They were standing four feet apart and looking at me with solid stares. I nodded but got no response.

The man on the left was leaning on a pushbroom. He was of average height, with a dark, bony face and a careless goatee. His nose was narrow and flat, his eyes almost Oriental in shape. A red knit cap was cocked on his head, filled high with dreadlocks. He wore a vest over a thermal shirt, and had the loose-limbed stance of a fighter.

His partner was a black albino with mustard skin and eyes the color of a bad scrape. There was one small braid coming from the back of his shaved head. He wore striped baggies, a faded denim shirt, and leather gloves. He was so tall that his posture and bone structure suggested deformity. There was a dead, soulless look in their eyes that I had seen increasingly on the faces of men in Washington's streets as the eighties dragged murderously on.

I walked towards them. When it was clear that they weren't going to move, I walked around them. I felt an inexplicable humiliation, like a child who later regrets walking away from a certain ass-kicking at the hands of the schoolyard bully.

I heard them chuckle behind me, and I turned. The dark one with the pushbroom blew me a kiss. Then they both laughed.

I walked out of the warehouse. In the parking lot I noticed that my fists were balled and shoved deeply in my pockets. Climbing behind the wheel of my car, I felt weak and very small.

Joe Dane lived in old Silver Spring, on a street where the houses were built very close to the curb and had large, open porches and deep backyards. I parked my heap in front of his place and was up on his porch in six short steps.

I knocked on the door, behind which I could hear children laughing and playing and falling harmlessly to the floor. After that came a woman's voice, raised halfheartedly to attempt sternness, then footsteps.

The door opened and Sarah Dane stood in the frame, wiping her hands dry with a dishrag. The lines around her eyes deepened as she smiled up at my face.

"Hi, Nick."

"Sarah." I leaned in and kissed her on the cheek.

Her baggy pants were frumpy and her sweatshirt featured a circular medallion of vomit centered between her breasts. Four kids and the raising of them had widened her hips and prematurely aged her face. But she had the relaxed beauty of contentment.

"Is Joe around?" I asked.

"He's in the backyard," she said, tugging gently on my jacket and pulling me through the doorway. "Come on in."

I followed her into the living room as she made a path through the toys scattered on the throwrug. The arms of the sofa had been shredded by cats. As we walked, she touched the heads of two children orbiting her legs.

We moved into the warm kitchen where a cat was haunched down, its face buried in a small yellow dish. Water boiled in a tall pot on the gas stove. Next to it sat an open box of pasta.

I looked through the screen of the dark back porch. Joe Dane was walking slowly through their garden, his hands in his pockets. Sarah folded her arms and leaned against the refrigerator.

"You look good, Nick," she said, focusing on the fading purplish area below my eye. "But I see you're not really staying out of trouble."

"I don't go looking for it," I said. "You look good too, Sarah."

"Don't bullshit me, Nicky. I look like hell." She grabbed some hair off her face and wound it behind an ear. It was fairly useless to tell her that I was being sincere.

"What have you all been up to?" I asked.

A small towhead, wearing fatigues and carrying a plastic machine gun, ran by. I tapped him on the shoulder. He ran back, socked me on the knee, and disappeared into another room.

"You're looking at it," she said, without a trace of regret.

"You're awfully lucky to have all this."

"All this," she laughed. "The funny thing is, I do feel lucky. This is what I want."

"How about him?" I asked, jerking my head in the direction of the backyard.

"Joe's the worrier of the family. Of course, he's out in the world every day, he sees other people with more than we've got. More money, that is. And this town can influence you, make you feel like if you're not wearing the four hundred dollar suit or driving the right import, you're lower than dirt. I'm insulated from all that crap, here with the kids." She looked me over. "How about you? You seeing anyone?"

"Not really."

"Talk to Karen?"

"No." The four of us had spent many evenings together in the early days of our marriages.

"Here," she said, handing me two cans of beer from the refrigerator. "Go talk to him. He could use it."

"Thanks, Sarah."

I stepped out onto the porch, which creaked beneath my feet, and pushed open the screen door. As I walked across the yard, I noticed the kids' Big Wheels had worn a semicircular track in the grass.

Joe Dane was a broad, bearlike guy whose gut had begun to creep unapologetically over his belt. Though he was only a few years my senior, his graying beard made him look much older. There was a look nearing relief on his creased face as I approached.

We had befriended each other early on at Nathan's. He came to me for advice on record purchases, and I to him on the latest films to catch. My opinions on music were solely based on taste, but his movie knowledge came from advanced studies and a Master's in Film Theory, a degree he had earned but never used professionally.

"Nick," he said tiredly. "What brings you out here to 'Pottersville'?"

I let that slide and said, "Just wanted to say hi. Your kid sick?"

"No, I just bugged out a little early."

I cracked both beers and handed him one. He winked and had a long swallow. I pulled on his shirtsleeve and brought him out of the garden to two ripped beach chairs that faced back towards the house. A calico cat slunk across the yard, brushed my shins, and settled into a ball beneath my chair.

"So, what's happening in music?" he asked, though he appeared uninterested. "I've been out of touch."

"You haven't missed much. This year it's the neo-folk movement, though there's nothing 'neo' about it. Tracy Chapman comes out doing the same shit Joan Armatrading was doing ten years ago, only Tracy's younger and has a funkier haircut, and she walks away with all the press and the awards."

"It's the same in film," he said. "There's very little in the way of originality right now. The film schools are cranking out mimics and technicians, but there isn't any soul."

"What about your boys, Scorsese and De Palma?"

"Scorsese's still a true visionary, a genius. *Good Fellas,* man, that was a piece of work. The first time I ever *saw* a cocaine high, visualized, up on the screen. And the violence was real, not stylized. Real. But De Palma?" Dane snorted and dismissed the director with a wave of his hand. "De Palma used to have that crippling Hitchcock fixation, and the critics hated him. I got a kick out of him, though. I mean, I had the sense, when I was watching his films, that I was witnessing the work of a madman. Then he does *The Untouchables,* and the critics love it. But it was pretty much just a straight narrative thing, don't you think? And the centerpiece of the film, the shootout at the train station—he managed to rip off both Eisenstein's Odessa steps sequence and himself at the same time."

"Rip-off?" I said. "You used to call that 'homage.' "

"Whatever. De Palma used that one hundred percent slow motion sequence once before, in *The Fury,* a much better film in my opinion, what with its theme of patricide and its dark humor. Godard called that the most honest use of slow motion he had ever seen on film." Dane rubbed his forehead and swallowed more beer, then said, "It's all bullshit anyway."

With that remark we sat in silence for several minutes. The calico emerged from under my seat, and with a low crawl slowly crept up on a group of sparrows that had lit in the middle of the yard. I watched as they scattered and flew away.

"I heard Jimmy Broda got it while I was on vacation," I said, a careful indifference in my voice.

"Yeah," he said, closing his eyes as he killed his beer.

"It surprised me, the fact that he was a gonif."

"Well, he was."

"You have to fire him yourself?"

"Yeah."

"You got a soft heart, Joe."

"What the hell are you talking about?"

I finished my beer and crushed the can. "I talked to our lady in personnel. She has his reason for termination down as 'job abandonment.' You told her that, so theft wouldn't be on the kid's record. Am I right?"

His face tightened. "Sure. He was clean, up until the time he tried to boost that box. No reason to have that on his permanent record."

A strong, stocky little boy ran from the side of the house and slowed to a walk as he neared us. He had his old man's pug nose and his mother's round eyes. Dane turned him around and locked him gently between his knees. He rubbed the kid's shoulders with his big hands.

"There's one thing I can't figure out about that whole deal," I said. "The kid's grandfather phoned me after the boy was fired. So I went to their apartment, and the grandfather shows me this VCR that the kid had bought for him."

"So?"

"So why would a kid lift an eighty dollar piece, then turn around and pay for a VCR worth two bills? Why not steal the more expensive item, if you're going to steal?"

Dane brought his child up into his arms and hugged him rather roughly. His eyes were closed and I wondered if he'd heard me. Then he opened his eyes and spoke.

"You're talking about a nineteen-year-old kid, Nick, and you expect him to do something rational." He put down his child. "You think too damn much."

"And you brood too much," I said, rising from my chair. "Why don't you go on inside. I've got to get going."

"Don't tell me not to brood. The hole is just getting deeper and deeper around here."

I looked at his beautiful kid, then at him, and said, "You're right. A single guy like me just can't understand your 'problems.' " I shook his hand. "So long, Joe. Thanks for the beer."

I walked across the yard and looked through the screen door. Sarah was stirring the pot of pasta, the child in the fatigues sitting at her feet. I went around the side of their house and to my car without saying good-bye.

When I entered my apartment, the top light was blinking on my answering machine. I pushed the bar. The tape rewound, then the unit made several noises that sounded like locks being turned.

The message began: "Mr. DeGarcey, this is Maureen Shultz. I reached John Heidel. He's not sure exactly where Eddie and his friends went, only he knows they went south. . . . He did give me some more information on the girl. Her parents are from Elizabeth City, in North Carolina . . . anyway, that's where she grew up. That's all I got out of John, I hope it helps. . . . If you talk to Eddie, tell him his father and me . . . tell him we said hello."

THIRTEEN

The day after Maureen Shultz left a message on my machine was the last Saturday I worked for Nutty Nathan's.

I woke that morning after a troubled night of sleep, a night in which I rose several times to wander around my apartment, sitting in different chairs and on my couch for long stretches at a time.

Sometime around dawn I lay awake in bed and watched my room begin to lighten, and the jagged, irregular lines of rainwater slide down my bedroom window. My cat stayed on top of the radiator, staring at the wall and listening to the rain.

At eight I got up, made coffee, and sat on the couch to read the *Post*. Two more people had been killed, execution style, in Northeast. The mayor denied allegations that he was a drug user, charged his accusers with racism, and said that all of this negative publicity was interfering with his "agenda" for running the city. There was a lengthy feature in Style on the outspoken and rather cartoonish wife of a freshman Southern senator (didn't they all come to town vowing to turn "buttoned-down" Washington on its ear?), and the main head in Sports dealt with the upcoming Skins–Giants clash, complete with the media-generated quarterback controversy.

When I was finished devouring the last section, I showered, shaved, and dressed. I put on light wool, faintly patterned teal slacks, a cream cotton oxford, a blue and beige Italian silk tie, and my twenty dollar sports jacket. I changed the litter box and filled the food and water dishes. My cat blinked at me from the radiator as I walked out the door.

The deep gray sky heightened the slowly emerging October oranges of Rock Creek Park as I drove west on Military Road. I was listening to Billy Bragg's "Talking with the Taxman about Poetry" on the box, and I turned the volume up enough to overtake the sound of my fraying wipers as they dragged themselves across the windshield.

When I entered the store and knocked the rain off my shoulders, the crew was in and standing around the front counter. They were drinking coffee from 7-Eleven go-cups and picking from a box of doughnuts iced in peculiarly unnatural colors.

McGinnes leaned against the counter with his arms crossed. Malone lounged beside him, coffee in one hand, Newport in the other. Lloyd was holding a doughnut up near his face, examining it as he chewed in slow, exaggerated chomps. Louie was spreading out newspaper ads on the counter.

"Black?" Lee asked, handing me a cup.

"You wish," I said, and took the coffee.

"All right, everybody," Louie ordered, "listen up," and we moved around him in a semicircle. McGinnes nudged me and pointed at the folds of fat at the back of Louie's head, which seemed to be fused onto his thick shoulders.

"Did you lose your neck, boss?" McGinnes asked.

"Shut up and look here, McGinnes." Louie pointed to the ads he had torn from the paper and spread on the counter. "Electric Town is running with the top-rated Sharp CD player for one nineteen. You boys know that that model has been discontinued—we don't have it and we can't get it. But they have a very sharp price on that Sharp." Louie looked back at us for recognition of his pun.

"We get it," Malone said. "You sharp, Louie."

Louie cleared his throat and turned back to the ads. McGinnes closed his eyes, dropped his chin to his chest, and began softly snoring.

"Anyway," Louie continued, ignoring McGinnes, "I called them up first thing this morning, and they don't have but one or two in stock. So now you know what to tell the consumers."

"Okay, Louie," McGinnes and Malone said robotically and in unison.

"Now," Louie said, "this one's tough," and he pointed to a Stereo Godfather's ("Our Competition Sleeps with the Fishes!") ad. "They're runnin' a VT290 for three ninety-nine. That's damn near cost. We can't meet the deal at that price. We've got to figure some way to get off of it."

"No problem," McGinnes said. "Isn't that the same model that caught fire in the customer's house last year?"

"Yeah," Malone said. "Killed a couple kids, too. Little itty-bitty motherfuckers."

"And we absolutely refuse to sell that model," McGinnes said, "until the manufacturer corrects the problem. It's a matter of principle."

"You know what the problem with that piece was," Malone said.

"What's that?" McGinnes asked.

"Fire in the wire."

"Really?" McGinnes said. "I thought it was shrinkage in the linkage."

"All right, girls," Louie said. "I don't care what you tell the customers. Just don't give the damn thing away. And we need some volume today. I figure we're about twenty-five grand down in pace for the month. On the for-real side, provided we get some traffic in here, I'd like to make up fifteen of it today."

"Shit, Louie," Malone said, "I'll write fifteen myself."

"Sellin' woof tickets, maybe," Louie said. "There's a case of beer for the top dog today. And five percent of your volume has to be in service contracts. Any questions?"

"Just one," I said. "What is the meaning of life?"

Lee laughed charitably but the others ignored me. Louie was already headed for the back room.

Lloyd said, "Did anyone see 'Mr. Belvedere' last night?"

"Too busy gyratin', Lloyd," Malone said. "How about you? You been doin' 'the nasty'?"

Lloyd gave Malone an awkward wink and raised his pipe to his mouth, hitting his teeth with the stem in a botched aristocratic gesture. Splotches of pink began to form on his pasty face.

"Well, Andre," McGinnes said happily. "I can almost taste that case of beer right now."

"Go on and taste it," Malone said, pointing to the front door as the first customer of the day walked in, "while I take this motherfucker to the bridge."

The morning was evenly paced with customers, mostly young couples with the type of money that affords residence in upper Northwest. Malone and McGinnes handled the floor nicely and closed most of their deals, as did Louie, whose strength on the floor I had forgotten.

The boys had instructed Lee to tell any customers who phoned, inquiring about small appliances, to "please ask for Lloyd" when they came in. This would keep him tied up in the low-commission department, and also keep him from blowing any major deals.

I took the overflow when the floor traffic became heavy and picked up my first customer of the day. She was an attractive woman in the last leg of her thirties, wearing colorful, gauzy clothing that attempted to conceal her shapeliness, but failed.

After my greeting she immediately pulled from her tote bag a copy of *Consumer Reports,* a legal pad on which she had neatly charted competitive prices, and a pen. She asked for the price of the top-rated VCR. I explained to her that, as is often the case, the top-rated model had been discontinued one week before the article was published; that top-rated models were usually a poor buy anyway, since manufacturers, upon receiving the rating, jacked up the cost of that particular model to their distributors, who passed it on to the retailers, who passed it on to the customers; and that the intelligent model to purchase would be one of the same brand and similar features but with a different model number and hence a lesser retail.

She wanted the model number that was printed in the magazine. Further, she thought *Consumer Reports* was *just great,* a protection against sleazy retailers who take advantage of unsuspecting customers. A smug smile appeared on her face. She looked me up and down, and her implication became clear.

I wanted to ask her why any person of even limited intelligence would choose to believe an article in a faceless magazine whose writers had looked at a product for a few days, over professionals who spent years working hands on, learning all the strengths and weaknesses of every model. I wanted to show her, through back issues, how *Consumer Reports* routinely top-rated a model one year, then turned around and gave the *identical model* a low rating the next.

I wanted to, but I didn't. This truly misanthropic breed of salesmen-baiters, who spend entire sunny weekends on retail floors with their magazines and pads, imagining themselves as crusaders in some made-up battle that is significant only to them, truly lie beyond conversion to humanity. And there is nothing more indignant than a salesman who is called a liar on those rare occasions when he is struggling heroically to tell the truth.

"I'm sorry," I said. "We simply don't have that model. It's been discontinued."

"I hardly have time," she said, "to bandy about on this matter with a *clerk.*" Then she walked quickly from the store.

Louie finished up with his customer and swaggered my way. He looked down at his shoes and scraped a fleck of dead skin off the bridge of his nose.

"That was pretty smooth, Nick. You didn't call her any names before you blew her out the door, did you, just so I know?"

"Nothing like that."

"Yeah, well. You been off the floor too long. Half the people come in here be actin' all superior—you can't let that bust on your groove. It's part of the job, man, it's what they payin' us for."

I looked at his sagging, tired face, and then at McGinnes and Malone, who were talking to each other in the Sound Explosion. The twelve-hour shifts, the standing on one's feet all day long on concrete floors and the varicose veins that resulted from that, the constant degradation from customers and management alike, the absence of praise or compliment, the cycle of work and drink and drugs and back again—it was taking its toll on all of them. The money became insignificant; ultimately the only reward was to get the deal, a small victory for its own sake that led inevitably to some suburban funeral parlor, where small groups of old men in stubbornly plaided polyesters stood in circles and said things like, "I remember the time Johnny stepped a customer off a giveaway RCA to a no-name piece of *dreck* that had a fifty dollar bill on it."

"I'm going to take a break, Louie."

"Go ahead," he said.

The rain was not abating. I crossed the Avenue and jogged south two blocks to an Amoco station, as the wet tires of slow-moving vehicles hissed past. I bought road maps of Virginia and the Carolinas in the office of the station and fitted them in the dry inside pocket of my jacket.

By the time I had run back up the block and entered the Golden Temple, I was heavy with rainwater. The matriarch of the family-owned restaurant seated me at a warm deuce in the rearmost corner. She set down a cup of tea and left the pot.

Her husband came out of the kitchen shortly thereafter, rubbing his hands with a rag. He was wearing a white uniform and had a white paper hat on his head. Straight gray hair shot out from underneath the hat in several directions. He clapped me on the shoulder. I said hello as he pulled the menu from my hands.

"You don't need," he said, and walked back to the kitchen after tossing the menu behind the register.

He returned five minutes later with steamed dumplings and some combination noodles that were mixed with thin slices of pork, shrimp, spring onions, and ginger. I ate while I studied the road maps I had spread out on the table.

Mama-san handed me the check when I was finished. I left fourteen on nine and walked to the entranceway, where I dropped a quarter into a payphone and dialed. Pence picked up on the second ring.

"This is Nick Stefanos."

"Mr. Stefanos," he said, bringing some phlegm up from his throat. "What's the word on your progress?"

I told him nearly everything I had learned in the last few days, soft-pedaling the character of Broda's companions and omitting entirely the theft and drug angles.

"Frankly," I said, "I think your grandson is just on a long joyride. He'll be back as soon as the money runs out."

"And you plan on leaving it at that?"

"Not entirely. But I believe he's safe right now." The old man picked up the doubt in my voice.

He sighed, said in a sarcastic manner, "You do what you can," and hung up.

I replaced the receiver and stood looking through the window at the rain, which was slicing at the road diagonally now, powered by a fierce wind. I pushed open the heavy door of The Golden Temple, stepped out onto the sidewalk, and let the stinging water hit my face.

FOURTEEN

The floor was dense with customers when I returned. Louie, who was hopelessly tied up with an elderly man, raised his arm over the man's head and pointed to a couple of live ones in the TV department.

I made my way towards them, ignoring a guy in a down jacket who was carrying a clipboard and demanding, for anyone who would listen, to see some "literature." McGinnes approached me in the aisle, doing his clipped goosestep and obviously in a hurry to get by. I grabbed his arm and stopped him.

"That guy over there needs some literature," I said, jerking my head in the direction of the professional stroker in the down jacket.

"I sell electronics," McGinnes said, loud enough for the customer to hear. "If he wants literature, tell him to go to the library." Then he rapped me on the dick with his fist and walked away.

The pain had subsided by the time I greeted my first customers. Louie had been on the mark by signaling me, as they bought within five minutes.

The rush was unusually long and steady, even for a Saturday, and continued unbroken for the next three hours. McGinnes and Malone did battle all afternoon. From the wide smile on Malone's face and from his energy level (at one point I saw him leap over a console to greet a customer), it was clear that he thought he was trouncing McGinnes.

But McGinnes was quietly writing some business that day. I knew he was booking from the way he rushed customers to the front counter as he closed and from the look of thought and determination on his face as he prioritized the floor. Louie basically handled the be-backs and took TOs from Lloyd. Between the two of them they probably popped five grand.

As for me, I found my rhythm. During one pitch I felt the adrenalin rush at that point where I realized I had succeeded in stepping a customer into a four-piece, high-profit, high-commission deal, though ultimately Malone's sales number would go on the ticket. And the day peaked for me when I attracted the audience of three separate couples during my pitch to one of them on a twenty-seven-inch stereo monitor set. Two of the three couples stepped up and bought. From across the room McGinnes smiled, crossed his arms, cocked his hip, and gave me a broad wink.

By four-thirty the crowd had dwindled to a few customers. My voice was nearly shot. Louie and Lloyd were waiting on the last people, while McGinnes, Malone, and I stood in the shadows of the Sound Explosion and popped three malt liquors. Lee came to us with several strands of adding machine tape in her fist. I handed her my can and she had a swig.

"So what's the total, darling?" Malone asked.

"We did twenty-five," she said. "Louie's going to be happy."

"Damn good Saturday," McGinnes said.

"What I do?" Malone said.

"Okay," Lee said. "Here it is. Louie and Lloyd wrote almost six between them. Nick wrote six, and gave you guys three each out of that."

"What I do?" Malone said again.

"You wrote ninety-two hundred, Andre. And Johnny did just over ten thousand."

"God*damn,*" Malone said, jumping up and half-spinning. "That last motherfucker was the only customer I had all day that walked on my ass. I would've had you too."

"You had a *day,* Andre," McGinnes said, and slapped Malone's hand. "You too, Nick. We all did."

Lloyd, wearing a nylon windbreaker and galoshes, waved good-bye to us, and left the store with Louie, who locked the door behind him. Minutes later he was back from Mr. Liquor and marching down the aisle with a case of Tuborg cradled in his arms.

"Here," he said, breaking the cans off the plastic rings and passing them around. "I don't care who the top man was today. *Everybody* smoked."

For the next hour we sat there, our ties loose at the collar, and killed the case of beer. Malone's cigarette smoke hovered around us as we told war stories of the day that became increasingly more dramatic with every beer. When the last empty hit the trash can, McGinnes suggested we shut down and walk up the Avenue to La Fortresse, a bar that he childishly insisted on calling "La FurPiece."

The wind and rain were against us as we crossed the street and headed up the east side of the block. Louie and Malone were ahead, trying to keep up with McGinnes as he motored up the slight incline. Lee huddled in as I turned up the collar of my jacket and put my arm around her shoulder.

La Fortresse was an alky bar with a French name and medieval decor that was owned and run by a Turk. It was one of the few bars in town that served a rocks glass full with liquor with a miniature mixer on the side. There was only one reason to come here, and that was to crawl deep into the bag.

A few old heads turned when Lee and I walked in, then returned to their drinks and the welterweight bout on the tube. We walked along the bar to the back room, which housed a piano, and where McGinnes, Malone, and Louie were already seated. The antique farm implements that hung on the wall resembled torture devices circa the Inquisition.

An easel holding an art card stood at the entranceway to the room, announcing the "Piano Interpretations of the Fabulous Buddy Floyd." Around Mr. Floyd's name were glitter drawings of a champagne bottle, bow tie, and several musical notes. We entered and sat with the others at a large corner table with a curved leatherette seat molded into the wall.

Presently a woman with an intoxicatingly crooked smile arrived to take our order. She had beautifully textured dark skin and spoke with a Caribbean accent.

Lee ordered an Absolut and tonic with a twist; I had an Old Grand-Dad, Malone took Courvoisier with a side of coke, and McGinnes asked for rail scotch with water. Louie ordered a draught.

"Make mine a double, honey," McGinnes said to the waitress as she began to walk away.

"They're all doubles," she said patiently.

"I know that, sweetheart. Just joking."

The drinks came and we toasted the day. The liquor was filled to the top of the heavy tumblers. I took a deep pull off the bourbon, one that ironed the dampness from my shirt.

McGinnes and Malone were building something with matches and straws on the table. Louie sat to my right and we listened to Lee tell us about the courses she was taking at AU and her plans for after college. Her arm was through mine, and she was refreshingly unconcerned about Louie's awareness of our relationship.

The waitress returned and we all ordered another round. McGinnes had not used any of his water to cut the scotch. Lee excused herself to go to the ladies' room.

"She's all right, you know?" Louie said, leaning in towards me as if we were conspirators.

"Yeah, I know. She's cool."

"Don't mess her up, man. When you have a young lady like that," he said, his hand cupped as if he were holding her in his palm, "you don't mess with it."

"Shit, Louie, give me more credit than that. Anyway, she already told me what was what."

"I bet she did," he said, smiling. "Her shit is more together than yours, man. And she's ten years younger."

The waitress brought our round. I took a sip and watched Louie down half his mug in one gulp.

"I'm a product of my generation, Louie. I guess it was all those Thoreau posters my junior-high hippie English teachers used to hang on the wall. 'March to a different drummer,' and all that. How many guys my age you read about, they're making a shitload of money, they decide to quit because they're not 'happy.' "

"I don't know whose product it is," Louie sad, "but you're right. Now the kids coming up, Lee's age, they *know* what they want."

"Like Ric Brandon?"

"Brandon's an asshole," he said, waving his hand. "You know what I mean. For instance, man, you don't mind my saying so, I been knowing you a long time. And you did a helluva job today. But, Nick, you fuckin' up."

"How so?"

"You sweat your ass off moving stock, you come up through the ranks in sales, you put yourself through college to get to that management position you're in, now you act like it don't mean nuthin'." He got right up in my face. "What's goin' on with you, man?"

"I don't know, Louie. I just can't convince myself anymore that what I do is important."

"Important? Come on, man, wake up. Where in the world did you get the idea that the work you do in life has to be important?" He took a swig of beer. "Let me tell you something, man. When I was young—you don't even remember the D.C. I'm talkin' about—this town was split black and white for real. I couldn't sit with you like this in a bar and have a beer. In the early sixties I went to work in the old Kann's department store downtown, and when the riots went down, they had no choice but to make me department manager."

Lee came back and sat next to me. We all had some of our drinks, and Louie continued.

"Well, you know they went out of business like everybody else down there. But I got hired as a manager at Moe's on New York Avenue. A couple of years later Moe died, his kids took over the business, and they went belly-up too. Then Nathan's put me on as assistant manager over in Arlington. It was rough for a while, but I hung with it and eventually they give me this store." He finished his draught and put it loudly on the table. "So I come a long way from the Colored Only section of this town to where I'm at. I don't just work here. I'm the *manager* of a store on Connecticut Avenue, understand what I'm sayin'? I own a house and every three years I buy a new ride. I got me a kid at Maryland, one at UDC." He paused and stared me down. "You want to know what's important."

A small man with a heavily veined nose wearing a tuxedo that fit like an afterthought walked into the room. He sat at the piano and placed his highball glass filled with straight liquor on a coaster.

"Welcome," he said into the mike, "to La Fortresse."

"It's La FurPiece," McGinnes shouted, and Lee jabbed me in the ribs.

"My name is Buddy Floyd," the man said, and began indelicately playing the piano intro to "Tie a Yellow Ribbon." With each chorus he turned his head in our direction and nodded in encouragement for us to sing along.

Mercifully, others began filing into the room, older couples over-dressed for this joint and out for their idea of a night on the town. Most of them were half-lit, and some of the women were elderly enough to be losing their hair, their pink scalps visible through their bouffants. For some reason I felt a tinge of sadness and kissed Lee on the cheek. Buddy Floyd was singing "They Call the Wind Maria."

"I'm pretty buzzed," Lee admitted, finishing her second vodka.

"So am I. You want to go?"

"Yes," she said. "Can we stay together tonight?"

"Sure. But let's go to my crib, okay?"

"Okay," she laughed. "But aren't you a little big for a crib?"

We settled up by leaving a twenty on the table. Lee kissed Louie good-bye. Malone, who was whispering something to our waitress, looked up long enough to give us a wink.

McGinnes was behind the piano, one arm around an older woman with raven black hair in the shape of a football helmet, his other hand clutching a precariously tilted tumbler of scotch. He and the others grouped around the piano were laughing and singing along loudly to the Fabulous Buddy Floyd's interpretation of "Hello, Dolly."

At the district line I stopped for a bottle of red wine, then headed towards my apartment. We sat in the car in front of my place, talking and listening to some old Van Morrison. When that was over, we went inside.

A half bottle of wine later our clothes were thrown about the living room and Lee and I were writhing all over my couch. We ended it loudly and in a sweat, with Lee inclined in the corner, the tops of her calves locked beneath my ears, the soles of her feet pointing at the ceiling.

Afterwards, I slid a pillow under her ass to catch the wetness, and watched the sweat roll onto her chest and break apart as it reached her large, brown nipples.

My apartment resembled a bombed-out laundromat. The cat had Lee's underwear on her head and was bumping into furniture. Lee pulled my face down and kissed me on the mouth for a long time.

"I had a good Saturday," she said sweetly.

"Yeah," I said. "Me too." Then I pulled a white blanket up from the back of the couch and spread it over us, and we slept, holding each other until morning.

FIFTEEN

Lee asked, "Where are we going?"

After a slow morning of breakfast and the Sunday *Post* at my place, we were heading south on Thirteenth Street, passing large detached homes with expansive porches. Ahead stood three-story rowhouses crowned with incongruously grand turrets.

"We're going to visit someone," I said. "A friend of my grandfather's."

I turned right on Randolph and parked halfway down the block of boxy brick houses. There was little color in the trimwork or shutters here. Dogs barked angrily from alleys. Even on bright and sunny days, this street seemed to remain dark.

"This is my Uncle Costa's place," I said. "He worked for my grandfather when he was a young man. When he wanted to start his own business, my grandfather helped him out."

"Let's go in."

"I just wanted to explain to you first, before you meet him. Let's just say that some of these guys didn't really assimilate themselves too well into the American culture."

"You're not ashamed of him, are you?"

"Not at all."

"Fine," she said, tugging at my arm. "Let's just go in."

As we walked up the steps, I waved to a man coming out of the next house who I knew to be a reverend. Behind us two gangly but tough-looking kids walked down the sidewalk, one wearing a Fila sweatsuit, the other with an Eddie Murphy "Golden Child" leather cap on his head.

A rusted metal rocker with moldy cushions sat on the concrete porch. Black iron bars filled the windows. I knocked on the door and waited, counting three locks being undone. Costa opened the door, looked at me, and smiled.

"Niko," he said.

"*Theo* Costa." I gripped his hand and kissed him on the cheek.

He was short and solid, with thick wavy black hair that was gray at the temples and slicked back, and a thin black mustache below his bumpy nose. Though it was Sunday, he wore a short-sleeved white shirt with two pens clipped in the breast pocket.

"Come on," he said, waving us in with both hands. As Lee passed him, he looked back at me and said in Greek, "Your girl? Very nice."

"A friend," I answered, but he winked anyway.

I introduced her and they shook hands. A couple of cats ran by us and into the kitchen. The curtains were drawn throughout the house. Costa switched on lights as we followed him through the living room and into the dining room. The air was dry and very still.

We sat at a large table in ornate chairs with yellowed cushions. On one wall was a mirror covered with a blanket; on the other hung a sepia-tinted photograph of a man and woman that had been taken in the early part of the century. The woman, even shorter than the short man and wearing a long black dress, was unsmiling. The man wore a baggy suit, a very thick mustache, and a watchchain from vest to pocket.

"You want coffee, *gleeka'?*" Costa asked.

"Thanks, Costa. Nescafe for Lee."

"One minute," he said in Greek, jabbing a finger in the air and stepping quickly into the kitchen.

"He's nice," Lee said. I nodded and she pointed to the wall. "What's with the mirrors? I noticed the one in the living room is covered too."

"His wife died last year," I said. "He covered the mirrors so he won't see her reflection." She raised her eyebrows. "I told you."

"It's just that it's so dark in here, and sad. He must be very depressed."

"I'm sure he's a little lonely and misses his wife. But this house was always closed up and dark, even when she was alive. They're old-timers, that's all."

Costa returned with a tray of two Turkish coffees, a cup of instant, and a small platter of sweets, which he set in the center of the table. On the platter were *koulourakia, kourabiedes, galactoboureko,* and *baklava.* He pushed the whole thing in front of Lee.

"Don't be shy," he said, moving his hands in small circles. "Eat!"

"I like baklava," she admitted, emphasizing the second syllable as most Americans do, and chose a slice. I took a *kourabiede* for myself.

We sat and talked for the next half hour, mostly about what we had been doing in the time since I'd seen him last. The tiny cup of coffee had given me quite a jolt. Lee eventually drifted away from the table and began to wander around the house. We heard her steps on the wooden staircase that led down to the basement.

She called upstairs excitedly, "Hey, Nicky, there must be twenty cats down here!"

"Twenty cats, Costa?" I said, and smiled.

"Maybe a dozen," he said sourly. "Lousy *gatas.*"

"If you'd quit feeding them. . . ."

"Aah," he said, dismissing me with a wave of his hand.

Now that Lee was gone we spoke in Greek. Though I understood everything he said, I kept my own sentences simple so as not to embarrass myself with my marginal command of the language.

Costa reached behind him and opened the door of an old wall cabinet. He pulled out a bottle of Metaxa and two shot glasses.

"Too early for you, Niko?"

"No." He poured a couple of slugs with efficiency and we knocked glasses. He sipped and watched as I threw mine back in one quick motion, returning the little glass to the table with a hollow thud.

"You drink like a Spartan," he said.

"Like my *papou.*"

"Your *papou* could drink. But he gave it up when your parents sent you to him."

"I miss him," I said.

"He would be proud of you," Costa said. Like most immigrants he equated my white collar with success.

"I'm doing fine," I said.

"It's time you found another woman."

"I'm not against the idea."

"The girl you're with. She's Jewish?"

"Yes. She's my friend, like I told you."

"Friends, okay. And the Jews are good people, very smart in business. But it's not good to mix, you found that out. Marry a Greek girl."

He finished his drink and poured two more shots. A gray cat with green eyes did a figure eight around my feet then jumped up onto my lap. Costa reached across the table and picked it off me, tossing it to the other side of the room.

"How is it here in the neighborhood now, *Theo?*"

"Not too bad," he said, and shrugged. "When Toula was alive, I worried more. They took her purse once, when she was walking home with groceries." His eyes were a faded brown and watery, more from long afternoons of drinking than from bitterness.

"It's not the same town it was," I said.

"You don't even remember how good it was," he said, suddenly animated. He pointed a finger at my chest. "When I first came here, your *papou* and me swam in the Potomac on hot summer afternoons. Now it's so dirty, I wouldn't even throw a photograph of myself into that river."

I laughed as he finished his shot. I turned the bottle around on the table and read the label.

"Five star, Costa?"

"Yes. Very good."

"Do you think you'll go back to Greece?" I asked, wondering why anyone would remain a prisoner in a house like this, in a city where the only common community interest was to get safely through another day.

"No, I plan on dying here. Believe me, Niko," he said, without a trace of irony, "there is no place in the world like America."

Later that day Lee and I drove down to Southwest and walked along the water, checking out the yachts in the marina. Continuing west, we ended up at the fish market on Maine Avenue.

Most of the good fish had been picked over by that time of day. I bought some squid, at one forty-nine a pound, from a cross-eyed salt who was attempting to stare at Lee. We took it back to my apartment.

After removing the ink sacks and the center bone, I sliced the squid laterally into thin rings, and shook them in a bag with a mixture of bread crumbs, garlic, and oregano. Then I fried them in olive oil in a hot skillet.

We ate these with lemon and a couple of beers as we watched the first half of the Skins game. For the second half we napped together on the couch in roughly the same arrangement as the night before. We woke as the afternoon light was fading. I drove her back to her car at the store and kissed her good-bye.

Back in my apartment I warmed some soup on the stove. From the television in the living room I heard the stopwatch intro to "60 Minutes" and felt that familiar rush of anxiety, announcing that my weekend was ticking away.

Two hours later I dialed the international operator and reached Greece. For the next ten minutes I was shuttled around to various women who worked the switchboards. Finally I reached my mother at her home in a village near Sparta. I had last spoken to my parents on the day my grandfather died.

We spoke superficially about our lives. She ended most of her sentences with, "my boy" or "my son." I tried not to confuse the ethnic inflection in her voice with concern or, especially, love. As our conversation pared down to awkward silences between pleasantries, I began to wonder, as I always did, why I had called.

I turned in early that night but lay in the dark for quite a while before I finally went to sleep. Though I forced myself to wake several times during the night, I was unsuccessful in stopping Jimmy Broda from haunting my dreams.

SIXTEEN

I was nearly done shaving my weekend stubble when Ric Brandon called early Monday morning. He instructed me to change my plans for working on the Avenue and report to the office.

I finished shaving and undid my tie, switching from an Italian print to a wine and olive rep. I changed my side buckle shoes to a relatively more conservative pair of black oxfords that had thin steel plates wrapped around the outside of the toes. I put on a thrift shop Harris Tweed, secured the apartment, and drove to work.

When I reached the receptionist's desk at half past nine, the office was already bustling with Monday morning's full fury. Calls from customers who had been stiffed on their weekend deliveries were automatically being forwarded to the wrong extensions. All terminals were printing, and everyone, though they were moving fairly quickly, carried Styrofoam cups of hot coffee in their hands. The usual line of delivery drivers and warehousemen had formed at the personnel office to complain about Friday's paycheck.

Marsha was screening the call of an angry consumer, but dug deep for a smile as I tapped her desk and set upright the "Elvis Country" plaque that had been knocked on its side.

Aside from a couple of new plants, the office had not changed in the week of my absence. There were several rows of used metal desks with laminated tops. The desks displayed photographs of children; notes written on small squares of adhesive-backed paper, stuck on the necks of clip-on lamps; rubber figurines from the fast food deathhouses, this year's being the California Raisins, running across the tops of computer terminals—all illuminated by the green glow of florescence.

I removed my jacket and had a seat at my desk. Marsha had arranged my mail in stacks, separated by solicitations, trade magazines, and important co-op advertising credits and checks. I tossed the junk mail after a quick glance at the return addresses, then went to the employee lounge for a cup of coffee.

When I returned, Ric Brandon was at my desk, his elbows leaning awkwardly on the soundtreated divider that separated Gary Fisher's cubicle from mine. He was wearing a boxy navy blue suit with a white shirt, and this year's popular tie among the fast-track M.B.A.s, a green print.

"Where's the funeral, Ric?" I said, and sipped my rancid coffee.

"No funeral," he said a little too cheerfully. He looked down at his black wing tips. "I'd like to see you in my office at eleven sharp."

"Sure, Ric. Eleven."

He put his head over the divider and told Fisher he wanted to speak to him "right now." Then Fisher followed Brandon down the hall into his office, where they closed the door behind them.

I checked my watch, pulled the accounts receivable file from my desk, and reconciled my co-op credits. After that I went through my messages. Karen had phoned twice. I took her messages, along with those from the radio and television reps, local newspapers and magazines, and direct mail houses, and threw them all away. I put the remaining stack of customer complaints under my phone, to be dealt with after my meeting with Brandon.

Fisher emerged from Brandon's office and shot me a dim glance. He walked in the direction opposite to our desks. As he walked, he stared at his shoes.

In the next fifteen minutes the office became strangely quiet. Though I had seen this many times before, I would not have expected to feel so oddly relieved when it happened to me. Nevertheless, the signs were all around me: the walking in and out of closed doors by management, the avoidance of eye contact, and the whispering into phones as word began to spread by interoffice lines.

I called Patti Dawson and a couple of the vendors with whom I had become close. Then I put on my jacket and walked to the receptionist's desk.

"I'm running out to 7-Eleven," I said to Marsha. "You want anything?" Her lips were pursed and there were tears in her eyes. She shook her head, unable to speak. I felt worse for her than I did for myself. "I'll be back by eleven."

I passed under the Nutty Nathan's caricature at the foot of the stairs and walked across the parking lot to my car. Then I drove to a hardware store on Sligo Avenue, had a duplicate made of my office key, and returned to headquarters.

At eleven I knocked on the door of Ric Brandon's office. He waved me in. I closed the door and had a seat. He lowered the volume of the news program on the radio, pulled out the bottom drawer of his desk, and rested the soles of his wing tips on the edge of it.

"Nick," he said, his delicate hands together and pointed at me as if in prayer, "this is a follow-up to our conversation in this office a week ago. Do you remember the gist of it?"

"Yes."

"I'd like to reiterate some aspects of it before we continue. In our conversation you basically agreed to play on the management side of the fence in this company, and to work more seriously at your position. This was definitely a fourth down situation, but understand that I allowed *you* to call the play."

I had spent many nights, lying awake in bed with fists clenched involuntarily, fantasizing about this moment. Usually the fantasy consisted of me firing off a string of cleverly vulgar obscenities, but on weirdly violent nights it ended with me pulling Brandon over his desk by his Brooks Brothers lapels.

Now, looking at his reddening face and hearing his feet slide nervously off the desk drawer that he had only moments before so coolly placed them on, I only wished he'd hurry up and get this done. I must have been grinning, because his plastic smile faded, leaving his fat upper lip stuck momentarily on one of his big front teeth.

"So it was my call, Ric. How did I blow it?"

"Don't think for a moment that I don't wish I was sitting here praising your performance. But when you went to work in our Connecticut Avenue store, you went as a representative of management. And you let us down."

"How so?"

"A very serious complaint was filed last week. A customer called and claimed that two salesmen, fitting the description of John McGinnes and yourself, were intoxicated during business hours. The customer also reported the smell of marijuana in the store. Can you explain this?"

I looked out of Brandon's tiny window, across the office and through the larger window on the south wall, at the brilliant blue sky. It was one of the last beautifully sunny days of the year.

"Are you letting me go?"

"I'm afraid so, Nick." His body relaxed in his chair.

"What about McGinnes?"

"I do only what's right for this company. McGinnes is an extremely valuable employee. I'm hoping that a very serious conversation with him will straighten things around. He's the engine that powers that store. Bates and Malone are decent employees, but they're in that store basically because I need some black faces on my D.C. floor. No, I definitely think McGinnes is salvageable."

"You didn't actually take that complaint yourself, did you Ric?"

"Mr. Rosen," he said unsteadily, "took the call when I was out. He suggested that there was no alternative but to let you go. Frankly, on this point I agreed. The nature of the complaint constituted a firing offense."

Through the window of the south wall I watched a flock of blackbirds pass across the blue sky. I rose from my chair. "Is that all?" I asked. I stared at him until he looked down at his desk, a little gray in the face but basically unmoved.

"I've written up your termination papers, effective immediately," he said coldly. "You're eligible for vacation pay, which will come in your final check. I'll pass this on to personnel."

I walked out of his office and softly closed the door behind me.

It didn't take long to clean out my desk. I was quite certain that I was through with retail. I left behind industry related materials, drawing implements, certificates from management seminars, sales awards, and all other evidence of my tenure in the business. Oddly, the things I put into the plastic bag that a tight-jawed Fisher had wordlessly handed me were the most memorable objects of my career at Nutty Nathan's: a book of matches, on the cover of which was printed "It Pays to Advertise," which opened up to a pair of paper legs that spread to expose a thick patch of female "wool"; a caricature of me that the office girls had commissioned, with what I thought to be a rather lecherous look in my eyes and with a cigarette hanging trashily out the side of my mouth, circa my smoking days; a set of pencils with erasers shaped as dickheads; and a file of vulgarities that is charitably referred to as Xerox "art."

All of these things I knew would end up in my apartment's wastebasket. But on that day, like some sentimental pornographer, I couldn't bear to leave them in my desk.

I dropped the duplicate key off with the woman in charge at the personnel office, who was busy cutting out clip art for the company newsletter, a waste of paper so heinous that as "editor" she should have been convicted of arboricide. Seaton, the controller who peed with his trousers around his ankles, stopped me in the hall to shake my hand and wish me luck. Though he was wrongfully despised by many employees for the cutbacks he was constantly forced to make, he was the only one that day with the guts to say good-bye.

A young woman wearing a Redskins jersey was sitting at the switchboard in Marsha's place. I gave her a questioning look.

"She's in the bathroom," she said accusingly, "crying." She popped her gum and looked me over.

"Tell her I'll talk to her later," I said.

"Sure, Nick. Take it easy."

I turned and walked down the stairs, out the door, and across the parking lot, the plastic bag of novelties (the summation of my career) in my hand, a weird grin on my face. It was only eleven-thirty, and therefore a bit early for a cocktail. A cold beer, however, would do just fine.

I was hammering my second can of Bud at the counter of the Good Times Lunch when I noticed a primered Torino parked on the east side of Georgia Avenue. Two men were in the front seat, and one of them was smoking and staring in my direction. Kim was pulling my lunch out of the deep fryer with a pair of tongs.

"I lost my job today, Kim," I said. He turned his head, looked at the can in my hand, then into my eyes. "I'm a free man."

A man seated at the end of the counter wearing an army jacket raised his beer to me in a toast. The radio was playing a half-spoken ballad by a teenage soul singer, barely audible above the jetlike sound of the upright fan.

My lunch was a breaded veal patty with a side of green beans and fries. I ate it quickly, especially rushing through the tastelessness of the veal.

After the lunch crowd had gone, I stayed and had another beer. Once, when Kim walked by, he almost spoke, but passed with only a nod. The primered Torino was still across the street, its occupants still staring into the Good Times Lunch. The last customer walked out as I finished my fourth.

The two men got out of the Torino. I watched them hustle across the street. They were very dark and wiry. They entered the store and moved quickly in my direction.

"What's going on?" I asked in a friendly tone, rising instinctively to face them.

The lead man threw a quick, hard right into my belly that dropped me to one knee. I coughed, fought for breath, and spit up a short blast of beer. I saw his foot coming but was unable to block it. The instep of his boot caught me solidly across the bridge of my nose. I felt the cartilage collapse and a needlelike pain as the force of his kick knocked me back into the base of a booth against the wall.

Kim must have made some sort of move. My attacker looked back and said, "Fuck you, Chang. This here is *our* business," then turned back to face me. I tasted warm blood pouring down over my lip and into my mouth.

"You can stop all that shit with the boy," the lead man said. "Understand?" My nose felt as if it were pointing upward, and the man in front of me got blurry and then it was black for a few dead seconds.

When my vision came back, Kim was vaulting over the lunch counter, a black snub-nosed revolver in his hand. Just as his feet hit the floor, he swung the pistol, striking the second man in the temple with the short barrel and dropping him to the floor. Then he quickly pointed the piece towards the stunned face of the man who had smashed my nose.

The guy seemed to contemplate a break but wisely froze. Kim backed him up to the wall, brought the gun to his face, and tapped the steel of the barrel on the man's front teeth, hard enough so it made a sound.

"You no fuck *me*," Kim said evenly. "I fuck *you*."

The man, hands up, moved slowly away from the wall with as much pride as he could fake. He helped his partner up and they silently backed out of the store. Kim kept the gun on them until they were gone, then locked the door from the inside.

I thought too late to read their plates. By the time I staggered to the door, their car was a fishtailing blur of smoke and burning rubber. I did notice that the plates were out of state, though all I could make out was a design something like a mushroom cloud.

"No cops," I said as Kim replaced the gun beneath the register. He nodded and pointed to the back room.

I lay on a cot next to a chest freezer, looking up at a shelf stocked with pickle spears and clam juice, holding a compress to my nose. The bleeding had stopped but the pain intensified.

"Help me up, Kim," I said as he entered the room. He put a hand behind my back and another around my arm, bringing me to a sitting position. The room caved in from both sides, but soon converged into one picture.

"Okay?" he asked.

"I think so. Thanks, Kim."

"No trouble in my place," he said with certainty, then smiled rakishly. "Bad day, Nick."

"Yeah. Bad day."

The doctor who worked on me at the Washington Adventist Hospital looked at my paper and asked if I was Italian.

"Greek," I said.

"Well," she said cheerfully, "now you'll have a classic Greek nose to go with your name."

"Helluva way to legitimize my name. Is it broken?"

"Not badly," she said, whatever that meant. She wrote out a prescription and handed me the paper. "These will help."

I took the script. "They usually do. They any good?"

She looked at me sternly. "No alcohol with these, understand?"

"Sure, doc. Thanks a million."

At my apartment I ate two of the codeines and chased them with a serious shot of Grand-Dad. Then I ran a tub of hot water and lay in it, everything submerged but my head and left hand, which held a cold can of beer.

A couple of hours later I awoke in the tub, now filled with tepid water. The empty can floated near my knee. My cat sat on the radiator and stared at my nose. It was still broken.

I got out of the tub, toweled dry, brushed my teeth, and switched off the light quickly so that I could not catch my image in the bathroom mirror.

The red light on my answering machine was blinking so I pressed down on the bar. The four calls, in succession, were from Karen, Joe Dane, Fisher, and McGinnes. All of the messages, except Karen's, were condolences on the loss of my job. Typically, McGinnes' was the only one with humor and without a trace of awkward sentiment. He ended his pep talk with what I'm sure he considered to be an essential bit of advice: "Don't let your meat loaf," he said.

Craving a black sleep, I chewed two more codeines and crawled into the rack.

SEVENTEEN

I first met Karen in a bar in Southeast, a new wave club near the Eastern Market run by an Arab named Haddad whom everyone called HaDaddy-O.

This was late in '79 or early in 1980, the watershed years that saw the debut release of the Pretenders, Graham Parker's *Squeezing Out Sparks,* and Elvis Costello's *Get Happy,* three of the finest albums ever produced. That I get nostalgic now when I hear "You Can't Be Too Strong" or "New Amsterdam," or when I smell cigarette smoke in a bar or feel sweat drip down my back in a hot club, may seem incredible today—especially to those who get misty-eyed over Sinatra, or even at the first few chords of "Satisfaction"—but I'm talking about *my* generation.

Because this club was in a potentially rough section of town, it discouraged the closet Billy Joel lovers and frat boys out to pick up "punk chicks." Mostly the patrons consisted of liberal arts majors, waiters who were aspiring actors and writers, and rummies who fell in off the street.

In that particular year the pin-up girl for our crowd was Chrissie Hynde. When I first saw Karen, leaning against the service bar in jeans, short boots, and a black leather motorcycle jacket, it was the only time that the sight of a woman has literally taken my breath away. With her slightly off-center smile, full lips, and heavy black eyeliner, she had that bitch look that I have always chased.

I felt sharp that night—black workboots, 501 jeans, a blue oxford, skinny black tie, and a charcoal patterned sportcoat—but when I approached her and offered to buy her a drink (hardly original, but I was, after all, in awe), she declined. I cockily explained that she was blowing a good opportunity.

"Then some day," she said solemnly, "I'll look back on this moment with deep regret." And walked away.

But soon after that I caught her checking me out in the barroom mirror.

A few beers later, keeping an eye on what she was doing and what she was drinking, I watched her walk out the back door, alone, to a patio behind the club. Hurrying up to the bar, I ordered her drink (Bombay with a splash of tonic and two limes) and a beer, and followed her outside.

She smiled and accepted the drink and my company. We sat in wrought-iron garden furniture, drinking and smoking cigarettes and some Lebanese hash I kept in the fold of my wallet for special occasions.

As the band grew trashier (a local female rocker who made up for a serious lack of tone by rubbing her crotch throughout the set) and the joint filled up, that time of night came when men were in the ladies' room pissing in the sink and several minor fights were breaking out. But at this point Karen and I were only concentrating on each other.

Two rounds later we were in the men's room stall, doing coke off the commode (a half Karen scored from the bartender), laughing because we couldn't even see the white on white. We dragged each other out of the place and, climbing into another old Chrysler product I was driving at the time, headed across town.

Then we were on the George Washington Parkway, screaming north at eighty miles per, all four windows down, and listening to Madness' "Night Boat to Cairo" at maximum volume with the radio dead set on 102.3, the old home of the then-ballsy HFS. We were twisted out of our minds and higher than hippies, and Karen had already unzipped my fly and dug in, and I knew it was going to be amazing, that night and maybe longer.

And it was, but only for about six months. By that time I had graduated from college and we had impulse-married and rented a portion of a house on the east side of the Hill. Soon Karen began wearing her hair differently and lost the eye makeup. She diagnosed me (correctly) as a childish romantic, and pushed me to be more assertive at work and "go for" management, which I grudgingly did.

We split up less than a year after we were married. Though it seems as if the explanation for our failed marriage should be more complicated, I know it to be just that simple.

When Karen opened the door of her apartment, located in old Arlington, the look of disappointment was plain upon her face. I had cleaned up early Tuesday morning, keeping the bandages on as an alternative to the damage underneath. But the area below both eyes had begun to swell and discolor.

"Don't look so happy," I said. "I thought you wanted to see me."

"I did, but not like this. What the hell happened to you, Nicky?"

"Can't I come in?"

"Sure," she said, waving me forward with her hand. "I'm sorry."

She had on jeans and an oversized pocket T-shirt, which she dowdily wore outside the jeans. As I followed her into the kitchen, I noticed that her hips and bottom were a little fuller, though she carried it well. The wedge cut she was sporting was shaven high and tight on the back of her neck, this year's stylish but not over-the-top hairstyle for the career woman.

There were many labeled cartons lining the hall but no furniture in the apartment. The kitchen was empty except for a live coffeemaker and one cup. There were no chairs so I sat on the linoleum floor, my back against a base cabinet.

Karen washed out the cup in the sink, then handed it to me, filled with fresh coffee. I took a sip and rested the cup on my knee. She had a seat across from me against the bare white wall, and crossed one leg over the other. She still had a look about her.

"Now I know why you've been calling," I said. "You're leaving, right?"

"Yes. The company's moving me to Philadelphia this week."

"Congratulations," I said, careful to omit any hint of sarcasm. "I assume it's a good move for you."

"It's an excellent opportunity. I got a substantial raise, and something like a signing bonus. I'm looking forward to the change."

"I'm sure you'll do well."

"I've been trying to call you," she said. "I mean, I wouldn't have left without saying good-bye."

"I'm sorry I didn't get back to you. There's so much been going on."

"I can see," she said. "Are you all right?"

"My nose is broken. In the last week I've been beaten up, twice. Yesterday I lost my job at Nathan's. I'm not exactly on the fast track."

"Shit, Nicky." She shook her head slowly. I hadn't meant to go for sympathy, but her news had made me bitter.

We sat for a while without speaking. I listened to the tick of my watch.

"You look good," I said, cutting the silence. We had often sat like this without awkwardness.

"Thanks. But I've put on a few."

She leaned forward to stand. I looked down her loose T-shirt guiltlessly. Karen had truly beautiful breasts. I remembered waking before her some mornings and admiring them, slightly flattened as she lay sleeping on her back.

I turned down her offer for more coffee. She washed the cup, and with her back to me said, "What are you going to do now?"

"I've got a couple of grand in my retirement account. That will get me through the bills for a while. In the meantime, I was hired by this old guy to find his missing grandson."

"That why you got beaten up?"

"Yeah."

"A detective now," she stated flatly, though she might as well have told me just to grow up. I must have looked pathetic, sitting on the floor wearing my little adhesive nose mask. She rubbed her hands dry with a paper towel. Looking down at her feet, she said, "I'm sorry, Nick. But I've got an awful lot to do today, with moving and all."

"Sure, Karen," I said, laboring to my feet. "I should get going too."

As she walked me to the door, I felt unsteady, as if another piece of my youth was being torn away. She faced me. The edge in her eyes, the dark side of her that had attracted me, was gone.

"Take care of yourself, Nicky," she said. "I'll write from Philly when I get settled."

"So long," I said, and kissed her mouth. I felt her warm exhale on my face when she withdrew.

I stepped out and down the walkway. The sound of her door closing behind me was final, like that of a vault.

I crossed the river via Chain Bridge and took Nebraska Avenue through to Connecticut, where I turned right and headed south a few blocks to Pence's building. One look at my battered face convinced him that I was indeed "on the case"; he stroked me an expense check without flinching.

"Good luck, son!" he shouted, as I bolted out the door.

I spent the remainder of my day doing laundry, listening to music, and taking codeine siestas. By evening I had spoken to my landlord as to the location of the cat food and litter box, and packed my knapsack and overnight bag. When I was done, I phoned McGinnes at his apartment.

"What's going on, Johnny?"

"I'm on vacation till the weekend."

"Brandon give you a few days off to think about things?"

"Yeah," he said, "but the little prick wants me back on the floor by Saturday, so he can make his numbers. How's your early retirement going?"

"Keeping busy. Some guys tried to warn me off the Broda thing yesterday. One of them put a boot to my face to make his point."

"What now?"

"I'm leaving town for a couple of days to check out a lead. I could use some company."

He thought it over. "It beats sucking down draughts in the Zebra Room."

"Good. I'll pick you up at eight, tomorrow morning."

"I'll pack the cooler," he said.

"Fine. And bring a swimsuit."

"Now you're talkin'. Where we headed?"

"Elizabeth City," I said. "North Carolina."

EIGHTEEN

By the time we neared Richmond, traveling south on 95, we had listened to Green on Red's *Gas, Food, Lodging,* and on the other side of the tape, Lou Reed's *Coney Island Baby.* I slid in a fresh cassette, an instrumental mix from the Raybeats, Love Tractor, and the Monochrome Set, and turned off onto 64, heading east towards Norfolk.

"Jesus Christ, man," McGinnes pleaded, "pull over! I gotta' pee like a racehorse."

"I'll pull over when your bladder's ready to burst."

"It's ready now. Anyway, I didn't know we were being timed on this trip. What is this, the fucking Cannonball Run?"

I found a Stuckey's on one of the turnoffs. He was out of the car before I stopped, running through the pounding rain across the parking lot to the store and rest area. I pumped gas into my Dodge under the sheltering overhang.

"Nice weather," I said to the attendant, an old guy who stood expressionless in his uniform, shoulders hunched up, hands in his pockets.

"For ducks," he said.

McGinnes trotted back to the car, a paper bag in his hand, and got in the passenger side. I pulled back onto the highway, turning up the volume on my deck to cover the scraping of my wipers.

"Man, that felt good," McGinnes said. "I'm ready now." He was pulling assorted candies and pecan logs from the bag.

"Careful. You might have bought something healthy. By mistake, I mean."

"I doubt it," he said. "You want a beer?"

"No."

But an hour later there was a cold can of Bud between my legs and McGinnes was working on his third one.

As we approached the Tidewater area, traffic increased and we crossed several small bridges. McGinnes rolled a joint, which we smoked while driving over and through the Hampton Roads Bridge Tunnel. We had been on the road for just under four hours.

At Route 17 I headed south along the Dismal Swamp Canal. The leaves on the trees had not yet begun to turn here. The rain had stopped and steam rose off the asphalt up ahead. We rolled our windows down. Jonathon Richman was on the stereo, telling his girl to "drop out of BU."

I looked over at McGinnes, who was wearing a Hawaiian print shirt with three pens in the breast pocket, a pair of twills, and Chucks. I had never seen him in sneakers.

"I like the shirt," I said.

"I'm on a holiday," he said with a Brit accent, holding the shirttail out and pointing it in my direction. "Do you fancy it?"

"Yeah, I fancy it. But what are the pens for? You plan on writing some business while we're down here?" We crossed the state line into North Carolina, and McGinnes tapped my can with his.

"Just a habit," he said.

"Hey, maybe you *could* get some work. Nathan Plavin's got a brother in the business down here, has a few retail stores of his own."

"Yeah, I know. Ned Plavin. Ned's World, it's called. Jerry Rosen worked for him before he worked for Nathan. But his stores are in *South* Carolina, smartass."

"Nutty Nathan's and Ned's World. Their parents must be proud."

"Anyway," he said, *"you're* the one out on his ear. I've still got a job."

"Thanks."

"I just hope you know what you're doing," he said. "I talked to Andre, told him the whole deal. Let's just say he's more familiar with the types of people you're dealing with now. He says the guys who worked you over aren't going to let that shit lie."

"What else did Andre say?"

"He said the next time you're in the way, your Korean buddy won't be around to protect you. And then they'll take you down, man."

"I'm not worried," I said, and pinched his cheek. "I've got you."

We reached the Elizabeth City area before two in the afternoon. McGinnes suggested we drive around to get a feel for the place. In certain residential areas of the city were large Victorians, some with wraparound porches on more than one level. Cypress trees stood handsomely on wide green lawns.

We drove by the waterfront, which seemed to be rundown to the point of decay in several sections. There was little commercial activity on the Pasquotank River that day, though there were a few pleasure boats heading out to the sound.

"This used to be quite a port," McGinnes said.

"It doesn't look like it was in our lifetime."

"Not in our lifetime. I'm talking about in the nineteenth century. Some serious Civil War shit went down in these parts. Naval battles. The Union ended up taking this place early in the war."

"How do you know so much about it?"

"I grew up in this state."

"Come on, man," I said. "You're not talking to one of your customers now."

"No, I'm serious. My old man was stationed at Lejeune. So we spent some time on the Carolina coast."

"Then maybe you can steer us to a motel."

"Is that an order?" he said, and wiggled his eyebrows.

We found a place off the bypass, a row of cottages that looked like toolsheds with stoops. The sign said Gates Motel. McGinnes kept calling it the "Bates Motel" as we approached it, and insisted we stay there.

The woman in the office had probably seen a few things. But she couldn't help staring when we walked in, announced by the sleigh bells that hung on the inside of the door. McGinnes had on his Hawaiian retailer outfit and a beer in his hand, and I my crisscross adhesive nose mask.

"We'd like a room, please," McGinnes said.

"Sure," she wheezed, her slit of a mouth barely moving on her swollen face. "Eighteen a night, checkout at eleven. How many nights you fellas plan on stayin'?"

"Just tonight for now," I said. I signed the book and paid her as she suspiciously eyed a smiling McGinnes.

"Anything else?"

"Is there a phone?" I asked. "I'll be needing to make some local calls."

She went into a back room and returned with a dial phone and directory, placing them both on the counter in front of me.

"There's a jack in the room. Number nine."

I took the key and handed her a ten. "This should cover the phone."

"That'll do."

"Any bars around here?" McGinnes asked sheepishly.

"Sure is, son," she said with a nasty grin. "But if you was to go into any of 'em, I wouldn't wear that shirt."

After a shower I sat on one of the twin beds in the room, with the phone in my lap and the white pages spread in front of me. McGinnes was out walking.

There were four Lazarus listings in the directory for the entire region. I began dialing.

My third call was to a T. J. Lazarus. The man who answered sounded old and either drunk or tired.

" 'Lo," he said.

"Mr. Lazarus?"

"Yes?"

"Kim's father?"

"Yes."

"My name is Nick Stefanos," I said quickly. "I'm a friend of your daughter's."

"Kim's away," he said.

"I know. But I was heading south on business and stopped in town for the night. Thought I might meet Kim's folks."

"Kim's mother passed on last year."

"I'm sorry."

"Don't bother yourself," he said. "But you just missed Kim. She was in town last week."

"I'd like to drop by and meet you anyway, sir."

"I don't know what the hell it is you want," he said bluntly. "But if you want to come by, come by. And stop and pick up some beer on your way out, will you?"

"Yessir." I took his directions, thanked him, and hung up.

I shaved and removed my bandages, deciding I looked more vulnerable and less intimidating that way. McGinnes entered the room.

"There's a train runs behind here," he said excitedly. "I walked into the woods out back and down a hill to some tracks." I didn't answer him. He looked at the keys in my hand. "Where you headed?"

"I found the Lazarus girl's father," I said. "I'm going to talk to him."

McGinnes drew a beer from the cooler at the foot of the bed. "Check you later," he said.

T. J. Lazarus lived on a street of old bungalows set on large pieces of land. His, a gray and white-shuttered affair, badly needed paint.

I crossed the walkway onto a wide wooden porch, where a black Lab rose clumsily to greet me. He sniffed at my jeans, then my hand, and gave me one perfunctory lick. Then he stood next to me and slowly wagged his tail as I knocked on the door.

The man who opened up and stood before me was well into his seventies. He was tall and thin and rawboned, and wore blue chinos with a faded yellow T-shirt. There was a gardening glove on one of his hands. His eyes were alert and a fluid blue.

"Well, come on in," he said, taking a good look at me before he shook my hand. "We'll walk through the house and out back."

His house was clean and furnished with worn, cushiony armchairs and sofas. A stereo television and VCR were set in the bookshelf, new models that made everything else in the place seem archaic. The dog stayed next to me as I followed Lazarus through the dining room to a back door that led to a screened porch.

"Been in a scuffle?" he said, his back to me.

"Yes," I said. "Like my grandfather used to say, I zigged when I should have zagged."

"Well," he chuckled, "no shame in taking a punch now and again."

We walked back deep into the yard to a garden that ran the width of his property. I pulled two cans of beer off the six I was cradling, holding the remaining four with a finger hooked through the plastic ring. He took them both and opened them, handing one back to me. Sipping the beer, he kept one eye in my direction.

"What was the name again?"

"Nick Stefanos."

"Okay, Nick. Mine would be T. J."

"I've been anxious to meet you," I said.

"You have?" he said almost mockingly. "Let's step into the garden. We can talk while I do a little work."

I followed him to a row of tomato plants, where he bent down and untied a stake, tossing it out of the garden.

"Good year?"

He nodded. "Steady rain last spring, hot and wet all summer. Great for tomatoes. I've cleared out most of the vine vegetables—squash and cucumbers and that sort of thing. Melons were no good this year—went rotten before I got 'em on the tiles." He waved his hand around the expanse of greenery. "Still pulling carrots and onions."

"Kim told me about this garden," I said, realizing how stupid it sounded as the words were coming from my mouth.

"She did, huh?" That mocking tone again. He squinted up at me. "Funny. She never took a bit of interest in it all the time she grew up here."

"Sorry I missed her. Was she alone?"

"No," he said, tired of the game. "She wasn't alone." He rose from his knees and stood to face me. "Why don't we set up on the porch and knock down these beers?"

On the back porch T. J. Lazarus moved two garden chairs together and pulled the remaining beers from my hand, setting them on a low aluminum table between us. He pulled a fresh one off the ring and popped it.

"Who *are* you, son?" he said. "You sure as hell didn't come here to see my garden, and I don't believe you're a friend of my daughter's. Now I don't appreciate the company of a liar, especially in my own house. But if she's in some kind of trouble, I want to know. You a cop?"

"Private cop," I said, my own words sounding unreal. I was getting tired of telling lies to honest people. Nevertheless, I handed him my phony ID.

He inspected it. "I didn't think you were a cop. Cops don't get beat up."

"So I've been told. I apologize for not being honest with you. But I'm not looking for Kim. I'm after one of the boys she was with. She *was* with two boys, wasn't she?"

"That's right. What's going on?"

"I was hired by the grandfather of one of the boys to find him."

He studied me. "Where you from, Nick?"

"Washington, D.C."

"Murder Capitol, huh?" I didn't answer. "You just get into town?"

"Yessir."

"Hungry?"

"I could use something to eat," I admitted. "I really could."

"Like it?"

"I like it fine."

We were sitting at his kitchen table, eating an early supper of grilled chops, fresh corn, and a tomato and onion salad. The late afternoon sun came in through the west window, brightening the colors on my plate. Lazarus brought a glass out of the cupboard and placed it next to my can.

"Here," he said. "Drink it like a white man."

I poured the beer into the glass. "What did you think of the boys Kim was with?"

"They only spent the night. The one boy said his name was Eddie, but the younger one called him Red."

"Redman," I said.

"That's right. This Redman was the tougher of the two, a brawler from the looks of him. And cocky, like everything was a joke."

"What about Jimmy, the other one?"

"He was trying to be tough, but it wasn't in him. You know what I mean."

"Where did Kim fit in with the two of them?"

"My daughter was way too old for both of them," he said bluntly. "This Redman character clearly thought he had a shot at her. Maybe something was going on between 'em, I don't know. But like everything else, she didn't seem to be too serious about the situation."

"What do you mean?"

He stared into his beer can. "Ruth and me had Kimmy late in life. That's not an excuse, but we were a little old to be raising a girl in these times. When she was in her teens, we thought her wildness was just something she'd grow out of, but she went through her twenties the same damn way. After Ruth passed on, I lost touch with her. She sends me expensive gifts on holidays now, but to me it doesn't mean much."

"Do you have any idea where they've gone?"

"They were headed to the Banks, I think."

"They tell you that?"

"I heard them talking about it."

"Where? Nags Head?"

"That would be a start," he said.

"She have friends there?"

"She worked there years ago, in restaurants. Worked in beaches all along the coast for a while, from Nags Head down to Cape Fear. Yeah, I suppose she's still got some friends on the coast."

"Where did she work in Nags Head? Specifically."

He tapped his empty can on the table while he thought. "It was a Mex place or Spanish. That's all I can remember. It's been a long time."

"That's plenty of information," I said, exaggerating. "Thanks." There couldn't be too many Mexican joints on the Outer Banks. I was beginning to get a picture of a smalltown girl, attracted to the resort towns by the money and drugs that came with northern tourists, elements that fed her natural wild streak.

"You like what you do, son?" Lazarus asked.

"I don't know yet. It's my first time out. I'm really just bulling my way through it right now. Anyway, it's not like you see on TV or in the movies, I can tell you that."

"I wouldn't know. I haven't watched either for years. But a man ought to like what he does."

We polished off the six, and Lazarus walked me to the door. On the way I stopped at a picture of Kim that was, from the looks of her hairstyle, probably ten years old. Lazarus caught my look.

"She got her beauty from my wife," he explained.

He shook my hand and wished me luck. I thanked him, feeling almost reluctant to leave. I stepped out into his yard. The dog followed me halfway to my car, where he turned and loped back up the porch steps. His tail was still wagging as he watched me drive off.

McGinnes was gone when I returned to our room. I washed up and put on a black sweatshirt over my T-shirt. Then I read the note that he had taped to the phone:

Nick—
    Behind our room are some woods. Walk straight in
and down the ridge until you come to a clearing. I'll be
by the tracks.

                                                    Johnny

NINETEEN

The ridge dropped gradually and was dense with pine and the occasional cedar. The ground beneath my feet was soft, in some places almost muddy.

At the bottom of the incline were a clearing and railroad tracks, just as McGinnes had described. A narrow drainage ditch ran along both sides of the track. The clearing looked to be only fifty yards in length. Then it ended and the tracks continued into the forest.

McGinnes was standing at the edge of the clearing, backlit by the sun, which was large and red and dropping quickly below the treeline. He was holding a pint bottle.

"Did you bring any beer?" he asked as I approached him. One of his eyes was covered by a wild strand of hair and the other one told me he was stoned.

I let the knapsack off my shoulder, opened the main flap, and pulled out a cold sixpack. McGinnes reached for one and popped the top. I did the same.

"You've been out here all afternoon?"

"Fuckin' aye," he said, waving his arm 180 degrees. "This is great. I haven't had a vacation in years. Here's to Ric Brandon." He saluted and took a swig from the bottle, then handed it to me. I hit it lightly, tasted peach brandy, and chased it with some beer.

"Where'd you get that?"

"I hitched to the ABC store," he said. "Any luck today?"

"A little. I'll tell you later."

We had a seat on the tracks. I listened as McGinnes described his day. Occasionally he would stand to illustrate a point, center stage as always.

Twilight came and with it bugs and the sounds of bats and small feet scampering through leaves and brush. I felt warm and relaxed.

A small sound like the ocean increased from a faint to audible rumble. McGinnes put his hand on the rail and led me back to the rightmost edge of the clearing.

"You ready?"

"For what?"

"A ride!"

"No way, Johnny."

"Why not?"

"It's stupid, that's why not."

"Don't be such a pussy," he said as the sound of the train grew louder. "You never did this before?"

"No."

"All right, listen up. All you do, you pick out a boxcar, an open one if you can, or a flatcar. Then you run alongside it, fast, and grab hold of the ladder or door. Swing up with it, don't try to let it pull you up. Otherwise, you'll go down. This run here is only forty, fifty yards before you hit the trees, so you've gotta be quick."

"I'm not doing this, man."

"Okay," he said. "Then watch me."

The train sounded loud enough to be upon us. But a half minute went by before the lead car emerged from the pines and passed. McGinnes dashed out as the lead car vanished into the woods at the other end of the clearing.

He reached it quickly, up the ditch and sprinting alongside the train. He grabbed the ladder of a boxcar and swung up, dragging a foot out first, then putting that foot on the edge of the open car and looking back in my direction. After that he put both feet on the ladder, held an arm out for balance, and let go, running alongside the train and slowing to a walk just as he reached the trees.

He spun like a dancer and bowed. As he swaggered towards me, he bent down once to pick up and toss a rock. I could see that he was stoked.

"Easy, huh?" he said. "Goddamn, that brings back some memories."

"You do that often?"

"I did," he said. When the caboose passed, we walked back on the high side of the ditch and took a seat on the tracks. "I rode trains all over this state when I was a kid. You had to be careful, though, even then. This was the early sixties. You'd here stories how these tough-ass railroad men would beat up tramps trying to catch trains out of the yards. Of course, in my old man's day, they'd throw you right in the chain gang if they caught you."

"You like growing up down here?"

"It was all right," he said, and passed me the brandy. "I lived in quite a few places, but I was a teenager in Carolina." He stared ahead and absently reached back for the bottle, a grin on his face. "I did some crazy shit, like any kid I guess."

But I had a feeling that he had been a little more out there than most. He had once shown me a photo of himself as a young man, standing balanced atop a split-rail fence, shirt off and arms crossed and flexed, with one eyebrow devilishly raised below a DI brushcut.

Time passed and the night was uncommonly bright. Black woods surrounded the moonlit clearing. As we killed the last of our beer and brandy, I felt a slight vibration beneath me and heard the low rumble begin.

"Come on," McGinnes said, and I followed him to the edge of the woods where there was no light.

He pushed down on my shoulder and we crouched in some leaves and soft earth. The rumble increased in volume. A swift wind rushed behind and through us, and I felt my adrenalin pick up.

"Talk to me, man." I was anxious and a little pickled from the booze.

"All right, Jim," he said, his hand on my arm. "When that first car passes and hits the trees, get out of here fast and run to the right side of the clearing, up the ditch and sharp left so you're parallel to the train. I'll be ahead of you. Just watch what I do. Remember, swing up that ladder, don't let it drag you."

I could barely hear him between the crush of sound that was on us now and the wind that had picked up and was blowing leaves past us into the clearing. My fists were tight as the first car came suddenly out of the trees. I remember feeling that I only wanted to be up and moving away from the blackness around me, up and out and into the light.

"Book!" he shouted, and we were in the clearing and sprinting towards the train, down and up the ditch where I stumbled, then regained my momentum, then alongside it, feeling its power and thinking it was much stronger than I had imagined. McGinnes was in front of me and moving his head back and forth from the train to the trees ahead, then quickly and fluidly grabbing the rung of a boxcar ladder and rising up upon it. He yelled back at me and I saw that the clearing was running out, and I grabbed, white-knuckled the ladder of the car behind him, and ran as he yelled again, and I put one foot on the bottom rung and pushed upward with my shoulders and I was on the machine, tight against the ladder, as the clearing ended and we all roared into the woods together.

I looked behind and the clearing was gone. Around us were only dark forms, and, ahead, the engine cutting a path through the trees. The cars were rocking wildly, and I kept a tight grip on the ladder.

McGinnes was silhouetted against the moonlight and climbing up the side of his car, which was swaying in an irregular pattern to mine. When he reached the top, he let go one arm and one leg, and released a yell and burst of laughter. His hair blew wildly about his head.

"This is great!" he screamed back at me. "Isn't this fucking great?"

"It is," I said, and realized I was smiling. My grip loosened and I took a deep breath. The time between the clanging of the rails shortened as we picked up speed.

McGinnes was attempting to open his boxcar with his free hand and foot. I tried the door on my car.

"It's locked," he shouted.

"So's this one," I called back. "What now?"

He looked around the side of the car. "Swing in between the cars. There's a small platform on either side of the link that you can stand on. And watch your feet."

I followed his lead and moved gingerly off the ladder and onto a two-foot-wide iron footing, taking my hand off the rung only when I was certain I was secure. McGinnes now faced me across the link that connected our cars. The ground below was a blur that rushed away.

We rode the train for a couple of hours, through smallish towns and low-activity yards and back through woods and clearings. When we crossed a bridge over a wide creek, McGinnes pointed to the moon's reflection on the still water. In one of the railroad yards a dog barked at us briefly. In another, an outline of a man waved slowly.

When we were again in the middle of a long stretch of woods, McGinnes suggested we get off the train. "It feels like we're slowing down," he said, and looked out from between the cars and back at me. "What you want to do is, move back out to the outside ladder. When I tell you, jump off and away from the train. Lean back to counter your momentum, and when you hit, take long strides until you slow down."

"I'll watch you," I said.

We moved out to the sides of our cars. The night air had grown cooler. McGinnes waited for a long while until the land gradually leveled out. Then he pushed away from the train, landed on his feet, and slowed to a jog.

I was concentrating on jumping away from the train—it seemed then to be the main objective—and threw myself way out, realizing as I did that my upper body was far ahead of my legs. My feet barely touched the gravel. I rolled until I was stopped by a log and some brush. When McGinnes helped me up, I was a little dazed but relieved.

"You okay?"

"Yeah," I said, though my back already ached and I could feel a deep scrape below my knee as it rubbed against my jeans.

The caboose passed and with it the noise, leaving only the quiet of the woods. We watched the last of it enter a curve ahead and disappear into the night.

We walked on the tracks in the moonlight, keeping in the direction of the train. He looked at the stars and claimed we were heading northwest. I didn't dispute it as it seemed irrelevant in any case. I was becoming tired and ornery.

"I don't know how you talk me into this shit," I said.

"Relax, will you?" McGinnes stopped me with his hand on my chest. "I bet you can't even tell me what you did a week ago today. But when you're drooling in your wheelchair in forty years, you'll remember this night—the way the woods smell right now, the sound of the train. That rush you got when you were running across the clearing. *This* is happening, man, *this* is what's important. Everything else is bullshit."

We walked on. I related the course of events from the day Pence had called to the present, leaving out nothing. McGinnes was unusually attentive as he listened. At one point he began coughing furiously, then retched and spit up something bilious. I sat on the tracks and waited until he was ready to continue.

Sometime after midnight we reached a railroad yard and found an office with a washroom, where an elderly man let us get some water and clean up. Then we walked into an adjoining town, found its main road, and put our thumbs out.

An hour after that the driver of a jacked-up Malibu slowed and pulled over. McGinnes looked in the passenger window, pointed me to the back seat, and hopped in front.

A young serviceman was behind the wheel. He checked me out in the rearview, looking slightly apprehensive at the sight of my marked face.

"Where you guys headed?" he asked.

"Elizabeth City," McGinnes said.

"Elizabeth City?" He laughed. "Hell, you're in Virginia!"

McGinnes looked back at me and then at the kid. "Where in Virginia?"

"Franklin area," the kid said. "What are you, lost?"

"We hopped a train," McGinnes said proudly.

"No shit!" the kid said.

"Damn straight!" McGinnes said, turning his head slightly so I could see his wink. "What you got in this thing, a three-oh-seven?"

"Yeah," he said sheepishly and added, "but it moves."

"Good engine. You in the navy?" The kid nodded and McGinnes told him of a base he had once been fictitiously stationed on. We were driving out of town.

"What was it like? Hopping a train, I mean."

"I'll tell you what," McGinnes said. "Let's grab some cold beer, and I'll tell you all about it."

I hunched down in the seat and folded my arms. I closed my eyes, confident that when I opened them next we would be parked in front of the Gates motel.

I woke early the next morning, hiked back into the woods, and found my knapsack in the clearing. Returning to the room, I woke McGinnes, showered, shaved, and gathered up our gear.

After checking out we stopped for coffee and juice, then got back on the highway and traveled east to 158, then south across a bridge over the intracoastal waterway, our windows down and the radio up.

Less than two hours later we crossed the bridge at Point Harbor and, announcing ourselves with a raucous whoop from McGinnes, rolled onto the Outer Banks.

TWENTY

"So, Johnny," I said. "Who's Virginia Dare?" We were driving down the beach road that bore her name. To our left were oceanfront cottages and houses on pilings.

"First child born in this country to English parents."

"I'm impressed."

"And I'm hungry. Let's get some breakfast," he said, and then, embarrassed, as if having knowledge of the state history was in some way a feminine trait, added, "Besides, I gotta' lay some pipe."

We switched over to the 158 bypass and pulled into the lot of a pancake house. It was warm as summer but there were few patrons. The town was in its off-season.

McGinnes ordered a pot of coffee, french toast topped with a fried egg, sausage, and practically everything else from the kitchen that would clog an artery. I had eggs over easy and scrapple.

When we finished, McGinnes grabbed a section of the *USA Today* he was "reading" and a book of matches and headed for the bathroom. I borrowed the phone directory and a blank sheet of paper from the cashier and wrote down the names and addresses of several restaurants.

Back in the lot I removed my sweatshirt and tossed it in the backseat. We drove to a variety store on the highway, where McGinnes bought sandwiches, beer, and ice for the cooler. While he did that, I pumped gas into my Dodge, then paid a young attendant who had a back wider than a kitchen table. He sang "Tennessee Stud" while I gave him the money and kept singing it as he walked back into the garage where he was working.

We returned to the Virginia Dare Trail and drove south out of Kitty Hawk, through Kill Devil Hills, past the Wright Brothers Memorial and into Nags Head. All of these towns were pleasant and indistinguishable from one another. Near the huge dune of Jockeys Ridge we stopped at a motor court named the Arizona and checked in.

We changed into shorts and walked across the road to the beach. We put our gear down in front of a white cottage on stilts that had boarded windows. The tide was receding and the swells were high at four feet and breaking far from the shore.

When I broke a sweat, I jogged to the shoreline and dove in the ocean. The water was pleasantly cold and clean. I swam parallel to the shore for roughly a quarter mile, then breaststroked back and rode in a few waves.

McGinnes handed me a cold beer as I toweled off. I drank it sitting upright on the blanket. McGinnes pulled another beer from the cooler and announced that he was going for a walk. I watched him go north, stopping to talk to an old man wearing long pants, a T-shirt, and a baseball cap.

When I finished my beer, I pulled another from the ice and walked up the wooden steps and onto the porch of the white cottage. The window frames were peeling and the rusted storm door was permanently weathered half-open. Wooden Adirondack chairs painted a bright green sat in front of the boarded bay window on the splintering deck. I turned one of them to face the ocean, sat in it, and put my feet up on the railing.

The constant crash of the waves was punctuated by the cries of a flock of gulls that sat on the gravelly beach. A young father was surf fishing a hundred yards down the beach, his tackle box, white bucket, and cooler by his side. His blond little boy looked for shells but stayed close by.

I pushed the hair back off my forehead and finished my beer. The area around my nose and under my eyes no longer ached, confirming my grandfather's claim that saltwater was a cure for every ailment. I crossed my arms and settled into the chair, then drifted to sleep.

McGinnes woke me with a shake. I was sitting half in shade now. I looked at my arms and their deep brown color, quickly regained from my vacation on Assateague three weeks earlier.

"Let's go, man," McGinnes said. "You're starting to look like a

Puerto Rican." I poked his red chest with my index finger and brought up a splotch of white.

We returned to the room. I showered and changed into a denim shirt, jeans, and running shoes. McGinnes put on his Hawaiian shirt and went into the bathroom, toothbrush in hand. He began to cough and shut the door.

I sat on the bed and ate one of the sandwiches as I looked over my list. McGinnes came out of the bathroom and wiped his mouth with the back of his hand.

"You all right?" I asked.

He smiled unconvincingly and chin-nodded the list in my hand. "What's up?"

"Restaurants that Kim Lazarus may have worked in. They should be open by now."

"Let me check out a couple," he said quickly.

"Based on what her father told me, I figure there's only three possibilities, unless the place she used to work in is out of business now." I ripped the bottom of the page off and handed it to him. "This place has a popular happy hour, judging from the ads, and it's Mexican. Skip the restaurant and check out the bar. I have a feeling they may be trying to off the drugs, and a bar with employees that use would be a perfect spot. If you get a bite, try and find out if they're still in town."

"No problem," he said.

"I'll drop you off and check out these other places. Then I'll swing back and pick you up after I've done that. You need bread?"

He put his hand out and I handed him some of my bankroll. He folded it and stashed it in his pocket, then pointed a thumb into his own chest. "Don't worry about dad," he said. "This kinda shit is like cuttin' butter."

I let McGinnes off in the parking lot of the Casa Grande, which was in a large, old oceanfront hotel in Kitty Hawk.

"I'll see you in the Big House," he said, and shifted his shoulders in a Cagneyesque manner. I watched him in my rearview as I drove away, feeling an odd sympathy for him as he strolled across the lot in his Hawaiian shirt and polyester slacks.

The first place I hit was in a strip center next to a cluster of movie theaters on the divided highway. It had been advertised as a restaurant but was little more than a carryout serving tacos and burritos.

The kid who was behind the counter when I walked in was busy playing air guitar to the Metallica that was coming from his box. I asked about Kim Lazarus and got a dull-eyed look and a negative response.

My next stop was a free-standing restaurant in Nags Head that was done in a stucco and adobe motif, one of those Tex-Mex chains that American families love specifically for their blandness. It was their dinner rush, and when I saw the waitresses' uniforms—green and gold dresses with some type of elaborate headgear more appropriate on a trotting horse—I had the feeling that Kim Lazarus had never worked here.

The woman behind the register, thin and sharp-featured, seemed to be the only one around not doing anything. I walked up to her and smiled.

"Hi."

"Hello," she said. "The hostess will seat you." She made a jerky, pigeon-like movement with her head.

"I'm not looking for a table. My cousin works here. I'm on vacation, thought I'd say hi."

"Everyone's kinda busy, sir. But what's her name? I'll see if I can get her attention."

"Kimmy," I said. "Kim Lazarus."

"There's no one here by that name," she said.

"I thought for sure she said this place," I whined. "Did she used to work here?"

"Honey, I've been on this station since we opened two years ago. No Kim ever worked here." She jerked her head again.

"Are there any other places like this?" I asked. "I guess I got confused."

"Casa Grande in Kitty Hawk. Or maybe she worked at Carlos Joe's. But they closed down last year. Had some trouble."

"What happened?" I asked, winking conspiratorially. Then I jerked my head like hers, for punctuation. "Taxes?"

She leaned in and whispered, "Owners got in drug trouble."

"Oh. Anybody work here who used to work at Carlos Joe's? Maybe they know my cousin."

She pulled back and buttoned up. "Not that I know."

"Thanks."

I walked to my car with my head down. Carlos Joe's was the type of place Kim Lazarus would have been attracted to. But it was closed now, and I had driven into a stone dead end.

The bar at Casa Grande was above the dining room and accessible by a staircase to the left of the hotel entrance. I picked a magazine up off the table in the lobby and went up the stairs.

McGinnes was seated at the bar when I entered. He was leaning across the rather appalled-looking woman to his left, showing her companion a trick involving a swizzle stick. He saw me but averted his eyes. I took a seat at a deuce near the window and the hors d'oeuvre station.

The young cocktail waitress who arrived at my table had that look of false health common to beach employees who party every night, then spend a couple of hours in the sun each day for recovery purposes. She had the scrubbed, Baptist good looks preferred by ACC frat boys, but her best days were already behind her. Her summer tan was fading like an Earl Schieb paint job.

"What can I get you?" she asked with a pained smile, and set a basket of chips and salsa on the table.

"A Dos Equis, please. And some *queso*."

The place was filled with older, successful men, stag or with younger women, gray-templed gents who tie the arms of their summerweight sweaters around their necks and drink single malt scotch or beer from green bottles.

McGinnes was doing an awful lot of buddying up to the bartender, one of those doughy ex-jocks who "parlay" a summer bartending job into a full-time career that leaves them forty-five at thirty.

The *queso* was spicy and hot. I ordered beef and chicken enchiladas with a side of sour cream and another Dos. I pretended to read the real estate magazine that I had brought up from the lobby.

The food arrived and was of the same quality as the *queso*. Someone in the kitchen obviously liked their job. I watched the bartender whisper something to his barback, then leave his station and walk into the men's room. Half a minute later McGinnes followed him in.

I finished my meal and the waitress removed the plates. The bartender returned to the bar, where he immediately lit a cigarette and drew on it hungrily.

McGinnes emerged from the head and took his seat at the bar, turning to his neighbors and quickly starting a conversation. Then he pulled the rope on a bell that hung from the ceiling. There was applause in the bar, as McGinnes had just bought the house a round.

I raised my bottle in a toast to McGinnes, via the bar mirror. He winked at me, a little too broadly, though he deserved to be somewhat reckless. Clearly he was on to something.

As I finished my beer, McGinnes was in close conversation with the bartender. He looked at me again, then stepped away from the bar, and said loudly, "What do I owe you, professor?" I left twenty on sixteen, walked down the stairs, and out to my car.

I turned the ignition key and knocked the ocean mist off my windshield with a stroke of the wipers. McGinnes bounded out of the hotel and goose-stepped to my car, settling in on the passenger side. He grinned the same cocky smirk when he closed a major deal.

"What's my name?" he asked childishly.

"Johnny Mac."

I pulled out onto Virginia Dare, heading south. McGinnes brought the snow seal out of his breast pocket, unfolded it carefully, dipped in with his pinky nail, and did a hit. Then he fed the other nostril the same way.

"What did all that cost me?" I asked.

"Call it a hundred. Thirty for the house round, seventy for the half."

"Seventy, for a half? You're pretty generous with my money."

"You got to ante to play the game, Jim. It was worth it, for what I got." He pointed ahead. "Pull in there. I'm thirsty."

"I'll bet you are."

He was out of the store quickly with a tall brown bag in his arms. He handed me a cold bottle of beer and took one for himself. We drove on.

"Spill it, man."

"All right," he said. "Soon as I walk in the bar, I can see everyone working the place is wired. I strike up a conversation with the barkeep and ask if he remembers Kim Lazarus, used to work there. I'm a good friend of hers from D.C. Not only does he remember her, she was in town last week. I steer the conversation to coke, and how Kim told me I could look him up if I wanted to cop. He gets suspicious now and I ease off. But I get him back on the track when I tell him I'm used to spending one-forty, one-fifty for a gram." He looked at me and smiled.

"Keep going," I said.

"This guy can't resist the high dollar. He offers to sell me a half for seventy. I gotta try it first, I say. We go into the john, he turns me on. Let me tell you, this shit is good. I know you've found Jesus and all that, but if this was the old days, you would *concur* on this, Jim."

"Get to the meat, Johnny."

"We go back out to the bar. I tell him this freeze is so serious, I've *got* to cop more. How can I get my hands on some quantity?"

"Kim and the boys, right?"

He nodded. "Let me tell it, man. The bartender, he's juiced now, he's my buddy. He tells me that it was my friend Kim that sold him the shit."

"Where are they?"

"This bartender was too small-time to take on quantities. There was another guy, though, a surf rat by the name of Charlie Fiora who used to work with Kim at Casa Grande. He's got his own gig now down the coast, a little bar called the Wall. He's the one that Kim and Eddie and your boy Broda went to see to sell their supply to."

"Where?" I said.

"Wrightsville Beach." He took a swig and looked at me out of the corner of his eye.

I slapped the steering wheel as we pulled into the lot of the Arizona. "Good job, man."

"I know," he said.

In our room I laid out maps and ferry schedules. McGinnes tapped out some lines on the mirror he had removed from the wall.

"You want a blast?"

"No," I said. But like any former cokehead, I really did.

He did a couple that had the width of fingers. "Let's go out and have a few."

"Not tonight. We've got a shitload of miles to travel in the morning."

"Wrightsville's *down* there."

"You want to go, go ahead. My keys are on the dresser."

"I think I will," he said. "For a short one."

"Thanks for tonight, Johnny."

"No sweat," he said casually. "See you in the A.M." He took my keys off the dresser and twirled them on his finger. He was coughing as he bolted out the door.

TWENTY-ONE

Crossing Whalebone junction, we passed the sign for Cape Hatteras National Seashore and blew down Route 12 very early the next morning. The sun sprayed over the dunes to our left, highlighting sea oats and myrtle.

We rolled our windows down as the dawn chill faded, and sipped our coffee from Styrofoam cups. I had a neo-country tape playing in the deck—Golden Palominos, Dwight Yokum, T-Bone Burnette, and Costello, with some Merle Haggard and Johnny Cash thrown in for tradition.

McGinnes was singing along to what he knew, and laughed at my voice as I joined him on the occasional odd chorus. The lines around his eyes crinkled out from behind his aviators.

"This is beautiful!" he said emotionally, his arm straight out the window, his palm catching the wind.

"Everything is Beautiful," I said.

"Ray Stevens, right? Worst Top Ten song ever recorded."

"Right about Ray Stevens. Wrong about the honors. They go to 'Daddy, Don't You Walk So Fast' by Wayne Newton. *That's* the worst song to crack the Top Ten."

"You mean, 'Daddy, Don't You *Hump* So Fast,' don't you?"

"Whatever you say, Johnny."

Soon we were on the Herbert C. Bonner Bridge over the Oregon Inlet. Scores of trawlers and charter boats were heading out into the ocean. On the other side of the bridge lay the Pea Island Refuge, where flocks of snow geese and shorebirds flew by at regular intervals. Egrets laced the wetlands to our right.

We drove through the nearly empty beachtowns of Rodanthe, Waves, and Salvo, then cruised a long stretch along the coast to Avon and beyond. Near Buxton, McGinnes had me stop at a windsurfing mecca on the soundside called Canadian Hole. He peed on the grass next to my car while I watched the brightly colored sails and their boards ripping across the chop. Then we pulled back onto the highway.

We stopped once more to fill the cooler in the town of Hatteras, then raced to the end of the highway to make the ferry. I pulled into spot number nineteen just as the khaki-uniformed park employees began to board the cars.

We were directed to an area behind a North Carolina Christian Academy school bus, where a tan woman wedged wooden blocks beneath my front tires. A fully restored black and white Chevy with red interior parked to our right. The New Jersey vanity plates read "57 Love." The driver was bearded and fat and wore an Alf T-shirt.

"Let's get out and enjoy it," McGinnes said, as the ferry finished loading and pulled away from the dock.

The crowd was an October mixture of elderly couples, young parents with preschool children, and a few tradesmen heading over to the island for work. The tourists began to congregate at the bow, where a woman was throwing bread to a few gulls. Those few gulls turned to dozens very quickly and stayed with the ferry for the entire trip.

McGinnes brought out two beers and handed one to me. I had intended to remain dry that day, but the weather was gorgeous, the final brilliant display of the long Carolina season. I took off my shirt, sat on the hood of my car, put my feet up on the iron rail, and popped the can.

McGinnes drifted away and struck up a conversation with a group of young men standing around a Bronco that had surf rods stuck in tubes mounted around the front fender. I folded my arms and enjoyed my beer and the view.

Forty minutes later we approached the island. The ferry ran parallel to the shore, which was crowded with all-terrain vehicles and fishermen, some of whom were throwing out nets. The family next to me waved at an old man motoring by in a Chris Craft, who waved back, mimicking them playfully. Finally we docked with a thud against the rubber-wrapped pilings.

We drove off the ferry and onto Ocracoke Island. The terrain was flat and covered with shrubs of myrtle, the two-lane road shoulderless and sandy. Many of the cars ahead turned off at beach access trails or state-run campgrounds.

The drive to the other end of the island took only ten minutes. But when we arrived, the Cedar Island ferry was full, and the next available was two hours away. I bought tickets and walked back to the car.

"Don't worry about it," McGinnes said. "We made good time getting down here. Let's relax, drive back to the village. I saw a place there."

We turned the car around and headed back up the road, where McGinnes directed me into the lot of what looked like an old house on pilings. The small gray sign, camouflaged against the gray house it hung on, read "Jacko's Grille."

"You coming?" he asked, out of the car before it stopped.

I shook my head. "I think I'll grab a swim. I'll swing back and pick you up." He waved me off and ran up the wooden stairs.

I drove to a small turnoff that I had noticed earlier, a place with no facilities and no tourists. I changed into shorts and walked on a path through the shrubs, over a barrier dune, and out onto a wide, white beach.

On my trek to the shoreline there were sandcrabs and shells and no footprints. The swells were small, like those in a bay. I walked out in two feet of water for what seemed like quite a distance. Small fish moved around my feet. I reached deeper water and swam, then walked along the beach until I neared a group of fishermen. I turned and walked back, stopping occasionally to put the more interesting stones and shells in my swimtrunk pockets. Some high clouds drifted in the sky but they never neared the sun.

I changed back into jeans and drove back to the bar. Inside were picnic tables and a jukebox and a small selection of domestic beer. McGinnes was talking to and drinking with a couple of old-timers. I ordered a burger and a beer and took them both out back to the screened-in deck that overlooked the wetlands and the Pamlico Sound.

The Cedar Island ferry was a two-hour trip. I grabbed the opportunity to nap on the hood of my car in the warm sun.

McGinnes shook me awake when we docked. As we prepared to disembark, I noticed the license plates on a car ahead. The "mushroom cloud" on the plates of the men who attacked me was the state tree of South Carolina. I told McGinnes.

"What difference does it make now?" he said. "You didn't get the number, so you still don't know dick."

As we drove off the ferry onto Cedar Island, I saw that the vegetation was more tropical. But the palmettos diminished, then disappeared as Route 12 became 70. We went through the lovely seaside town of Beaufort, then passed the more conventional Morehead City and turned off on 24 south. At two o'clock we entered Camp Lejeune, where McGinnes saluted the MP at the gate and told childhood stories all the way through the grounds and beyond. Then we were on 17 south along the coast, passing billboards advertising surf shops and hamburger stands.

At nearly four in the afternoon we reached Wilmington, a large city in the midst of revitalization, which was still filled with examples of old Southern architecture. McGinnes informed me in the same breath that Wilmington was once the premier city of the state, and that it was the birthplace of Sonny Jurgenson.

Wrightsville Beach was just across the bridge over Bank's Channel. Driving onto its main strip, I saw the large hotels and general congestion of concrete that I associated with the Delmarva Peninsula and the

Jersey Shore. We checked into a clean and expensive motel near the fishing pier.

McGinnes was sleeping when I came out of the shower. I dressed quietly, slipped out the door, and walked up to the pier. At its entrance was a snackbar that overlooked the beach. I sat on a red stool and ordered a tuna sandwich with fries and a coke.

The teenage girl behind the counter had black hair and thick eyebrows and wore a Byzantine cross. I asked if she was Greek and she said yes. Her parents owned the concession stand and the adjoining restaurant. I asked her if she knew a place called the Wall.

"It's a surf-rat place," she said. "In the summer they rage, but now in the off-season only the hardcores hang out there. If you're not a local and you're not in that crowd, it's not too cool." She told me where to find it, up near the Strand. I thanked her and left eight on four.

Traffic was light. I found the Wall on the soundside corner of the intersection the girl had mentioned.

The place appeared to be a converted service station. It stood alone on a shell and gravel lot. I was the only one parked in the lot. I sat in my car for half an hour and listened to top forty radio and beach commercials. Then a modified, black VW with two shortboards racked on the top pulled in. The doors opened and two guys got out.

They walked across the lot. The taller one of the two was in oversized baggy shorts and a tie-dyed T-shirt and wore a red duckbilled cap, out of which came white blond hair. He was tall and in swimmer's shape. The smaller one was dressed similarly but had a weak frame and the overly cocky strut of the insecure.

I got out of my car quickly and ran to the door of the bar, just as the tall one was turning the key. I startled him as he turned and for a moment he looked vulnerable, but only for a moment. He had thin eyes and a cruel, thin mouth.

"Hey," I said, "how's it going?" He didn't answer but gave me the once-over. "Is Charlie Fiora around?"

"That's me," he said in a monotone. "What do you want?"

"I'm a friend of Kim Lazarus," I said. His eyes flashed for a second, an emotion that he quickly shut down. "I heard she was in town. Heard you might know where she's staying."

"You heard wrong, ace. I don't know any Kim Hazardous," he said, and his little friend giggled. "Now I gotta get my place opened up. So later."

The two of them walked in and shut the door behind them. I heard the lock turn. I stood staring at the door and the painted cinderblocks around it. Then I turned and walked back to my car. I sat there for a while. Nothing happened and I did nothing to make it happen. Finally I turned the ignition key and drove back to the motel.

McGinnes was cleaned up and waiting when I returned to the room. We walked to the restaurant above the arcade and concession stand and had a seat at the bar, which afforded us a view of the pier below. The ocean shimmered orange and gray at dusk. I told McGinnes of my experience at the Wall. Afterwards, he put down his Pilsner glass and looked at me dourly.

"I didn't want to bring this up," he said, "but I've got to be at work tomorrow morning. If I don't post, I lose my job."

"I know."

I settled the bill after finishing only half my meal. We walked down the stairs and out onto the pier. I turned my collar up against the wind as we neared the end, where some kids were spinning a cast-iron telescope on its base.

"What are you going to do?" McGinnes asked. His hair was blowing back to expose his scalp.

"They're here in Wrightsville," I said with certainty. "I didn't go through everything and come all the way down here to drive back to D.C. now with my fucking tail between my legs."

"You want company?"

"No, not this time. But get everything together at the room. I'll be back in an hour to pick you up."

He nodded sadly and looked away. I left him there at the end of the pier and walked back, passing a small group gathered around a sand shark that was floundering and dying on the wooden planks.

I found my car in the motel lot, pulled out onto the highway, and headed for the Wall.

TWENTY-TWO

When I pushed open the heavy door to the Wall, they were blasting *Led Zeppelin IV* through the speaker system.

The place was one big unfinished room, with a couple of pool tables, pinball and video machines, scattered chairs, and a bar. Some of the people that night looked to be underage. It was difficult to pick out the patrons from the employees.

Charlie Fiora was standing outside the service bar area and recognized me as I entered. He said something to his sidekick, who then looked at me and grinned. I walked across the concrete floor to the bar, where I took a seat with my back to the wall on a stool in the corner.

When the bartender was finished ignoring me, he dragged himself down to my end. He was tall with long brown hair and wire-rimmed glasses, which gave the probably false impression of intelligence. I ordered a bottle of Bud and gave him three on two. He didn't thank me but accepted the tip.

I drank the beer and looked around. There were no windows. The area that had once housed the service station's bay doors had been bricked up. The decorations were sparse but effective. Tiny white Christmas lights laced the walls and bar mirrors. Posters, replicating album covers of groups like Siouxsie & the Banshees and the Meat Puppets, hung on the cinderblocks. Styrofoam Flintstone Building Blocks were spraypainted and glued to the ceiling to better the acoustics and insulate the noise. Tie-dyed bedsheets hung like inverted parachutes, and held in their pockets still more Christmas lights. Fiora was nothing if not resourceful.

The crowd here was the dark side of the myth of healthy, bronzed surfers out for clean fun and the perfect wave. The young people who lived in beachtowns like this, long after their peers had returned to school for the fall semester, were strangely joyless hedonists, bitter poseurs who were capable of unrepentant violence.

Fiora was staring at me and I could feel it. I got up and walked across the room, past the pool tables and pinball machines, and into the men's room.

There was one sink, two urinals, and a stall. I stood at one of the urinals and peed. Above me on the wall were two lines of graffiti: "Michael Stipe sucks my pipe" and "Any friend of Ted Bundy's is a friend of mine."

I washed up and returned to my barstool. There was a pretty young blonde in a powder blue sundress standing next to Fiora now. Fiora whispered something in her ear. She looked at me and smiled, then kept her eyes on me as she kissed him on the cheek. They both laughed.

I ordered another beer. They were now well into the second side of the Zeppelin tape. A loaded kid sitting next to me said to his friend on the right, "I'm tellin' you, dude, the way to get a babe to like you is to make her drink."

I began to read the cassette titles that were racked behind the bar. There were hundreds of them, arranged alphabetically. When I was finished doing that, I looked at my watch.

Bonham's drum intro to "When the Levee Breaks" kicked in, followed by harmonica. I finished my beer, got up from my stool, and walked back into the men's room.

I rewashed my hands. I was drying them with a towel and looking in the mirror when Charlie Fiora and his buddy walked in behind me. I threw the paper in the trash and turned to face them.

Fiora had removed his cap, making him appear less boyish. In the blinking Christmas lights his tan skin was drawn tight. Veins popped on his biceps below the rolled-up sleeves of his T-shirt. His right fist was balled.

"All right, ace," he said. "What do you want?"

I glanced quickly at his skinny little partner, who was struggling to look tough, then back at Fiora, whom I addressed.

"Tell your girlfriend to beat it," I said. "Then we talk."

The kid took half a step towards me out of pride but stopped short. I thought I saw the beginnings of a grin at the edges of Fiora's mouth.

"Go on, Robo," Fiora said.

Robo left after giving me one more hard stare. Fiora and I studied each other for a minute or so. The music was thin and distorted, coming through a cheap speaker hung above the mirror.

"I told you earlier what I wanted. Kim Lazarus is in town with two guys and I want to talk to one of them."

"You some kind of cop?"

"Private," I said. Fiora relaxed.

"Then why don't you just get the fuck out of here?" he said.

"I could make trouble for you, Charlie. I know Kim sold you some shake, and I know you're dealing it out of this bar." I shifted my weight to my back foot.

"You want some more?" he said, and pointed his hand very close to my bruised face. I was tired of him and all of it. Most of all, I wouldn't be touched like that again.

I grabbed his outstretched wrist and twisted down, and at the same time yanked him towards me. Then I kicked him with my back foot, pivoting the heel of my front foot in his direction and aiming two feet behind him, as I connected at the bottom of his rib cage.

The sound of it was like that of a hammer through a carton. He veed forward, coughed once, and opened his eyes in pain and surprise. I stepped behind him, one hand still around his wrist, and with the other pushed down violently on his elbow.

His face hit the floor before the rest of him. A sickening sound, like stone against stone, echoed in the bathroom. When a puddle of blood spread between his face and the floor, I knew he had broken his teeth on the concrete.

"Where are they?" I growled. I had pressure on his arm and held it pointed at the ceiling.

"Beachmark Hotel," he said, and coughed convulsively, adding more blood and phlegm to the floor.

"Where in the hotel?"

"I don't know the number," he said, and I believed him. But I pressed harder on his arm. "Last room on the right. Oceanfront."

"Floor?"

"Second floor." He made a gurgling sound.

"Repeat it," I said, and his answer was the same. I let go of him and stepped away without looking back. I pushed the door open and walked quickly across the main room.

Fiora's friend was shocked to see me emerge first. He moved back from my path and stopped against the wall. I felt numb, and a foot taller at the same time. Robert Plant was shouting the blues.

I walked over to the blonde in the blue sundress, took the bottle of beer out of her hand, and drank deeply. I put my other hand behind her neck and pulled her mouth into mine. When she began to kiss me back, I pushed away.

Then I was out of the bar, out in the cool and wet air. I got into my car and watched my hands shake before I tightened them around the wheel, then laughed for no reason. I pulled out of the lot and screamed down the strip, to pick up McGinnes, and, from there, to get Jimmy Broda.

"What's going on, man?" McGinnes said, and looked at me strangely as I entered our room.

"You turn in the room key yet?"

"Yeah."

"Let's get going, then."

We were out on the street quickly. I unintentionally caught rubber pulling out of the lot. I felt McGinnes' stare.

"I guess you got your information," he said.

"That's right."

"There's blood on your shirt," he said.

"I know," I said, pressing down on the accelerator. "It isn't mine."

TWENTY-THREE

The Beachmark was a tan, three-story hotel on the ocean near the Wrightsville Holiday Inn. It was highlighted with green awnings and a diagonal green sign with white lettering announcing its name. I parked and looked over at McGinnes.

"You coming?" I said.

"You want me to?"

"Yeah."

"What's the plan?"

"There isn't one. Let's just go in and get him."

There were few cars in the parking lot, and the area around the hotel was still and quiet. The pool's green light tinted our clothing as we walked around it and on past a Coke machine and ice dispenser.

We ascended a metal stairwell, then went through a concrete hall and onto a walkway around the second floor. We walked along the north-side wall and turned right at the oceanfront, where the temperature immediately dropped, the air became damper, and the sound of the surf more pronounced.

I found the last door on the right and tried the knob. It was locked. To the left of the door was a small rectangular window and, through it, darkness. My first thought was that I had been had by Fiora. But McGinnes whistled and directed me to the next door in the row.

The door of that room was ajar. Out of it fell a bar of light and the sound of a radio playing AOR at a very low volume.

I knocked on the door and shouted "Hello." No response. My knock opened the door halfway. I finished it with a push and stepped onto the green carpet of the living room. McGinnes followed me in.

We walked slowly past the standard bamboo and plastic beach furnishings and the seaside prints that hung on the wall. There appeared to be two bedrooms. I pointed to one, and McGinnes walked in. I walked into the other.

At first I did not recognize the figure lying on the bed. He did not look much like the defiant kid in the photograph his mother had shown me. In the photograph, Eddie Shultz had been alive.

They had gagged him and tied his hands and feet together behind his back, laying him on his side on a dropcloth. Then they had cut his throat down to the windpipe, from left to right. His shirt and jeans were soaked halfway up in blood. Rope burns marked his wrists and his eyes were open. He looked something like a frog.

I fell back against the door, tasted the bile of my dinner, and swallowed my own puke. I felt the blood drain from my face and I thought I heard Maureen Shultz's voice on my answering machine. I stumbled into the other bedroom.

McGinnes was on the bed, cradling a woman in his arms. Her eyes were barely open and her lips were moving but there was no sound. He pushed some hair out of her face.

"She was unconscious when I walked in," he said. "I've almost got her around." He turned his head to look at me and dropped open his mouth. "What the fuck . . . ?"

"Eddie Shultz is dead, man. Murdered in the other room."

"Hold her," he said, and I absently put my arms around the woman as he rushed out. I heard him say, "Jesus Christ," then walk around the apartment until he came back, pasty-faced, into the bedroom.

"Is Jimmy Broda . . . ?"

"Nobody else in the apartment," he said.

"We've got to. . . ."

"We don't have to do shit," he said, his voice shaking. He reached out and grabbed a handful of the front of my shirt. "Now listen. Did you touch anything besides the front door?"

"I don't know. I mean I don't remember. Probably."

"You walk downstairs, now, and bring the car around to the stairwell we came up. I'm going to wipe this place down and get her walking. I'll be down in a few minutes. Understand?"

"Yes," I nodded.

"Do it," he said, and released my shirt.

I let the woman down gently on the bed, forcing her hand off my back. I walked out of the apartment, around to the north side of the hotel and down the stairwell.

I moved the car past the pool and into the spot nearest the stairwell. I kept the windows rolled up, listened to the tick of my watch, and wiped sweat off my forehead.

McGinnes came down the stairs ten minutes later with the woman. She was walking, supported by his arm. In his other hand was a suitcase. He put her in the back seat, where she immediately lay down. He stowed the suitcase in the trunk and got into the passenger side.

"I think I got everything," he said to himself, then looked at me. "Come on, let's get out of here."

I found the bridge over Bank's Channel, left Wrightsville Beach, and drove into Wilmington. At a convenience store I parked far away from the entrance.

I bought three large coffees and a pack of Camel filters. I returned to the car, handed McGinnes two of the coffees, and tore a hole in the lid of mine. Then I opened the deck of Camels, shoved one in my mouth, and lit it. I had not smoked in more than three years. The raunch hit my lungs and burned. I kept it there, finally exhaling a stream out the window.

"She know where Broda is?" I said, jerking my head in the direction of the backseat, where she slept.

"No," McGinnes said. "Drive."

He directed me to 421 heading northwest. It was past midnight and there were few cars on the highway. I kicked on my hi-beams with a tap on the floorboard.

"We blew it," I said, after a long period of silence.

"Bullshit," he said angrily. "Everything that's happened has had nothing to do with you. And everything that's going to happen, whether they catch up with the kid or not, you can't change that either. The boy got his hands on some shake that wasn't his, and the guys he took it from, man, they are not to be fucked with. You're way out of your league, Nicky. Forget about it."

"What about the woman?"

"She'll be all right. I don't think she was hurt bad. I've got to figure that half of her condition right now is from all the drugs they were doing. Take her back to D.C., drop her off, and wash your hands. Then pray we don't get implicated in all this."

We drove for a couple of hours on 421. When we neared the signs for 95, McGinnes had me pull over.

"I'm going to switch with her and try to get some sleep," he said. "It'll do her good to open her eyes for a while."

We urinated on the shoulder of the road. McGinnes rousted the woman and walked with her down the highway for a block, then back to the car. She slid in next to me on the passenger side. McGinnes lay down on the backseat.

At Dunn, past Fayetteville, I turned off onto 95 and headed north. I offered her a cigarette. She took two from the pack and lit them both with the lighter from the dash, then handed one back to me.

She smoked while staring out the window. Her shoulders began to shake, and I could see that she was sobbing. I turned the radio on to a country station and left the volume very low. When she had stopped crying, she turned her head in my direction.

"Who *are* you guys?" she said. There was that slight Southern accent.

"We're taking you back to Washington. I'm Nick Stefanos. The guy in the back is John McGinnes. Who are you?"

"My name is Kim Lazarus." She took another cigarette from the pack and lit it off the first. She still had the long brown hair from her father's photograph, and large, round, blue eyes.

"You feel well enough to talk?"

"I think so," she said, but again began to cry. She shook her head. "Fucking Eddie. Why?"

I let it go again for twenty minutes. She drank the cold coffee we had saved for her and smoked another cigarette. I kept my eyes on the road.

"I'm not interested in anything other than Jimmy Broda," I said finally. "I want you to know that . . . so you can speak freely. I was hired by his grandfather to find him, and that's what I was trying to do when I caught up with you. I know he had coke that wasn't his, and I know you were selling it off as you traveled. But I don't care about any of that."

"What can I tell you? We were partying for two weeks straight. We had sold most of it, and we were doing the rest of it like a last blowout." She dragged on her cigarette.

"Keep going," I said.

"Jimmy went out for some beer late in the afternoon. Pretty soon after that two guys came into our room. I don't remember much after that. Either I hit my head backing up or they knocked me out. Anyway, the next thing was, your friend in the backseat was waking me up."

I thought about that for a while. "You recognize the guys?"

"Black dudes," she said meaninglessly. I didn't ask her any more questions, and after a short time she fell back asleep.

I drove on through the night, into Virginia and around Richmond, stopping once more for gas. Kim slept through, though her body jerked occasionally from speed rushes.

McGinnes awoke outside of Springfield and sat up. He stared out the window for the remainder of the trip. We rolled into D.C. just after dawn on Saturday morning. McGinnes grabbed his gear from the trunk and walked back to the driver's side, leaning his forearm on the door and putting a hand on my shoulder.

"I'll be talking to you," is all he said. Then he turned and walked into his apartment building, stoop-shouldered and slow, and suddenly old.

I woke Kim Lazarus and got her into my place. While she showered, I put fresh sheets on my bed. She came out looking clean but still drawn. She had only enough energy to thank me and get into bed. I closed the bedroom door and walked out into the living room.

The light on my answering machine was blinking. I let it blink. I lay on the couch and pulled the blanket over me. My cat jumped up and kneaded the blanket. I went to sleep.

I did not dream. But I woke two hours later, thinking of a redheaded boy who looked so horrible in death that I was grateful for never having known him alive. And there was still Jimmy Broda. Either he was caught now, or he was running. I knew with certainty that he was frightened and he was very much alone. The thought of it made the comfort of my apartment seem obscene.

Unable to return to sleep, I rose, and with great impotence, paced the rooms of my apartment.

TWENTY-FOUR

On the television news there was no mention of the out-of-state murder of an area youth.

I erased the tape on my answering machine without listening to the messages. The phone rang twice during the day but I did not pick it up. In the afternoon I gathered all the liquor, beer, and wine from my apartment and made a gift of it to my landlord.

Kim Lazarus woke up at around six in the evening. I cooked her an omelette, fried potatoes, cut a salad, and served it with juice and tea. She ate it and returned to bed, where she slept soundly through the night.

On Sunday morning I prepared a huge breakfast. She came to the table, a bit swollen around the eyes, but with color back in her face. She was wearing Levi's and a blue sweatshirt.

"Thanks," she said as I poured her some coffee. One side of her mouth rose as she smiled, her thick upper lip arching lazily above her slightly crooked teeth.

"You've been thanking me an awful lot. It's no bother having you here. I figure we both need to chill out for a few days."

"What day *is* it?" she asked.

"Sunday."

She ate her breakfast and cleaned her plate with pieces of toast. I refilled her plate and she kept going. She was a big-boned woman with little body fat but plenty of curves.

When she was finished, the cat, who had already taken to her, jumped up on Kim's lap.

"Do you mind?"

"No," she said, rubbing behind the cat's ears. "I like it. How'd she lose her eye?"

"Catfight, I guess. That's how I found her. She was hiding outside behind some latticework, and her eye was just hanging out, hanging by a nerve. I got her to a vet, and he took it out, then sewed the lid shut. After that she stuck around."

"Kind of like how you adopted me."

"Until we figure this whole thing out, yeah."

"Don't you work?" she asked.

"I lost my job last week."

"Where?"

"I did ads for a retail outfit."

"Really. Which one?"

"Nutty Nathan's," I mumbled.

"I know that place," she said. " 'The Miser Who Works for you.' "

"That's the one."

"Your friend John work there too?"

"Yeah, how'd you guess?"

"He looks like a salesman. You don't."

"Well, I was—for years. Johnny and I worked the floor together for a long time."

"Hard to stay friends and not fight over ups and things like that."

"Oh, we fought over ups, believe me."

"How did that happen?" she asked, reaching across the table and touching the faded purple area around my nose.

"Looking for Jimmy Broda."

I refilled our coffee cups and put a fresh pack of smokes on the table between us. She shook one out and lit it, then blew smoke at the window. Her mouth turned down at the edges and her eyes watered up.

"Have you heard anything yet?" she asked.

"Not yesterday. Not on the news today or in the Sunday paper. Frankly, I'm beginning to think that the ones who killed Eddie went back and cleaned up." I thought of the dropcloth they had placed beneath him. "I don't think anybody's going to find Eddie, not for a while anyway."

"And you're not going to report it?"

"Not yet," I said. "Can I ask you something?"

"Go ahead."

"How did you get involved with those guys?"

"Cocaine," she said. "The same way I get involved with every guy I know." She butted her cigarette and lit another, then looked back at me. "When I moved up to D.C., I didn't have a job, but I had money. I was dealing for a guy. Then we had a falling out, and my supply and income got cut off. I started hanging out in the clubs. One night at the Snake Pit I met Eddie and Jimmy."

"And Jimmy was holding."

"Bigtime. And he was generous with it. I think it made him feel like a bigshot, but at the same time he was real nervous about it."

"Did you know it was stolen?"

"I suspected it at first," she admitted, "and then after a while I was certain. But I'm an addict, Nick. I didn't care *where* it came from, only that he had it, and that he didn't mind handing it out."

"Where did Eddie fit in?"

"He wanted me," she said.

"Why did the three of you leave town?"

"Like I said, Jimmy was paranoid. I told him how we could off it and take a vacation at the same time. So we drove south."

"Did he ever say where he got the drugs?"

"No."

"Come on, Kim, think. Something must have been said. With all the shit you were putting up your noses, there must have been quite a bit of talking going on."

"I'm certain," she said bitterly.

I stood up and washed our cups in the sink. I could hear her crying behind me. When I turned, her arms were outstretched.

"I'm sorry," I said, and put my arms around her.

"I'm so fucked up," she said. Her tears felt hot on my neck. I was aware of her breasts crushed against my chest, and of my erection. I eased her away.

"You can stay here for as long as you like."

"I could use a glass of wine or something."

"There isn't any booze here," I said. "I was thinking maybe it would be a good time to start drying out. I could stand it myself."

She nodded. "If you're willing to put up with me. But I'll need a few things from my place."

"Where do you live?"

"I have an apartment in Southwest."

"I'll take you there."

"Thanks, Nick."

Her place was in a low rent hi-rise near the Arena Stage, two blocks back from the river. We rode the elevator up to the eighth floor.

Her apartment seemed to be a part-time residence. There were chairs and stereo equipment and a television, but no tables. The walls were bare. Magazines and newspapers were scattered on the floor, along with several full ashtrays.

As she walked towards the bedroom, she said, "I'll be out in a minute."

I had a look in before she closed the door. A sheeted mattress lay on the floor. Next to it was a small reading lamp and a telephone, and another ashtray.

I walked out onto her narrow balcony and lit a smoke. Her view faced north and looked out over other bunker-style buildings. I crushed the butt on the railing and reentered the apartment.

I could hear her muffled voice through the bedroom door as she talked on the telephone. I browsed through her small record collection, a typically seventies example of dead-end rock: Boston's debut, REO Speedwagon, Kansas, etc. Her stereo equipment was high-end; her television, state-of-the-art.

"You ready?" she asked cheerfully, coming out of the room with the suitcase she had emptied, then refilled.

We got on the freeway at Maine Avenue and headed east for a couple of miles, turning off past the Capitol and driving down Pennsylvania. I parked near the Market.

We walked to a restaurant near the strip, one of those places that does a huge Sunday brunch business on the Hill. The television set over the bar was already fired up and set on "The NFL Today." They were moving plenty of mimosas and Bloody Marys, though there was also a fair amount of draught beer being sold to those who were past kidding themselves.

We lucked into a window deuce and ordered burgers and coffee. When the coffee came, Kim lit a cigarette.

"Is this going to be your first winter in D.C.?" I asked.

"Yes." The sun was coming through the window, finding the three or four strands of silver in her long brown hair. "When does it start getting cold around here?"

"Sometimes this month. Sometimes not till January."

"How long have you lived here?"

"Practically all my life."

"Your folks alive?"

"My parents live in Greece."

"Were you born there?"

"Yes. But I don't remember it." I sipped my coffee. "I met your father, you know?"

"When you were following us?" Her eyes narrowed, then softened. "He's a good man."

"He is. That home in Elizabeth City might be the right place for you to start again."

"My childhood's over, Nick."

"It was only a thought."

"How about you?" she asked. "Any plans for a new start?"

"No," I said. "I think I'll just hang around."

"And what?" she asked.

"See what happens."

After lunch I drove across town and picked up Rock Creek Park just above the Kennedy Center. The leaves on the trees had turned completely. With everything, I had not noticed the change of season.

A car that had been behind us since we entered the park stayed with us as I veered right on Arkansas Avenue. When I made a left onto Thirteenth Street, the car turned right.

The rest of the day I watched football and paced around the apartment while Kim napped. At one point I pulled a chair up to my bed and watched her sleep, then spent the next fifteen minutes wondering why I had done that.

I drove to a Vietnamese fish market on New Hampshire and Eastern Avenue, bought two pieces of flounder, and returned to the apartment. I brushed them with butter and lemon and wrapped them in foil. Kim put them on a small hibachi she had set up outside near the stoop. I sat on the steps with my cat and we watched her grill the fish.

After dinner she washed the dishes while I watched the news. Still no word on Eddie Shultz. Kim entered the living room. She looked healthy and almost beautiful.

"You're nearly there," I said.

"Goodnight, Nick." She kissed me on the back of my cheek, where the neck meets the ear. Then she turned and walked into the bedroom. I watched her walk.

That night I slept on the couch. The cat slept on my bed, with Kim Lazarus.

The next morning I used my room to change clothes while Kim showered. She had reorganized my dresser into a makeup stand. Moisturizing creams, eye shadows, and lip glosses were mixed in with barrettes and odd pieces of jewelry. A wallet-sized, aged black and white photograph of a German shepherd was wedged in the frame of the mirror that hung over my dresser.

"I guess I kind of took over," Kim said as she walked into the bedroom wearing my bathrobe. Water dripped from her hair onto her shoulders and over the top curves of her full breasts. "I'm sorry."

"Don't be," I said. "I like a woman here. The difference of it, I mean. When I was married, my wife was always putting fresh flowers and plant pieces around our place. It's something I would never think to do myself. Now it's one of the few things I remember about our marriage." I pointed to the picture of the dog on the mirror. "Who's this?"

"Rio," she said. "A shepherd I had when I was a kid."

"How do you feel?"

"Really good," she said. "The mornings are great. I feel so proud waking up, knowing I made it through another day without doing drugs. But the nights are really rough, Nick. I just associate the nighttime with getting fucked up."

"You feel like going for a ride today, look at the leaves?"

"Yeah," she said, smiling. "I'd like that."

We drove out 270 and turned off at the Comus exit, parking in the lot on Sugarloaf Mountain. We hiked the mile to the top.

It was Monday but crowded due to the peak foliage. We found a rock on the edge that was unoccupied, and had a seat. The air was cool and there was a strong breeze. As the clouds moved across the sun, we watched their shadows spread over the trees below.

The temperature began to drop. We didn't speak for quite a while. Kim found my hand with hers and held it. I was thinking of Jimmy Broda and I know she felt it. But she let the afternoon drift by and didn't say a word.

That night I fell asleep on the couch shortly after Kim had gone to bed.

She woke me sometime after midnight with a long kiss on my lips. She was wearing only a T-shirt. She was kneeling beside me, and the T-shirt crept above her pale, round ass as she leaned in.

"Aren't you tired of this arrangement?" she said.

"Yes."

"Me too."

She pulled down my blanket and straddled me, easing me into the folds of her dampness. I pushed her breasts together and kissed them, then her neck. Her hips moved with an even liquidity. I let her take me to it, and when I was there, it was if she were tearing a piece from me to keep in her lambent belly.

Afterwards I remained inside her. She laid her chest on mine and I listened to her breath.

We slept in my bed that night, with the cat between our feet. I woke early, showered, and dressed. I shook her awake and told her I was leaving to run some errands, then kissed her. Her eyes had closed again by the time I reached the door.

When I returned two hours later, she was gone. Her suitcase had been taken, as had all of the makeup and jewelry on the dresser. The rest of the apartment was orderly. There were no signs of struggle.

The photograph of the German shepherd still hung crookedly on the mirror, the only item Kim Lazarus had left behind, like the last discarded fragment of a childhood long since past.

TWENTY-FIVE

The weather that morning suddenly turned, to the kind of gray, windy October day that is a harbinger of winter. I put on my charcoal wool sportjacket over a blue denim shirt, filled the cat's dish, secured the apartment, and headed downtown.

I had the desk clerk ring up Kim's apartment from the lobby of her building. There was no answer and she had not been in to pick up her mail.

Out in the street, I turned my collar up and walked into the wind down the two blocks that ended at the river. I entered a seafood restaurant on the waterfront that was just opening for lunch, and had a seat at the empty bar.

The bartender was a thin man with a thin mustache wearing black slacks and a stained white shirt. He stopped cutting limes, idled over, and dropped a bev-nap on the bar in front of me. Then he ran a waxy fingernail along the edge of his mustache.

"What can I get you?"

"A bottle of Bud. And an Old Grand-Dad. Neat."

He served me and returned to his cutting board. I downed the shot and lit a smoke, then drank deeply of the beer. When the bottle was empty, I ordered another and a shot to keep it company.

I watched a yacht leave the marina while I killed my second round. I settled up and walked back out, up the street and to my car. Heading northwest, I stopped at a liquor store and bought a sixpack and a pint of Old Crow.

Before my next stop I slammed two cans of beer and had a fierce pull off the bottle. I wasn't really sure where I was going, but it didn't much matter. I knew at that point that I was spiraling down into a black binge.

I parked in front of May's, a glorified pizza parlor on Wisconsin between Georgetown and Tenley Circle. To the left of the dining room was a bar run by a fat Greek named Steve Maroulis. Maroulis also made book from behind the bar.

"*Ella, Niko!*" he shouted when I walked in.

"Steve," I said, and took a stool at the bar next to a red-faced geezer in an Orioles hat.

"What'll it be?" Maroulis asked cheerfully, with a smile on his melon-like face.

"A Bud and a shot."

"You still drinkin' Grand-Dad?"

"Yeah."

He put both in front of me and I drained the shot glass. I lit a smoke and put the matches on top of the pack, then slid them neatly next to my bottle of beer. All settled in.

"Sorry to hear about Big Nick," Maroulis said.

"He had a life."

"Tough sonofabitches, those old Greeks."

"That they were."

"Not like us."

"No," I said. "Not like us."

I drank my beer and watched a soap opera on the bar television. A pretty-boy actor was doing his impersonation of a man, while the young actress opposite him was trying to convince the audience that she could love a guy who wore eye makeup.

I ordered another round and finished watching the show. When the next one came on, the same garbage with different theme music, I asked Maroulis to switch the channel.

"Anything," I said. "Christ, even 'The Love Boat' would be better

166

than this shit. How about a movie?" I was looking at the stacks of tapes Maroulis had lined up next to the VCR.

"No movies!" the geezer next to me declared, and pounded his fist on the bar to make his point. "Haven't seen a movie since *Ben Hur.* Don't plan to either. They're all shit."

"All right, old-timer," I said. "No movies."

And, I might have added, "Welcome to the '90s." I thought of T. J. Lazarus, another senior who claimed he hadn't seen a movie in years. But there had been a brand-new television and VCR in his house. Probably one of the gifts from Kim that he had mentioned. I thought of Kim's state-of-the-art equipment in her barren apartment. But from the looks of her collection, she hadn't purchased a record since Don Kirschner's heyday. And I thought of Pence, with his unconnected recorder, a pathetic reminder of the gift from his missing grandson. Gifts.

The geezer next to me was still talking. I don't know if he was talking to me. I smoked another cigarette and moved the ashes around in the ashtray with the lit end. In my other hand I held the empty shot glass and made circles with it on the bar. I finished my beer.

"Steve," I said, calling him over. "You still got that phone in the office upstairs?"

"Yeah?"

"I need to use it."

"Go ahead."

He handed me an unsolicited beer as I stepped away from the bar. I put the Camels in my breast pocket and passed the kitchen, tripping once as I went up a narrow staircase. I found the small office and had a seat at a government-issue desk that faced a dirty window overlooking the alley. The phone directory was under the desk.

I looked up the number for the local authorized Kotekna service center and dialed it. After two rings a friendly voice picked up.

"Service," he said.

"Hi," I said. "I've got a problem with my VCR."

"Is it in warranty, sir?"

"Yes, but it's been serviced twice already. I'm not interested in having another serviceman look at it. What I need from you, is there some sort of eight-hundred number, a customer service line or anything like that?"

"Hold on," he said, a little less friendly. He got back on the line and gave me the number. I thanked him, hung up, and dialed the number he had given me. A recorded voice instructed me to wait for the next available operator. Before the message ended a live voice broke in on the line.

"Kotekna Video. Customer service."

"Customer service?" I said lamely. "I'm sorry. I'm a retailer, not a customer. I was trying to get the sales manager for the mid-Atlantic region. What's his name again?"

"Bruce Baum," she said.

"Yes, of course. Could you connect me please?" There was a click, then a couple of rings.

"Mr. Baum's office," a sweet voice said.

"This is Gary Fisher," I said, "with Nutty Nathan's in Washington. Can I speak to Bruce, please?"

"Let me see if he's in. Hold, please." A click, more waiting, then, "I'll connect you."

"Bruce Baum," a smooth voice said.

"Bruce," I said, "Gary Fisher, the merch manager with Nutty Nathan's."

"Gary," he said with false warmth. "What can I do for you?"

"I'm really calling for some advice on one of your products."

"Go ahead, Gary."

"My company purchased a hundred sticks from your people at the CES show in Vegas, a closeout I think."

"That's right. The KV100, wasn't it? Your GM, Jerry Rosen, cut the deal himself."

"Yes. Anyway, to be honest with you, I'm having some trouble moving them. I don't know if it's a problem with price point, or if I'm not promoting them correctly, or what?" I heard the slur of my words and let him talk.

"Well," he said, "I hope you're not trying to make the full mark on them. After all, even considering they were defects, I practically gave them away."

"Defects?"

"Yes. Didn't you know?"

"No."

"Well, then," he said with a chuckle, "there's your problem right there. Miscommunication in your office. I had this load of KV100's with defective boards. Jerry Rosen came out to the show and decided to take them off my hands for practically nothing. He said he was going to have your service department order the new parts, fix the units themselves, then blow them out at a strong retail to make an impression in your market. He probably hasn't gotten the parts yet. *That's* why they're still sitting in your barn."

"The units are shells right now, is that what you're saying?"

"That's right."

"Thanks, Bruce."

"*Thank you.* Let me know how you do with them. We've been trying to get our foot in your door for years. Frankly, I cut this deal with Rosen as an entrée."

"I'll let you know, Bruce. Thanks again." I hung up.

I put fire to a Camel and leaned back in my chair. A bird flew onto the window ledge, saw me, and flew off. I exhaled a line of smoke and watched it shatter as it hit the glass. I heard cynical laughter and realized it was mine.

There was one more call to make, a detail done so that I could put it all away and return to my cleansing binge. I got South Carolina information on the line.

I contacted the personnel director for Ned's World. I identified myself as a the personnel manager of a large retail chain in the Baltimore–Washington corridor. After a couple of questions my suspicions were confirmed.

Then I was downstairs and spilling money on the bar. Steve Maroulis yelled something to my back as I walked out. The temperature had dropped and the sun was buried in a thick cover of clouds. Still, the light burned my eyes. I put on shades and got behind the wheel of my car.

I cut down Thirty-Eighth to Nebraska, across Connecticut and right on Military to Missouri, then left on Georgia. I pulled over and parked across the street from the Good Times Lunch.

Kim shot me a look when I walked in. Some heads turned in the gray-haired group seated near the upright fan and the malt liquor poster featuring Fred "The Hammer" Williamson. I sat on the stool nearest the front door. Kim walked over with a pad in his hand.

"No food today, Kim. Just give me a can of beer."

He brought one, set it down, and walked away. I drank half of it in one swallow and lit a cigarette. The fan blew my smoke in the direction of the front door. I killed my beer and shouted for Kim to bring me another.

I dozed off or blacked out for a minute or so. When I opened my eyes, Kim was setting a fresh beer in front of me. I popped the top and drank deeply. Some of the beer ran down my chin.

"Last one," Kim said.

"Sure, Kim."

"Go home, Nick." There was something approaching sadness on his face.

I left the remainder of the beer and a pile of ones on the counter. I stumbled out and stepped off the curb. A group of kids yelled something from a car that nearly grazed me. The kid riding shotgun flipped me off.

My Dodge came to life. I swung a "U" on Georgia and headed back downtown. I undid the top of the pint with one hand and took a burning slug. I cracked another beer and wedged it between my thighs.

The car next to me honked and someone yelled. I turned the radio louder. I passed what was once a movie theater and was now a Peoples Drug Store. My thoughts moved back twenty years.

I am ten years old in this summer of 1968. I'm on the bus, the J-2, on my daily trip down Georgia Avenue to F Street, where I'll transfer to another bus that will take me crosstown to papou's carryout. I bag lunches there behind the counter.

The D.C. Transit bus, with its turquoise vinyl seats and orange striping, is not air-conditioned. The ones they commission to this part of town never are. By ten in the morning, when I ride, the bus already reeks with the sweat of working Washington.

This summer things feel different. Georgia Avenue is not the worst of spots, but the fires of April have lapped at this street. Every week I notice more businesses have closed. There seems to be a tension on the bus between blacks and whites, though I'm not afraid. Something is happening and I'm there to see it. Women wear large, plastic florescent earrings that read, "Black Is Beautiful" over the silhouettes of Afro'ed couples. Lawyers have long hair and wear wide, flowery ties. The ultra-square DJ, Fred Fiske on 1260 AM, is playing the Youngblood's "Get Together" in heavy rotation.

I read the changing marquees of the neighborhood movie theaters that line Georgia Avenue: Eleanor Parker and Michael Sarrazin in Eye of the Cat*; George Peppard and Orson Welles in* House of Cards*; Alex Cord in Harold Robbins'* Stiletto. *Downtown, at the Trans-Lux,* The Great Bank Robbery, *with Clint Walker and Kim Novak, has just opened.*

At three in the afternoon, after the lunch rush is over at papou's store, a man drops a stack of Daily News *on top of the cigarette machine. I take one to a booth and read the reviews of the films whose titles I have seen splashed across the marquees earlier in the day.*

I look behind the counter at my grandfather. He is slicing a tomato that he holds in his hand. The juice of the tomato stains the yellowish apron he wears around his ample middle. There is a Band-Aid on his thumb from his accident on the meat slicer earlier in the day. He sees the tabloid open in front of me and knows my daily ritual.

"Anything good today at the movies, Niko?" he shouts across the store.

"Nothing much, Papou."

"Okay, boy," he says, and continues to slice the tomato. There is a smile on his wide, pink face.

I threw my head back and killed another beer. More horns sounded. I pulled back within the lines of my lane and turned left on Florida Avenue, heading east.

I ran the red at North Capitol and bore left onto Lincoln Road. I passed houses with rotting back porches, alleys littered with garbage, and packs of young men grouped like predators on street corners.

Then I was veering left, passing under the black, arched iron gate of the Glenwood Cemetery. I pulled the top on another beer and stayed to the right, driving slowly around long curves and lazy inclines, by rows of headstones and monuments crammed together, their symmetry broken only by the occasional dogwood or pine.

As the names on the headstones changed from Protestant to ethnic, I slowed down. When I reached a section that only contained the graves of Greeks, I stopped the car.

I remained seated and drank my last beer. When I finished it, I crushed the can, tossed it into the backseat, and slipped the pint bottle inside my jacket. I got out of the car and staggered onto the grass.

Spartan immigrants had chosen to lie here. They were buried on a long hill overlooking the road and a junior-high playground. A few of the headstones mentioned their native villages and the year in which they came to America.

I recognized many of the family names. Some had been friends with, or had known my grandfather: Kerasiotas, Kalavratinos, Stathopoulos, Psarakis. On the headstone of a guy named Vlatos, the inscription read, "I Wish I Was in Vegas."

I had a seat under an oak tree across from my grandfather's headstone. I reached into my jacket and pulled out the pint, tilted it back to my mouth, and watched bubbles rise to its upturned base. I swallowed, toasted my grandfather with the bottle, and replaced the cap.

Though it was probably very cool, I felt comfortable. I listened to the faint laughter and yells of the boys playing ball on the playground at the foot of the hill. The wind blew small yellow leaves around my feet. And I stared at the headstone that bore my name: Nicholas J. Stefanos.

I stayed in that position for the remainder of the afternoon. I was unable to focus my thoughts on any one thing; all of my emotions seemed to flow through me at once. In the end there were only a few pathetic certainties: I was thirty years old, unemployed, and sitting dead drunk in a graveyard, an empty pint of rotgut bourbon in my hand.

Sometime after the skies had darkened and the sounds of the playground had died away, a man in a caretaker's uniform walked towards me. He kicked the soles of my shoes lightly. The name stitched across his chest, on a white patch, was Raymond.

"You better get on up," he said. "They'll be lockin' the gates, and just before that the police cruise through."

"Thanks," I said, using his arm to help me up.

"You all right, man?"

"Yeah, Raymond. Thanks a million."

I don't remember the ride home, except that there was shouting and more hornblowing. There was also a nasty bit of business at the National Shrine, where I attracted a small crowd when I pulled over to vomit.

I woke up early the next morning, halfway on my bed and fully clothed. There was some puke splashed across my denim shirt, and a dried clump of it on my chin.

I had a cold shower. After that, I put on side two of the Replacements' *Tim,* the most violently melodic rock and roll I owned. I cleared the room and forced myself to jump rope.

By the time Bob Stinson's blistering guitar solo kicked in, on "Little Mascara," my eyes were closed and I was working the rope, my body soaked with sweat and alcohol.

I took another shower, as hot as I could stand it, and shaved. I cooked breakfast, made a pot of coffee, and finished them both. I put on clean clothes and ran fresh water into the cat's dish.

Then I climbed into my Dodge and pointed it in the direction of James Pence.

TWENTY-SIX

The buzzer unlocked the glass doors automatically. I stepped into the building, past the security guard and the woman at the switchboard, and into the elevator. I rode it to the tenth floor and walked the narrow carpeted hallway to Pence's apartment. The door was open as I arrived.

The final drag of Pence's cigarette burned between his fingers. The familiar smell of Old Spice and whiskey drifted towards me.

"You look like hell," he said.

"May I come in?"

"Certainly." He stepped aside as I passed.

I walked into the living room, hearing his padded footsteps behind me. I turned to look at him. The grief of the last weeks had taken years from him, years he didn't have.

"Coffee?" he asked.

"No coffee. Why don't you just get me a screwdriver. A Phillips head, can you do that?"

"Yes," he said. "I own one."

"Then do it."

I heard him rummage through a drawer in the kitchen. I picked up the VCR from the lower shelf of the television stand and moved it over to the dining room table. It felt very light.

Pence brought me the screwdriver. I took it and worked on the back of the recorder. He lit another cigarette and sat watching me from the end of the table. His face was reddening from embarrassment, but there was also a look on him something like relief.

When the screws were off, I lifted the back panel and put it aside. I reached in and felt around, then looked it over with a perfunctory glance. I sat back in my chair and stared at Pence. He looked away.

"It's empty," I said. "But you knew that."

"Yes." He looked at his lap boyishly and blew some smoke at his knees.

I walked over to the window and raised the blinds. Then I cranked open the casement window and breathed cool air.

"Is my grandson alive?" Pence said in a small voice.

"I don't know."

"What *do* you know, Mr. Stefanos?"

I turned and looked at him angrily. "I know now what you've suspected for weeks. The people I used to work for are involved in some sort of drug trafficking. They're moving the drugs through the warehouse in these VCRs. I think that Jimmy stole one and brought it home. Do we agree so far?"

"Yes."

"When he got it home and saw it was dead, he opened up the back and found its contents. He was never fired from Nathan's, he just never went back. But he knew they'd figure out eventually who took the VCR. So he got scared and left town with the drugs and a couple of friends he made along the way. You figured all this out and came to me for help. Then you put the VCR out where I could see it, knowing I'd notice it, right?"

"That's right," he said. "Believe me, I'm not proud of how I got you into this. Playing on your sympathies, and so forth."

"So forth. You mean *lying*, don't you?"

"Yes. I'd do more than that, to protect my grandson. When you have children, you'll understand."

"I'm not interested in understanding your motives." I shook a cigarette out of his pack and lit it, then dropped his Zippo on the table. "Why did you come to me?"

"After I found the empty recorder in Jimmy's room and linked it with his rather erratic behavior and the company he was keeping, I didn't know what to do. Going to the police seemed out of the question. After all, Jimmy was involved, in a criminal sense. I went to Mr. McGinnes for help—he was the only one in the organization I knew—and he suggested you. When he said your name, I recognized it. Jimmy *had* mentioned you to me, several times. It wasn't all a lie, Mr. Stefanos."

"But why didn't you come clean with me from the beginning?"

"Obviously there's more than one person at Nutty Nathan's who's dirty," he said. "I wasn't sure if I could trust you."

I raised my open hand without thought, then lowered it. My voice shook.

"You stupid old bastard," I said slowly. "You just don't understand, do you?" He stared at me blankly. I butted the cigarette, walked to the door, and turned the knob.

"I'd like to help," he said weakly.

"No."

"What are you going to do?"

"Finish it."

McGinnes watched me enter Nathan's on the Avenue, and kept watching, his arms folded as he leaned against a microwave oven display.

Lee was behind the counter to my right. She was wearing a jade green shirt, buttoned to the top, and a jean skirt, out of which came her stout little wheels. First she smiled, then her brow wrinkled.

"You look terrible," she said.

"So I've been told."

"Sorry about your job."

"Don't worry about it, Lee. Listen, I've been awful busy."

"You don't have to explain," she said.

I glanced back at McGinnes. "Lee, I don't mean to cut you short, but I've got to talk to Johnny."

"Go ahead," she said. "We'll talk later."

I head-motioned McGinnes. We walked the length of the store through the back to the radio room.

"You want a beer?" he asked.

"No."

"Suit yourself," he said, and pulled a malt liquor from his usual spot. He popped the tab and drank.

"Where's Andre and Louie?"

"Andre's off. Louie's out making a deposit. What's up?"

"Can we talk for a few minutes?"

"Yeah, the floor is dead. If this is about the Broda thing, I can tell you that I've been keeping an eye on the news, and that Shultz boy was never found."

"I know. But there's more."

I told him everything that I was certain of, and some of my guesses. He whistled softly when I was finished and then stared at his feet. Some color had gone out of his face.

"What do we do now?" he said.

"I only wanted you to be aware of the situation, in case they think you're involved. They haven't made any kind of play on me yet. Maybe they think the Shultz murder scared us off."

"What happened to the girl?"

"She's gone," I said. "Listen, Johnny, I need one more favor of you, man, then it's over for you."

"What is it?"

"I know you keep a few pieces that you collect, the unregistered kind. I'll be needing to borrow one."

He looked at me as he finished his beer. He moved the can around in his hand and then crushed it.

"You come in here," he said, "and tell me all this shit, and I haven't even got it all digested yet, and now you want a gun? You're fuckin' nuts, man. Why don't you just ask me to put one to your head and pull the trigger?"

"Listen," I said. "I'm going on with this thing. I don't *have* any options, Johnny. And I need something behind me if I'm going to get this kid."

"I don't think so, Nick," he said, and shook his head as he walked away. "I gotta get back out on the floor."

"Think about it," I yelled to his back. But he was already out the door.

Late in the afternoon I stopped in the Good Times Lunch and had a seat at the counter. Kim came over with a pad in his hand.

"The special, Kim," I said sheepishly, "and a coffee, black."

He nodded and returned shortly with a fried-fish platter. I shoveled it in and had a cigarette with my coffee. After that I paid the check that Kim laid in front of me.

"Kim," I said, and he turned back around. "I'm sorry about yesterday. I was out of control. It won't happen again."

"No problem, Nick," he said. "But you should get rest. You don't look so good."

The red light on my answering machine was blinking when I entered my apartment. I pushed down on the bar.

The first message, from McGinnes, told me to meet him at the store tomorrow. He would have what I wanted. The second message was from Joe Dane. I called him at home, and he picked up on the third ring.

"Hello?"

"Joe, it's Nick, calling you back."

"Nick, we need to talk."

177

"I think it's time. How about right now?"

"No, not now. I'm busy tonight. Tomorrow morning in the park."

"Tomorrow's fine, but not in the park. Someplace more public."

He hesitated. "So it's like that."

"That's right," I said. "Tomorrow morning at ten, in the bell tower at the Old Post Office downtown."

"Okay, Nick," he said. "Ten o'clock."

TWENTY-SEVEN

To get into the tower of the Old Post Office at Twelfth and Penn, one has to take the tour. I stood amid a group of eight tourists on the ground level, around a brightly lit, U-shaped counter.

A gangly Park Service employee was giving us a brief history of the Post Office. He mumbled into a microphone in a barely intelligible, nasal voice. The man next to me was taping him with a video camera.

After his speech we were ushered into a glass elevator and began our ascent to the tower base. The checkerboard floor of the Pavilion fell away rapidly as we rose higher. A little girl near me said to her father, "Daddy, if we fell now, we'd be dead, right?" An older woman who already looked a little frightened touched her collar and laughed nervously.

The doors opened and we walked out to a circle of white and red ropes that rang the Congress Bells. A rotund guide informed us that the bells, a gift from Great Britain, were rung on the opening and closing days of Congress, and on all national holidays. The only other instances when they were rung, she said, were in honor of the Challenger's crew, and "when the Redskins won the Super Bowl."

Then the guide herded us into another elevator. She reached in and pushed the floor button from the outside. "You picked a great day for the tower," she said, as the doors closed and her fat, bespectacled face disappeared.

When the doors opened again, the group walked out into the open-air tower and scattered. The clock mechanism was housed in a raised platform in the center. A Park Ranger sat on the platform and looked through binoculars.

A circular walkway afforded a view of the city in all directions. Three of the sides were strung with narrowly spaced wire to discourage jumpers. The south side had a Plexiglas shield. Joe Dane was standing on the east side, looking out. I tapped his shoulder.

He turned without surprise. Though his clothes were clean, he looked as disheveled as always. There was a dead look to his watery brown eyes.

"I don't really like this view," he said, turning his head towards the expanse of Pennsylvania, Constitution, and the Capitol.

"We can move," I said.

We walked past the southern view of the Potomac and the Jefferson Memorial, and over to the west wall. Dane stared through the wires. The curving lines of the Federal Building below were like a horseshoe framing the Mall and the Lincoln Memorial.

"All those tourists," he said. "They waste their time standing in line to get up the Washington Monument, when the best view of D.C. is right here." He smiled. "Remember when you and me and Sarah and Karen used to come down here on Sundays? Smoke a joint out in the car, then come up and take pictures with our heads through the wires and shit like that? After that spend a couple of hours munching our way through the eatery downstairs."

"Joe," I said. "Let's just get down to it, all right?"

"All right, Nick," he said softly. His smile faded, and he buried his hands in his pockets.

"Give it to me straight up. Did they get Jimmy Broda?"

"Yes."

"Is he alive?"

"Yes."

I smiled and slapped the wall. The ranger and a couple of tourists looked my way. I wanted to hug Dane but didn't show it. I wasn't finished with him.

"Why are you here, Joe?"

"Last shot at redemption, I guess." He shook his head. "I don't know."

"Are you still with them?"

"No. But they don't know that."

"Tell me about it."

He shrugged. "It's not all that complicated. It's a small operation, smaller than you think. Only a few people involved. And this was their first time at this sort of thing. At least it was for Rosen."

"Jerry Rosen in charge of it all?"

"On the D.C. end."

"What about Nathan Plavin?"

"No. It was easy to keep him out of it. Rosen had him insulated from the day-to-day aspects of the business, anyway."

"Who else at Nathan's? Brandon?"

"No."

"How did you get in, Joe?"

"Rosen knew I was hard up for money," he said. "He came to me with a proposal. Supervise the shipment, in and out, and keep an eye on it while it was in the barn. The payoff was pretty sweet. And I rationalized it with that old mentality you and I grew up with—drugs are innocent, done by innocent people."

"That was a long time ago."

He looked down at his shoes. "When one of the warehouse guys tipped me that the Broda kid had stolen the VCR, I knew things were going to fall apart. Then you started to poke around. I wanted to tell you and get out then, but I had to make a choice. . . . I had to make a choice between warning you and looking out for Sarah." He spread his hands out.

"Keep talking," I said.

"I went to Rosen," he said, still looking at his shoes. "He had Brandon fire you, then had his boys beat you up to warn you off. They followed the kids south. The Shultz boy was killed. Then they caught Broda and brought him back."

"Why didn't they kill Broda too?"

Some tourists walked by. Dane stopped talking until they passed. "They don't know *what* to do with him," he said. "Listen, Nick, I know you feel like a sucker. But the reason that kid is still alive is you. They know you've stuck with this thing, and that you're not going to leave it alone. They *can't* get rid of the kid while you're still looking, and they can't let him go. It's a stalemate now."

"Don't bullshit me, Joe." I eyed him suspiciously. "Let me get this straight. Jerry Rosen was a fair-haired boy when he worked for Ned's World in South Carolina. When he moved to D.C. to work for Nathan, he saw the drug market up here and decided to get a piece of it. Those two guys who roughed me up—did he recruit them from the South Carolina warehouse?"

"Yes."

"Who else?"

"There's the Jamaicans who work with me."

"I met them," I said. "A tall albino and his shadow. So there's them, Rosen, the two from Carolina, you—and the man who bankrolled the whole deal. Ned Plavin, right?"

"That's right."

I thought for a minute. "Are the drugs out of the warehouse yet?"

"Not entirely," he said. "It was a hundred sticks to start out with. They moved fifty in two consecutive nights last week, and another twenty-five on Tuesday. Tomorrow night they move the last twenty-four."

"How?"

"What do you mean?"

"The setup. Where, who comes for it, how it's done, the money, all of it."

"Shit, Nicky." He studied my face. "The way it was done the other times, two buyers come. They bring a hundred-fifty grand in a suitcase. We meet in the back of the warehouse, where the VCRs are stacked. Our guys load them up, they leave the suitcase."

"Guns?"

"Yeah, everyone."

"What time does it go down?"

"Ten o'clock."

"Are you going to be there?"

"I'm gone, Nick. Sarah and I packed last night. I called in sick today. We're leaving this afternoon, all of us."

"Just walk, then everything's all right."

"No," he said, "it's never going to be all right. I was part of something that got a kid killed. Maybe someday I'll put a gun in my mouth to help me forget. Probably not. But for the time being my job is to protect my family."

"You'd better get going then, Joe."

"One more thing," he said, and grabbed my arm before I could pull it away. "These guys are just a bunch of dumbshit cowboys. You go up against them, man, you're gonna die."

"You know where they've got the kid?"

"No." He took his hand off my arm. "I'm sorry, Nick. I really am."

"So long, Joe."

He turned and headed for the stairwell. When the door closed behind him, I wished him luck.

Louie was behind the front counter when I walked into the store. He gave me a nod with his chin, then stared at me over the tops of his reading glasses.

"How's it going, Louie?"

"Oh, I'm makin' it, Youngblood. How about you? Anything goin' on?"

"I'm weighing the possibilities."

"Well, you got all the time in the world now. To find out what's *important*."

"Is Johnny in?"

"In the back, takin' his medicine."

I negotiated the maze of floor display and passed under the BB-riddled caricature of Nathan. I took the stairs down to the stockroom.

McGinnes was sitting on a carton in the back. Malone was standing next to him, a live Newport between his long fingers. I walked through a stagnant cloud of tobacco and pot smoke to get to them. I shook Malone's hand and shot a look at McGinnes.

"Andre knows everything," McGinnes said unapologetically.

"He ran it all down to me," Malone said quickly, "in the hopes that the two of us could talk you out of whatever it is you plannin' to do." He gave me the once-over, dragged on his cigarette, exhaled, and threw me a hundred dollar smile. "You really stepped in some shit this time, didn't you, Country?"

"It's deeper than you think."

I told them just how deep it was. Malone's brow was wrinkled the entire time I spoke. When I was finished, he ran a thumbnail between his front teeth, keeping his eyes on mine.

"So," McGinnes said. "They've got the boy."

"If you don't mind, Johnny," I said, "I'll take what I came here for."

McGinnes went to the corner of the stockroom, moved some boxes, and returned with something in his arms. He unwrapped the oilcloth it was in and brought it out.

"I wasn't sure what you wanted," he said. "So I brought a solid automatic. Nine-millimeter Browning Hi-Power. Push button magazine release." With a quick jerk of his wrist the clip slid out into his palm. "Holds thirteen with one in the chamber. Right here is the safety—you can operate it with your thumb while your hand's still on the grip. If you're not sure the safety's on, try cocking the hammer."

"Thanks." I held out my hand.

"I brought an extra clip." He pulled that out, placed it with the pistol, and put them both in my hand. "It's your up, man."

I rewrapped everything in the oilcloth and put it in my knapsack, then hung it over my shoulder.

"You guys coming upstairs?"

"I am," Andre said.

"I think I'll hang," McGinnes said. "Catch a buzz."

Malone and I climbed the stairs. As we neared the landing, we heard McGinnes coughing below. Malone stayed with me all the way to the front door, where he stopped me with a grip on my arm.

"Hey, Brother Lou," he shouted at Louie, who was still behind the counter. "I'll be takin' a break."

"You already had a break," Louie said tiredly.

"Then I'll be takin' another."

"What's up, Andre?" I asked.

"Let's go for a ride," Malone said. "I got a proposition for you, Country."

TWENTY-EIGHT

Malone said, "Pull on over, man."

We were in the southbound lane of North Capitol, near the Florida Avenue intersection. I pulled over and cut the engine. Malone rolled the window down, leaned his arm on its edge, and put fire to a Newport.

On the east side of the street was a casket company, a beauty parlor, and a sign that read, "FISH, UBS." Hand-painted on the door, in dripping, wide red brushstrokes, was, "Closed for Good." To our right stood a Plexiglas bus shelter on a triangle of dirt that the city called a park. A man in a brown plaid overcoat slept in front of the shelter's bench, where another graybeard sat and drank from a bagged bottle. Further down the street, near P, a Moorish carryout and a "Hi-Tech" shoeshine parlor graced the block.

The sidewalks were teeming with activity. Those not seated on stoops paced within the confines of their block. A woman in a two-piece, turquoise jogging suit stood with her hands on her hips and yelled gibberish at the unconcerned people walking past. Her flat buttocks sagged much like her sloping shoulders. Straight ahead, less than two miles down the strip, rose the Capitol dome.

"Look at it," Malone said. "This is our city, man. Just *look* at it. Right in the shadow of the motherfuckin' Capitol. And they be throwin' eighty million dollar inauguration parties."

"You came from a neighborhood just like this," I said, "and you made it out. It's no different than it was twenty years ago."

He chuckled cynically and blew out some smoke. "Don't tell me it's no different, man. On these streets they kill you now for a ten dollar rock. And the media, all they be talkin' about: 'The Mayor Snorts Coke.' But nobody really cares about these people, because it ain't goin' down in Ward Three. It's just niggers killin' niggers. Meanwhile, you read the *Washington Post*—they supposed to be 'the liberal watchdog of the community,' right?—well, check it out. Some white woman gets raped in the suburbs, it makes page one. Now go to the back of the Metro section, where they got a special spot reserved for the niggers. They call it "Around the Area," some shit like that. And it's always the same little boldfaced type: 'Southeast Man Slain, Northeast Man Fatally Shot.'" He tossed his butt out the window. "One little paragraph, buried in the back of the paper, for the niggers."

"You and me have talked about this a hundred times, Andre. What's it got to do with today?"

He looked out the window and squinted, then ran a finger along the top of his thick mustache. "I remember my first day of work at Nathan's. I got dressed that morning, real sharp. When I walked out of my place that day, I *knew* I was serious, I was so hooked up, I was *proud.*"

"I remember," I said, and smiled at the thought of it. But I wondered where he was going with it.

"Anyway, I was all fired up, like anyone on their first day of the job. After a year, I had me enough to rent my place on Harvard, out of the old neighborhood. But then I started to notice some shit. The company was always sending other guys to seminars, putting other guys in management training. When the big dogs came into the store, I got no recognition, man, nary a nod. I doubt they even knew my name. And then they started cutting our commissions, changing payplans every six months. I woke up one day, I saw I was sliding back to where I came from."

"What are you telling me?"

He waved his hand the width of the block. "I don't want to come back to these streets, man. I *won't* come back to these streets, understand?" He lit another smoke and pitched the match out the window. "When I was listening to you earlier, I started to think. We both got a problem we need to work out. How could we take that situation they got down in that warehouse and turn it around to our advantage?"

"And?"

"I ain't got it all nailed down yet, see what I'm sayin'? But it would involve other people."

"Not McGinnes," I said quickly. "There's something wrong with him. I mean he's not well."

"Yeah, I think he's getting ready to bottom on out. Besides, all the man wants is to sell televisions."

"And what do you want?"

"I'm still thinkin' on it," he said. "Hold up a minute while I make a call."

He left the car and walked to a payphone at the gas station on the intersection. I had a Camel while he talked on the phone. By the time I finished it, he was back on the seat at my side.

"We got an appointment to see some fellas," he said.

"Who?"

"Just younguns, that's all. They all right."

"This is getting too complicated," I said.

"Not complicated. Simple. Look here." He slid closer to me on the seat. "You want the boy, that's as plain as the light. But you got nothin' to deal with. When that last shipment of goods leaves the warehouse tomorrow night, and they tighten up the loose ends, they gonna do that boy just like they done the one down in Carolina."

"I could go to the cops," I said, "like I should have done from the beginning."

"Too late for that. You might get the boy killed, and take a fall yourself. No, man, there's a better way."

"Talk about it."

"Twenty-five percent of the man's goods," he said. "That's a big bargaining chip to sit down with at the table."

I thought about that. "You mean, steal the rest of the cocaine."

"That's right, Country. Then trade it back to Rosen for the boy."

I lit another cigarette and tossed the match, taking a deep lungful of the deathly smog. Then I watched my exhale stream out the window and disappear as it met the wind.

"What's your angle?" I said.

"My angle? A way out. All the way out. The way you tell, there's gonna be some money changin' hands tomorrow night. The money will be mine. A hundred-thirty for me, twenty for the boys I just called."

"So you think we can just walk in and grab it—all of it, the money and the shake—from these guys? You said yourself, these people don't play."

"Then neither will we."

"You'd have to leave town. You'd never work or live in D.C. again. Have you thought about that?"

"This shit goes down in the street every day. As for work, well, a hundred and thirty grand is quite a start. For me, some things I've wanted for my mom. Yeah, I've thought about it."

"It's too fucking crazy, Andre." I dismissed the idea with a motion of my hand. But even as I did so, I was picturing in my mind the layout of the warehouse.

Andre pointed to the key in the ignition. "Kick this bitch over," he said. "I want you to meet my boys."

We veered off of Florida and climbed sharply up Thirteenth Street. On our right was Cardoza High School; to our left were the Clifton Terrace apartments. At the crest of the hill, just past Thirteenth and Clifton, I made a "U" in the middle of the street and pulled the car over to the curb at Andre's command.

Children kicked a ball around the glass-covered courtyard of the apartments. Boys walked from the high school, hunched and slower than old men. The downtown skyline rose below us majestically.

"Top of the motherfuckin' town," Malone said without emotion. He pointed left to the Highview Apartments. "They'll be coming out of there."

"You grew up right around here, didn't you?"

"Yeah."

We sat there for about ten minutes without speaking. Then Malone tapped me on the shoulder and I looked left. Two young men were crossing the street.

They were still in their teens. The taller of the two was lanky and wore a red sweatsuit with high-tops, and walked with an exaggerated downstep. There was a fixed scowl on his face. The other one was short and slender at the waist, with a boxer's upper body. He wore Lee jeans and a T-shirt. Both of their heads were shaved close to the scalp, with off-center parts like scars. They climbed into the backseat of my car.

"All right, Home," the short one said to Malone, and they touched knuckles.

"Tony," Malone said to the short one. "Who's your friend?"

"His name's Wayne," Tony said. "He in my crew."

"This is Nick," Malone said. Tony nodded slightly. Wayne did nothing. We stared at each other in my rearview. "Where's your big brother at, Tony?"

"You mean Charles?" Tony said and tilted his head.

"Yeah."

"Chillin' in Lorton."

"What happened?" Malone asked.

Tony said, "Charles always be tellin' me, 'Don't be shakin', messin' with guns and shit.' One day this nigger dissed his ass in the street. Charles steals the motherfucker in the jaw. The nigger gets up for more. Charles double-steals the motherfucker. Nigger hits his head on the street. Dead. Charles doin' six to twelve, second degree."

Wayne said to Malone, "What'd you call us for, Home?"

"A job," Malone said slowly. "Tomorrow night."

"What kind of job?" Tony asked.

"Robbin' a cocaine deal."

"Where?"

"A warehouse, just over the line."

"Talk about the pay," Wayne said.

"If it goes down right, twenty thousand for the two of you," Malone said. In the rearview I saw Wayne grin and tap Tony's hand with his own.

"How many guns?" Tony asked.

Malone said, "We lookin' at maybe six." If this impressed them, they didn't show it.

"What about the 'caine," Wayne asked.

"The cocaine goes to Nick."

"Who?" Wayne said and smiled.

Malone glared at him. "You heard me. And he's in charge." Wayne and Tony stared back but didn't speak. Malone continued. "We're going to need guns, and a van."

"We got guns," Tony said. "We can get a van."

I cleared my throat and spoke for the first time. "The guns are for show, understand? They're not to be used." My voice sounded awkward and lily-white.

Tony said to Malone, "You better tell your boy what time it is. If a man holdin' a gun on you, and he willin' to use it, you *got* to fire down on his ass."

"He knows that," Malone said unconvincingly.

"That's all for now," I said abruptly, and turned over the ignition. I could feel their stares. "We'll let you know tomorrow if it's going to happen. We'll let you know."

Tony and Wayne slid out of the car. Tony leaned in the passenger window.

Malone said, "How the pay sound?"

Tony said, "Pay sound good, Home."

"I'll call you tomorrow," Malone said, "first thing."

I yanked the column shift down into drive and pulled away from the curb. Fifteen minutes later I dropped Malone at the door of the Avenue.

That evening I drew a diagram of the warehouse and studied it. After that I phoned Malone.

"Andre, it's Nick."

"Nick. What's up?"

"It's on for tomorrow night."

"Good."

"Call Wayne and Tony. Tell them to meet us, with the van, on top of the Silver Spring parking garage, the one next to and on the same side of the street as the Metro station. All the way up, at seven-thirty sharp. You got that?"

"That it?"

"You want out, I mean up to the last minute?"

"I'm in, Nick."

I hung up and smoked a couple of cigarettes at the kitchen table. The cat sat on the radiator and watched me smoke. When I was finished, I washed up, locked the front door, and went to bed. I fell asleep quickly and did not dream.

I rose early the next morning and got permission from a high school friend to visit his property out around Thurmont, north of Frederick. An hour and a half later I was parked in front of a padlocked barn. I walked across a plowed field and into the woods.

I found the clearing where my friend kept his personal garden of vegetables and marijuana. Both had been harvested by now. I pulled a few rusty beer cans from a steel drum on the edge of the clearing and set most of them upright on stumps. I hung the remainder on the low branches of trees.

I walked to the middle of the garden, removed the Browning from my knapsack, loaded it, and undid the safety. I took my time firing at the beer cans. Eventually I emptied a full clip. When I was done, I had a reasonable approximation of the sight, and a good feel for the kick.

I replaced the gun in my knapsack and walked back into the woods. I came across a deer blind and climbed up into it, using the wooden blocks that had been hammered to the tree trunk.

For the next hour I sat in the blind smoking cigarettes and listening to the silence. There were not many birds this time of day. A rabbit bolted across some dry leaves, then down the bluff of a nearby creek.

I climbed off the tree and walked through the woods and across the field to my car, then drove back to D.C.

In my apartment I cleared out the center of my bedroom, turned my stereo up, and began to jump rope. Twenty minutes later I removed wet clothing and had a hot shower.

I shaved and dressed in jeans, a black sweatshirt, and running shoes. I had a sandwich, a cup of coffee, and, with that, a smoke. I put some dry food in the cat's dish. I loaded the Browning and placed it in my knapsack. Then I left the apartment to pick up Malone.

We drove onto the roof of the parking garage at about seven-twenty. A thin, purple line of sunset ran between a thick mass of clouds on the western horizon.

"That would be them," Malone said, pointing to a green, windowless Ford van parked in the far corner.

"Is it stolen?" I asked, and drove towards it.

"That's a bet," he said. I pulled up next to them.

We got out of my car and locked it. Malone walked around to the driver's side. They were up front in the buckets, both wearing jeans and blue, zip-up windbreakers.

"Give me the keys and move in the back," Malone said. They did it, but slowly. Malone got behind the wheel, and I took the passenger seat. There were no seats in back. Tony and Wayne sat with their backs against the interior walls, a blanket-covered mound between them at their feet.

"All right," I said, pulling the diagram from my knapsack and crawling back with them. "Andre and I have already gone over this, so listen up." They moved in close and looked at the drawing. "I have a key to the office, and I know the alarm code. But the code to the warehouse is different. We'll have to wait until they come to make the transaction before we can enter the warehouse."

"Where they gonna be?" Tony asked.

I pointed to the diagram. "The goods are in the rear left corner. Here. Wayne, you're going to go down the center aisle and cut left at the break in the row. You just move in and cover them from the side. Andre and me are going to walk right in on them, straight up the aisle they're in. That way they'll be covered on two sides. The other two sides are walls." Wayne nodded and concentrated on the diagram.

"Where am I?" Tony asked.

"You enter the warehouse from the loft. Here. Then you climb over the railing and drop down to the top of the stock in the center aisle. Crawl along the top of it until you get to where the deal is happening, in the back. You cover us all from above."

"What you gonna do," Wayne said, "ask 'em, 'Please, can I have the 'caine?' " I didn't answer.

Malone said, "What about the guns?"

"Right here, Home." Tony pulled back the blanket and tossed it to the side. He reached in the pile and handed Malone a blue steel pistol. "Three-eighty Beretta, holds eight rounds. Bad little gun, too."

Malone felt the weight of the piece and checked the action. I watched Wayne slide a nine-millimeter Colt into his jacket. Tony held up some sort of semiautomatic assault pistol.

Malone said, "What you plan on doin' with that, Tony?"

"Spray the motherfucker," Tony said, "if I have to. MAC ten. Thirty-two rounds in the clip. Can't *nobody* fuck with it." The short barrel passed in front of me as he moved the gun to his other hand. I grabbed the barrel and glared at Tony.

"Remember what I told you," I said.

"Sure, chief," Tony said, and Wayne chuckled joylessly.

Malone turned the key in the ignition, and the van came alive.

We parked in the body shop lot across the street from the Nutty Nathan's headquarters. The trucks near the warehouse were closed and locked. The showroom doors stood open. A couple of employee cars sat parked near the entrance. The office windows above the showroom remained dark.

"How long?" Tony said.

"They'll be leaving any time now," I said. "Then we go."

Night came quickly. The air was heavy with the smell of rain. A salesman left the showroom and drove away. Moments later the lights went out and the store manager emerged. He locked the glass doors, walked to his car, and was gone.

"Okay," I said, exhaling a nervous breath. "I'll go in through the employee entrance. When I signal, the three of you follow. Move quick and low, and keep the guns in your jackets."

Malone tried to smile, then shook my hand.

Wayne said to Tony, "You ready, man?"

"Yeah," Tony said, and they tapped fists. "Let's get paid."

TWENTY-NINE

I walked to the curb with my knapsack slung across my back. A car approached, and I turned my face in the direction it was heading, letting it pass. When the car disappeared around a curve, I ran quickly across the street, through the Nutty Nathan's parking lot to the double glass doors of the employee entrance.

I felt my hand shaking a bit as I put the key in the lock. The key began to turn but then stopped. I pulled back slightly on the door and put pressure on the key. It caught and turned.

A high-pitched note sounded as I entered. I pressed the numbers one, two, four, and three in sequence on the keypad of the alarm box. The red light above the keys turned to green and the sound stopped.

I pulled a penlight from my pocket, pointed it at the van, and flashed it twice. A car drove by on the road and then another. I stepped back into the darkness of the stairwell.

The three of them were running across the road as the second set of taillights passed. Malone was in front, the others close behind. As they passed through the light of the parking lot, their features became more distinct. Malone's face seemed to be stretched back. Wayne and Tony were expressionless.

I pushed the door open enough for them to slide in. Though it was a short sprint across the lot, Malone was fighting for breath. Wayne coolly unzipped his jacket and drew the Colt. Tony's weapon hung over his shoulder by a strap. I relocked the door and motioned them up the stairs with my thumb. We passed under Nathan's caricature on the way. At the top of the stairs I halted them with my palm.

Though the florescents were off, the office was drawing light from the crime bulbs out in the lot. Some of the terminals had been left on, their amber screens displaying blinking cursors. The office was nearly unrecognizable in its stillness and in the faint yellow glow.

I crouched down and moved along the wall towards my old cubicle. The others were behind me. When I reached my desk, I sat on the floor near my chair and put my knapsack beside me. Malone sat close by.

"Relax," I said unconvincingly. "Five minutes."

Tony and Wayne were whispering behind the divider that separated Fisher's cubicle from mine. There was also the low, unidentifiable hum that exists in all commercial buildings late at night. I stared up at the drop ceiling.

The alarm company phoned ten minutes later. I gave the woman my employee ID number and explained that I would be working for a couple of more hours. She thanked me and hung up. Though I had been gone more than a week, our personnel director had not called the alarm company to have my name stricken from the list. I had counted on her inefficiency.

"All right," I said, "let's go."

We were back against the wall and retracing our steps. At Marsha's desk I made a right, the others following. I turned the knob on the third door to the left, opened it, and stepped in.

Except for a block of light that fell in from a large rectangular window on the eastern wall, the room was black. The window looked out into the warehouse. Next to the window was a door, which led to the stairwell landing, which led to the door of the loft. At the bottom of the stairs another door opened to the warehouse itself.

I tugged on Tony's windbreaker and pulled him closer. I pointed out to the loft and then to the second row of stock that rose up to meet it from the warehouse below.

"Tony, when I let you into the loft, get over to the railing and drop down onto the boxes in that row. You've got a long way to crawl to get to the back of the warehouse, but you've got time, understand?"

"Yeah," he said, staring out the window with his mouth open. "When?"

"They should be here soon."

"What then?" Wayne said.

"There's an office downstairs with glass walls. We'll go down the stairwell, out the door to the warehouse, then get into that office—as far back into it as we can. When they're all together in the back, we make our move." I pointed to the break in the middle row. "That's where you cut in, Wayne."

"Ain't no thing," he said, and looked at Tony.

After fifteen minutes a sound came up from below, far away but heavy. We stepped back from the light of the window. One drop of cool sweat rolled down my back.

A figure emerged from below the loft and walked slowly towards the left aisle. The loose-limbed Jamaican was wearing his knit cap and vest. The grip of a pistol stuck up above his rearmost beltloop. He was followed by the tall albino with the single braid. The albino was cradling a shotgun that had a pistollike grip.

"Check that shit out," Wayne mumbled.

"Mossberg," Tony said. "Twelve gauge." For the first time there was a hint of apprehension on his young face.

"When it goes down," Malone said, his eyes straight ahead, "I'll be coverin' that yellow motherfucker. Everybody got that?" The others nodded.

"I go now?" Tony asked.

"No," I said. "There's two more, be along soon."

As I said that, two others followed from beneath the loft. The first man was the one who smashed my face. Both wore heavy jackets that stopped at the waist. I could not see if they were armed.

"Wayne," I said, before they left our sight. "The man in front has killed before. When you step out, you cover him."

"They all look like they done some killin', chief," Wayne said.

"Maybe so," I said. "But I'm sure about him. Let's go, while they're in the back."

They followed me to the door in the left corner of the room. We moved out to the stairwell landing. The steel below our feet gave off a soft echo. My key unlocked the next door. I opened it a few inches and looked out at the loft and the warehouse. I jerked my head to Tony in the direction of the railing.

Tony tightened his gunstrap. The MAC hung snugly against his back. He looked back at Wayne, tucked in his head, and was out the door.

He moved quickly across the loft. He climbed over the railing above the second row of stock. He stepped off about two feet to a console carton below. The carton moved under his weight. Then it stopped moving and he was on his stomach, crawling towards the back of the warehouse.

I eased the door closed and pointed down the stairs. The rain had begun, and muffled the vibration of the steps as we descended. I reached for the knob, and turned it slowly until there was a small click. I cracked open the door and looked out.

I heard faraway voices and the rain. I slid out the door and moved along the wall to Dane's office door. The knob turned in my hand. I left the door ajar as I moved into the darkness.

Malone and Wayne followed me in. Wayne closed the door behind him. They found me in the rear of the office, sitting on the floor with my back to the wall. They sat near me. I felt clammy and wet. I pulled the gun from my knapsack and tossed the knapsack aside.

A motor kicked in. The sound of it grew louder. A spinning shaft of yellow light approached with the sound. I held the Browning tightly between my legs. Then the sound diminished and the light faded.

"Forklift," I said quietly and saw Malone nod.

There were more voices. I crouched up on the balls of my feet. Two tallish, thin men I didn't recognize were standing with the albino thirty yards from the office. They would be the buyers. One of them wore his dreadlocks long and out, and carried a briefcase in his right hand. He kept his other hand in his jacket pocket. So did his partner. The albino and one of the buyers traded unsmiling nods, then were gone behind the last row of stock.

"All here now," I said.

We listened to the rain and each other's breathing. Some time went by like that, then Malone spoke.

"We best go, Country," he said quietly.

"Okay," I said.

I stood up and moved to the door. I undid the safety on my gun. I looked out, saw no one, and opened the door.

Wayne was out without a word, bolting across the floor to the center aisle. He held his gun up next to his head and pressed his back against the cartons. He began to edge his way to the back of the warehouse. I could see sweat reflecting off his forehead.

I walked out and moved quickly to the end cap of the second row. I felt Malone move with me. We glanced at one another. He moved his pistol from his left to his right hand. I wiped my palm across my jeans, got that hand around the grip of the Browning, and jacked a round into the chamber.

The rain had intensified. It beat against the metal roof with a steady rumble. Below that sound was the bass of their voices. We stepped away from the boxes, moved into the aisle, and walked towards them.

They were standing in a group at the end of the aisle. The buyers had their backs to us and the briefcase was at their feet. The other four were facing them. Everyone was armed.

We came within twenty yards of them. Then the loose-limbed Jamaican, the one who had blown me a kiss, locked his eyes into mine and stiffened. I stopped and raised my gun, pointing it in his direction. The buyers turned to face us.

"Don't nobody move," Malone said evenly.

Wayne appeared suddenly from the right, stepped in quickly, and put the barrel of the Colt to the head of the South Carolinian who had broken my nose. He pulled back the automatic's hammer. It locked with a click that rode over the sound of the rain. The man dropped his gun from his left hand and let it fall to the concrete floor.

The Jamaican seemed to study me and then grinned. I squinted and looked down the sight of my gun to his chest, but it wasn't enough. A cowboy, just like Dane said.

He began to raise his gun from his side. He must have crouched down into a shooting position just as I squeezed the trigger.

The slug tore into him above his shirt collar, on the Adam's apple. A small puff of white smoke and some fluid shot away from his neck as he was blown back to the floor.

Wayne squeezed a round off into the head of the South Carolinian. His scalp lifted and his forehead came apart like an August peach. Then Wayne moved his gun to the face of the man's startled partner and shot him twice at close range. As he fell back, I saw a nickel-sized spot steaming above the bridge of his nose. His mouth was moving as he went down, but he was dead before he hit the ground.

Malone had shot the albino twice in the chest. The tall man stumbled, and still standing, pumped off two loads in succession from his shotgun. Malone screamed. In my side vision I saw him falling backwards in a "V," still firing. The albino was tripping forward. I emptied two more rounds into his long torso.

The dreadlocked buyer was spinning slowly from the rapid fire of Wayne's automatic. The second buyer raised his gun in my direction. I screamed Tony's name.

I saw fire spitting down from above. I covered my face with my arms. There was the sound of ripping cardboard, splintering wood, and concrete ricochet. Glass exploded around me, and I went to my knees.

Then there was only the sound of the rain hitting the roof. I stood up. Tony dropped the empty clip from above. It hit the floor and bounced once. He slapped in another clip.

Wayne walked towards me through the smoke, his feet crushing glass. He stopped at the second buyer. The man was kneeling with his head tucked between his knees. Wayne pointed his gun at the back of the man's neck and looked at me. I shook my head.

The powder smell was heavy. I waved smoke from my face and turned. Behind me someone screamed out for Jesus and moaned, then stopped moaning. I knelt down over Malone's body.

He had taken a blast low in the abdomen and one in the chest. The gutshot had opened him. His upper lip had curled up and stuck on one of his teeth, so that it looked as if he were sneering. I pulled the lip away and down. Then I closed his eyes.

"Let's move, chief," Wayne said.

I reached into Malone's wet trouser pocket and pulled out keys. His blood stained my fingers. I tossed the keys back to Wayne.

"Get the van," I said. "Pull it up to the warehouse door."

Wayne walked away. I held my gun on the buyer until Tony made it down to the floor. He nodded, saw Malone, and looked back at me. I picked up the suitcase and turned to the man still kneeling on the floor.

"Get the forklift going," I said, "and load the van with the goods. Do it and you'll live."

He got started. I sat against a carton and smoked a cigarette while he moved the bodies to the side. Tony rode the forklift with the man for several trips until the VCRs were all loaded. Tony walked back and stood over me.

"It's done," he said. "What now?"

"Put him in the van," I said, motioning towards Malone. "Tie the other one up and wait for me. I'll be out in five minutes."

I switched on the light in Dane's office, found my knapsack, and pulled a phone number from its front compartment. I put the Browning in my knapsack and carried it and the briefcase to Dane's desk. I lit another cigarette and dialed the phone number.

"Hello."

"Jerry Rosen, please."

"This is he." The voice was deep and rich.

"This is Nick Stefanos."

"I'm sorry, Nick, but it's very late. If this is about your termination—"

"Shut up," I said. "Don't say a word, understand? Just shut up and listen." I heard him swallow. "I busted up your deal tonight. All four of your employees and one of your customers are lying dead in the warehouse." He cleared his throat. "I own the remainder of your supply now. If you want it back, bring Jimmy Broda with you to the roof of the Silver Spring parking garage tomorrow morning at nine o'clock sharp. We'll make the trade there."

"I don't—"

"I told you, no talking. Now you'd better get down here. Someone will be waiting for you to confirm everything I've told you." I hung up and stubbed out my cigarette. I grabbed my knapsack and the briefcase, and left the warehouse.

The wipers struggled to clear the rain from the van's windshield. I was driving south on Eleventh Street, into the darkest center of the city. The liquor and convenience stores were closed now and few of the streetlights were lit. People walked through the rain, drenched and unprotected, in slow, druggy steps.

The briefcase was next to me on the seat. Tony and Wayne sat in back, on opposite sides of the cartons. Malone lay between them, covered by the blanket.

Tony pointed me into an alley near a Bible Way church. I stopped at the head of it and cut the lights. A stream carried small bits of trash down the center of the alley.

Tony said, "Wait for me in there, Wayne."

Wayne exited the van through the back door. He walked into an open garage and was consumed by its blackness. I continued down the alley with the headlights off until Tony told me to stop.

"What you gonna do with all this 'caine?" he asked.

"I've got plans for it."

"You make more at the cookin' house," he said, and looked me over slowly. "You got plans for Homeboy's money, too?"

"Yeah," I said, and stared him down with all the energy I had left.

"I'll take mine," he said.

I counted twenty thousand in worn bills from the briefcase. He shoved the stack into his jacket. I looked at the lumpen figure in the back and then at Tony.

He nodded and pulled the blanket off Malone. I grabbed him under the arms and lifted. Tony held his feet. We stepped out of the back of the van and carried him into the rain.

"Set him down," Tony said, and we placed him in the middle of the alley.

For some reason I straightened Malone's shirt. I looked up from where I knelt. Tony was standing over me, dripping wet and staring into my eyes.

"Just another dead nigger," he said. "Right?"

He turned and walked away. I watched him meet Wayne at the door of the garage. They passed under the glow of the alley light, then disappeared into the night.

I let go of Malone's hand and returned to the van. I drove slowly to the end of the alley and began to turn out. In my side mirror I saw Malone's body shift and move, carried by the stream. Then it stopped moving. I accelerated out of the alley.

I drove to upper Northwest and parked on a side street in a residential neighborhood. I moved to the back of the van.

I didn't sleep. For the rest of the night I stared at the cartons and listened to the rain. And with one wringing hand I clutched the blanket that was smeared with Malone's blood.

THIRTY

The rain had tapered off by dawn. I started the van and drove north. Just over the district line I stopped at a convenience store that had a public rest room.

I cleaned up in the rest room, then bought two coffees, an orange juice, a bag of nuts, some beef jerky, and a deck of Camels. I returned to the van, drank the orange juice and one of the coffees, and ate the nuts and jerky.

After that, I drove the half mile to the parking garage and took the van up to the roof. I parked next to my Dodge and locked the briefcase in my trunk. I shoved the barrel of the Browning in my jeans and covered the grip with my sweatshirt. Then I drove the van to a sub-roof four floors down and locked it up. I walked back up the open-air stairwell to the roof.

I leaned against my car and drank the second coffee. I had a cigarette with the coffee, then another. The sky was already clearing though the wind carried quite a chill.

A long, late-model Cadillac rolled up the ramp and onto the roof, passing me slowly. Rosen was driving. The buyer we had left in the warehouse was in the backseat. Next to him sat Jimmy Broda. He glanced at me blankly as they passed.

They parked in the far corner of the roof. I remained against my car. A few minutes passed, then Rosen got out of the car and walked towards me. I blew out the rest of my smoke and crushed the butt under my shoe.

Rosen was a heavy man of medium height with a tendency to put on pounds. His scalp showed through his thin permanent, and he wore a beard that only partially masked the fatty rolls of his neck. There were dark semicircles beneath his eyes.

Rosen extended his hand as he reached me. He had on one of those diamond horseshoe rings that are impressive only to the pompous shitheels who wear them. I refused his handshake. He placed his hand back in his cashmere overcoat.

"Nick," he said solemnly. "Let's make this civil, shall we?"

"Is everything in order?"

"The warehouse, you mean? Yes. Though you left me quite a mess. Fortunately, the man you left behind decided to join me rather than return to his people empty-handed. He handled most of the mop-up work. No one will miss them. As for the inventory that was destroyed, I'll have my accountants write that off as pilferage." He stroked the tip of his beard. "What are you going to do with all the money, Nick?"

"It's already gone," I lied.

"That's right," he said. "You had to pay off your little army. But you lost one, didn't you? From my man's description, that would be your friend Malone, from our Connecticut Avenue store, correct?" I didn't answer. "My sympathies. Of course, no one had to die. They should have let you take it. We would have settled it later. But they had to make a play. Fucking *Schwartzes.*"

"You talk too much," I said.

"I'm sorry. It's because I'm nervous. This is all new to me."

"Why'd you get into it in the first place, then?"

"I *wanted* it," he said. "When I saw that Ned Plavin's ambitions were in line with mine, I convinced him to bankroll the operation up here. I chose D.C. for the same reason all the gangs come down from New York. Law enforcement here—face it, Stefanos, it's a joke. The cops are passing out jaywalking tickets downtown. And the mayor? Well, maybe he could take care of things. If only he could pull his head up off the mirror."

"Get back to our business," I said.

"You're going to think I'm blowing smoke up your ass, but frankly, Nick, you did me a favor last night. I've been wanting this whole thing to end. I know where I made my mistakes. It was stupid to try and move the goods through the warehouse. Plus, those guys who worked for me"—he waved his hand in front of his face—"*they* killed that Shultz boy, on their own. I never ordered that. And I didn't know what to do with the Broda kid." He spread the fingers in both of his hands out to suggest helplessness.

"What else?"

"Like I said, in a roundabout way you did me a favor. I'm going to get my goods back, but nobody has to know that, understand what I'm saying? Now I can turn this last batch over on pure profit. That makes me an independent. Which is what I wanted all along."

"Let's go to the car." We walked in the direction of the Cadillac. "Is the boy all right?"

Rosen shrugged. "He's an addict, I'm sure of that. Some associates of the ones you took down last night were keeping him busy in a crackhouse. He'll need treatment."

"That kind of treatment is expensive," I said. "And often it doesn't take."

"He's lucky to be alive." Rosen stopped walking and narrowed his eyes. "So are you."

"We should get something straight before this is over. Because when I take that boy out of here, it *is* over. I've written several identical letters to my contacts at the *Post,* explaining in detail the history and players of your operation. These letters won't be read, unless something happens to me, or the boy, or his grandfather, or anybody I know for that matter. That includes John McGinnes, and Joe Dane, *and* Dane's family."

"McGinnes," he said, "will have to be terminated. He can't continue to be employed at Nathan's. You can understand that."

"McGinnes can make a living anywhere. He's a salesman. But he's not to be touched."

"Anything else?" he asked, irritated.

"One thing," I said. "Where's the girl?"

He chuckled. "You're so predictable." He shook his head, but gave me the address.

We reached the car. Rosen signaled his new ally, who got out, threw me a requisite, half-hearted, hard-guy look, and walked around to the other side of the Caddy. He opened the door and helped the boy out.

Jimmy Broda's color was just short of gray. His trousers were crimped at the waist by a severely tightened leather belt. His jean jacket fit his shoulders as if it were hung on a wire hanger.

The buyer walked him towards me. Broda's eyes widened almost imperceptively as recognition seeped in. He quickened his step and reached out in my direction. I pulled him in with one hand and put my arm around his shoulder, holding him up. He had the weight of a paper bag.

"You've got him now," Rosen said impatiently. "Where are my goods?"

"Follow me," I said. "The van is parked a few floors down. Your boy here knows which one it is." I tossed the keys to the buyer.

Rosen said, "Don't even consider fucking me."

I let him have the last word and, with Broda under my arm, walked slowly across the roof. I was aware that they were still standing by the Cadillac, watching us. I instructed the boy to continue moving in the direction of my car.

I let him into the passenger side and got behind the wheel. His hands were folded in his lap, and he was staring straight ahead. I reversed out of my spot and rolled down the ramp.

They were tailing me slowly. Jimmy turned his head back, saw them, became startled, and looked at me.

"Just look ahead," I said. "We're almost out of here."

We wound around the garage. Four floors down I stopped my car, rolled down the window, and pointed my arm out to the sub-roof. Then I continued down the ramp. I saw them in my rearview, veering off to the right.

I accelerated when I reached the ground floor and blew off the stop sign at the exit. I lit a cigarette and turned down North Portal at the Sixteenth Street circle. WHFS was playing Graham Parker's "Howling Wind," and I kicked up the volume. An Afghan hound was running alongside our car, and Broda watched him until he broke stride. Orange leaves blew out of our path as we entered the park.

* * *

Between the double glass doors of the apartment house on Connecticut Avenue, I dialed up Pence's number.

"Yes?" he said.

"Nick Stefanos. Buzz me in, will you?"

"Certainly. Would you like me to meet you?"

"No," I said. "I'll be right up."

We exited the elevator at the tenth floor and followed the carpeted hallway. Pence opened the door on the second knock. His eyes widened and both hands reached out. He pulled Jimmy Broda through the door and into his arms.

The old man shut his eyes and mumbled something as they held each other. Their faces crushed together. I stood in the hallway, my hands shoved into my pockets, and looked down at my shoes.

"Please, come in, Nick," Pence said finally over the boy's shoulder.

"I can't right now," I said. "But call me later at my apartment. There are some things you need to know."

"Your compensation. Of course."

"That, and other things. Good-bye."

Before he could object, I pulled the door shut from the outside. I stood there for quite a while and listened to the muffled cadence of their voices on the other side of the door. Then I stepped away and walked slowly down the dimly lit corridor.

Early Monday morning I dialed the number for Ned's World in South Carolina.

"Ned's World, how may I help you?"

"This is Roy Lutz," I said, "regional director for Panasonic, confirming my lunch appointment with Ned Plavin. Is he in, please?"

"I'll see if he's at his desk. Hold please." A click, some whale music, then another click. "I'll transfer you now."

A gravelly voice answered after two rings. "Roy!" Plavin said with forced excitement. "I didn't know we were on for today."

"This isn't Roy," I said.

"Well, then, our lines must have gotten crossed—"

"Our lines didn't get crossed. This concerns the Kotekna VCR deal that got soured up in Washington, D.C., over the weekend."

"I'm not familiar with any 'deal' in Washington," he said thickly. "Who is this?"

"If you're not interested in what I have to say, hang up now. If you are, I'll continue." There was a silence while he thought it over. "Can we talk on this line?"

"Go ahead," he said.

"I'm not sure what you've been told about the events of this past weekend. I suspect you know only part of the truth. I'll condense it for you. I was one of the group that stopped the deal in the warehouse. We took the merchandise and the money. I kept the money. I traded the merchandise back to your people in exchange for a boy they were holding."

Ned Plavin cleared his throat. "My people?" he said. "Who did you give my goods to?"

"Jerry Rosen," I said. I watched my cat chase a large bug that was crawling across the rug to the safety of the baseboards.

"Do you have any proof of this?" Plavin asked.

"No."

"What do you want?"

"I don't trust Rosen," I said. "I want this all to be over with, now. I want Rosen out of Washington. And I don't think *you* want a business partner who plans on going solo with goods that you bankrolled. He's the proverbial loose cannon, Ned. Do something about it."

This time the silence was longer. My cat trapped the bug under its paw, examined it, then walked away. The bug continued on its path to the wall.

"I'll look into it," Plavin said. "If what you say is true, I'll act on it."

"Do it quickly, Ned. Good-bye."

I hung up the phone and lit a cigarette. I dialed the number for the Connecticut Avenue store and got McGinnes on the line.

"What's happening, Nick?"

"Too early to meet me for a cocktail?"

"Hell, no," he said. "But things are a little hectic right now. Andre didn't post on Saturday, or today. Louie's ready to can his ass. I don't think I can get out till eleven."

"Eleven's fine," I said.

"Where?"

"La Fortresse, in the back."

"La FurPiece?"

"Yeah, Johnny. La FurPiece."

THIRTY-ONE

The bartender was fanning out cocktail napkins with a tumbler when I entered La Fortresse sometime after eleven. I passed him with a nod and walked towards the back room.

McGinnes sat at a deuce, halfway into a cold bottle of beer. He saluted mockingly and shook my hand as I sat down. I put the briefcase on the floor, between our feet.

"What'ya got in there," he asked, "a bomb or something?"

"Something like a bomb," I said cryptically.

He waved a hand in front of his face and finished the beer left in his bottle. Our fine-skinned waitress came over to the table. Her white shirt had a start-of-shift crispness. She smiled.

"What can I get you, Nick?"

"A Coke," I said. "Bottled, please, not from the gun. Thanks."

"One more for me, darling," McGinnes said, pointing at his bottle. He frowned at me. "You on the wagon, man?"

"No."

The waitress brought our order. I poured from the bottle to a glass full of ice and waited for the foam to retreat. By the time I took the first sip McGinnes had killed much of his second beer. Some of his straight black hair fell across his forehead as he set his bottle down.

"You seen Andre?" McGinnes asked.

"Yeah."

"He'd better drag his black ass back to work. The man is in some shit. And you know what it's like to work with Void, full time? That shit-for-brains can't close one deal—hell, he can't even close his fly."

"Andre's not coming back, Johnny," I said. "He's dead."

McGinnes' mouth opened, then the corners of it turned down. One tear immediately fell from his left eye and rolled down and off his cheek. He swept the bottle off the table with the back of his hand, sending it to the floor. Foam poured from its neck. McGinnes made a fist and dug knuckles into his forehead.

Our waitress came back into the room. She saw the bottle and McGinnes, then looked at me.

"Bring him another," I said. She nodded and left quickly. She returned just as quickly, set a fresh beer in front of McGinnes, picked the old up off the floor, and left the room. McGinnes stared straight ahead with watery eyes and slowly shook his head.

"You stupid bastards," he muttered. "You stupid, stupid bastards."

I waited until he looked at me again. "Andre and me," I said carefully, "and a couple of guys from his old neighborhood interrupted the tail end of Rosen's drug deal on Friday night. The idea was to heist the money and the drugs and trade the drugs back to them for the boy. Andre was to keep the money. But Rosen's people turned out to be gunslingers. When it was over, most of them were dead. Andre died quickly." I drank some soda. "On Saturday morning I got the boy back. He's safe, Johnny. He's with his grandfather."

"That's it, huh?" he said emotionally. "The boy's safe, Andre's dead, you and me just walk away into the sunset."

"Nobody will touch us," I said vaguely. "I fixed it."

"You fixed it," McGinnes said, and snorted. I slid the briefcase along the floor with my foot, until it touched his own. He looked down, then back at me.

"There's a hundred and twenty grand in that case," I said. "It goes to Andre's mother. I think that's what he was planning to do with it, regardless of the outcome. Do me a favor and see that she gets it."

"How much did you skim?"

"I took ten, to keep me on my feet. Until I figure out what's next."

McGinnes chugged the rest of his beer and slammed the bottle on the table, loud enough to cause the waitress to poke her head back into the room. He signaled her for another. She served it without looking at either of us.

"So, Nicky. Was it worth it?" McGinnes squinted at me. His voice shook as he spoke.

"I don't know."

"How did it feel to deliver the kid?"

I thought about it and said, "It felt good."

"You know what I mean," he said impatiently. "Did you find *your* parents, too? Did you say good-bye to your grandfather?"

I stood up and reached into my pocket. I found a five and dropped it on the table.

"Make sure Andre's mother gets the money," I said.

"To Andre," McGinnes said, and raised his bottle in a toast. "The only hero in this whole damn thing."

I grabbed a handful of McGinnes' shirt and pulled him up out of his seat. When I looked into his frightened eyes, I let him down gently but still held on. His breath was sour and sickly, like an old man's.

"Andre's no hero," I said softly. "He was, when he was alive. But he died, and then he was nothing. I dumped him in a fucking alley, like a sack of shit. So don't romanticize it, understand?" I released my grip on his shirt.

"Sure, Nick, I understand." He tilted the bottle back to his lips.

I wiped tears off my face with a shaky hand. "Try not to sit here all day," I said.

"The stuff tastes awful good today, Nicky." I walked to the doorway. "So long, man," he said behind me.

I looked back to the table. "So long, Johnny."

I left him there, staring into his bottle. I crossed the dark barroom, passed through the door, and stepped out into the light.

The corridor I had entered marked the beginning of the hospital's original wing. I followed its worn carpeting as it snaked towards the ward. Small hexagonal windows had black bars radiating spiderlike from their centers, and were spaced at intervals on the yellowing walls to my left.

At the end of the corridor I pushed open one of two swinging metal doors and stepped into the ward's reception area. I signed my name and recorded the time in a notebook on the desk. Behind the desk sat a young man wearing a flannel shirt and a brush mustache. I asked him for her room number.

"She stays in eight-oh-two," he said. "But this time of day you might try the rec room."

"Thanks," I said, and headed down the hallway.

I had visited friends on several occasions in places such as this. The alky wards were usually populated by middle-aged individuals who drifted slowly and deliberately, like ghosts, in and out of doorways. In this place they separated the boozers from the druggies. The k-heads and cocaine kids moved about these rooms like hopped-up insects.

I passed a large room that had a shield of gray smoke at its entrance. There were Ping-Pong tables and board games, but everyone was seated in vinyl furniture watching a television mounted high on the wall. A couple of them were laughing.

I stopped at eight-oh-two and knocked on a partially closed door. She told me to come in. I pushed the door open.

There were two cots in the room, with a night table and reading lamp in between. On the night table was some propaganda, and under that a notebook. Next to the notebook was a flat aluminum ashtray filled with crushed filters. She sat on the edge of the bed nearest the window, a live cigarette between her fingers.

"Nicky," she said, without emotion.

"Kim. May I come in?"

She nodded and I entered. She was wearing jeans and a T-shirt, with a sweater vest over that. Her hair had been cut short and spiky, which made her big eyes even more pronounced above her hollow cheeks. She had the pallid color of the very ill.

"Cigarette?" she asked, rustling the pack in my direction.

"No thanks. I won't be staying long."

She took a drag and blew some my way. "I knew you'd be by, eventually. You're not particularly bright. But you are persistent."

I let that go and asked, "How's it going?"

"I've been through all this before," she said with a small sweeping gesture of her hand. "Several times. They tell you to surrender your will to a higher being. Trouble is, I don't know if there *is* one."

"Let's assume there is," I said. "But then you still would have a problem. There's certain people, even He has no interest in saving."

She calmly shook a cigarette out of her pack and lit it off the one still burning. She butted the shorter one of the two and exhaled a wide cloud that spread around me.

"How did you get on to me?" she asked.

"Nothing set right with you from the beginning," I said. "Like what you were doing with those kids in the first place. And the fact that you were barely hurt, much less alive, when we found you. I buried those suspicions, though, as I became more attracted to you. At that point I was letting my dick do all the thinking." I waited for a reaction to the twisting knife. There wasn't one. I folded my arms and leaned against the wall. "After you left me, I met a geezer in a bar who reminded me of your old man. I started to think about his unused video equipment, and the new stereo in your apartment. And how Maureen Shultz told me that you had worked in some stores in the South before coming up here. Then there was the time you asked about me and Johnny taking 'ups.' Only a retail salesperson would know that expression. I made the connection to Rosen and called Ned's World in South Carolina. You had been on the payroll at one time."

She nodded. "I was a cashier in one of the stores down there when Jerry Rosen was sales manager. It wasn't long before he was fucking me, and supplying me with all the coke I needed. We moved up to D.C., I got heavier into drugs, and he lost interest in me. In the end, he only kept me around to help out with his business."

"He had you hook into Jimmy Broda," I said, "when he discovered the missing VCR. You were to keep an eye on him and the drugs, maybe take him out of town, someplace where Rosen's boys could take care of things without much scrutiny, right?"

"Yes," she said, and looked away. "I didn't know anybody would be hurt. It was just another free party for me. And for a change, I didn't have to sleep with anybody to do it."

Tired laughter ebbed briefly from the television room down the hall. "Back to Wrightsville Beach," I said. "Jimmy never went out for beer like you said. He was there when Rosen's boys came in. You must have signaled them somehow. But why didn't they kill Broda too?"

She blew some smoke at her feet and spoke softly. "After you fought, Charlie Fiora called me at the motel to tip me off that you were on the way. They had just killed Eddie. There wasn't time to do anything but take Jimmy and leave me behind, to slow you up." She looked up at me with pleading eyes and began to cry, but I stopped it.

"You can save the crocodile tears," I said coldly. "I don't think I'll ever forget the way Eddie looked, tied up on that bed. His throat had been cut, left to right. You could tell by the entry wound on the left, and by the direction of the skin as it folded out from the slice. Assuming he was killed from behind, that would have to be done by a right-handed person." I stepped away from the wall and unfolded my arms. "The other night, I faced the man I thought had killed Eddie Shultz. He proved to me that he didn't have the stomach for that sort of thing. In fact, before his brains were blown out, he dropped his weapon. And he dropped it from his left hand." I paused and stared at the cigarette in her right hand, then into her eyes. "You cooled Eddie Shultz."

The silence between us was heavy and long. Finally she spoke just above a whisper and with her eyes down. "They couldn't do it," she said. "They were tough, but even they couldn't do that, not to a kid. They didn't know Redman like I knew him. Him and his Nazi friends. They would have queered the whole deal, believe me. He *had* to die."

"Everybody has to," I said. "But nobody has to like that. What were you going to do about me?"

"Nothing," she said, her voice rising. "Jerry just wanted me to keep you occupied until he could figure out what to do."

"Relax. I'm not going to turn you in. They'd only treat you and set you free. I'd only be doing you a favor."

"I know what I did was horribly wrong," she said. "But this program here. . . . I'm going to clean up."

"There isn't going to be any program. Not much longer. Your benefactor is going to be leaving town any day now. When the well dries up, you're out. You're a junkie, Kim. That's your future."

"I'll make it," she said.

"I don't think so."

My landlord had wedged my mail in the screen door of my apartment. The cat nudged my calf as I carried in the letters and sorted them out.

There was a phone bill, which I kept, and a credit card offer, which I tossed. The last item in the stack was from the D.C. government. My application for a private investigator's licence had been accepted. The notice instructed me where and when to pick it up.

I fed the cat, brewed some coffee, and took a mug of it and a pack of smokes out to the living room. I settled on the couch to read the Monday *Post.*

Andre Malone's two little paragraphs were buried in the back of Metro, under a group head called "Around the Region." He was "an unidentified N.W. man." He died of "gunshot wounds to the chest and lower abdomen." Police believed the killing, the article said, to be "drug related."

One week later, McGinnes phoned.

"Nick?"

"Yeah?"

"Johnny."

"Hey, Johnny. Where you at, man?"

"The Sleep Senter," he said.

"That the place that spells *Center* with an *S*?"

"The same."

"Uh-huh," I said.

"The way they explained it to me, it has a double meaning. The sleep *sent-her,* get it? Like this place really sends her, it's some kind of out-of-body experience."

"Clever."

"Yeah," he said. "This place is okay. They got a bunch of *schmoes* on the floor, but they're an all right bunch of guys. And dig this—they put

213

a fifty dollar pop on the reconditioned mattresses. Fifty big ones, man, for something that's recession proof. Everybody's gotta sleep, right, Jim? Anyway, mattresses, electronics, what the hell's the difference? I could sell my mother if they'd tack a dollar bill on her."

"When did you make the move?"

"Today's my first day. The last day I saw you, I kinda fell into a black hole. When I crawled out the next day, I quit my job at Nathan's. Good thing I did. I talked to Fisher—they had some serious shake-ups after I left."

"Such as?"

"Rosen resigned on Wednesday, effective that day."

"Who's running the show?"

"They booted Ric Brandon up to general manager. You believe that shit?"

"The cream always rises to the top," I said.

"Yeah." He laughed briefly, then coughed into the phone. "Listen, Nick, I gotta go take an up. I don't want these *putzes* to think I'm weak. Talk to you later, hear?"

"All right, Johnny. Talk to you later."

The next morning I was folding my clothes from the laundromat when some shells and stones fell from the pockets of my swimtrunks. An hour later I was driving south on 95, headed for the Outer Banks and Ocracoke Island.

The ferry was nearly empty that early November day, as was the island campground. I pitched my tent on a spot near the showers and, wearing a sweatshirt beneath my jean jacket, unfolded a chair on the beach.

I spent the first day reading the rather seedy biography of a relentlessly hedonistic musician, a story I lost interest in long before the inevitable overdose. Later I wrote a long letter to Karen that took two hours to compose and only a few seconds to shred. In between those activities I walked on the beach and stopped occasionally to talk with fishermen who were wading in the surf. In the evening I cooked hot dogs and ate a can of beans, and then crawled into my sleeping bag as soon as it was dark, as there was little else to do.

By the middle of the second day, I realized once again that being away from home clarifies nothing. Despite romantic notions, that's been the case in every instance that I've left town to "think about things."

An approaching northeaster shook me out of my stupor late in the afternoon. I broke camp as the slate sky blew in, and was packed and in my car when the rain came down, suddenly and quite violently, from the clouds.

I started my Dodge and drove through the storm to the gray house on pilings with the small gray sign. Running through the rain and up the wooden stairs, I entered Jacko's Grille.

The door slammed behind me when I entered and most of the heads in the place turned my way. There was a group of older locals in plaid flannel shirts and dirty baseball caps, all sitting at a couple of picnic tables that they had pushed together. Empty cans of beer dotted the tables. Full ones were in the men's hands. Water dripped down through holes in the roof into more than a few spots in the room, though no one was taking much notice. The sound of the rain competed with the country music coming from the jukebox.

I nodded to the men and pushed wet hair back off my forehead. A couple of them nodded back. One of them smiled and said, in a startling island accent more northern European than American South, "Wet enough for ya?" I said it was and stepped up to the bar, where I ordered a burger and a beer.

I took the beer out to the screened-in deck and drank it while I watched the hard rain dimple the wetlands as it blew across the sound. The beer was cold but warmed me going down, and I ordered another when I picked up my burger.

I ate the burger and drank the beer out on the deck. When I was finished, the first, beautiful verse of "Me and Bobby McGee" came from the juke, and the men inside began to sing. I listened as their drunken voices welled up on the achingly true chorus. When I went to the counter for another beer, one of them waved me over and I joined them.

I bought what was the first of many rounds. The water was coming in now all around the bar, and someone had turned up the jukebox to its maximum volume. One of the men produced a fifth of whiskey and some glasses, and we started in on that.

The corners of the room bled into the walls. There was laughter and it was warm and I was away from my world, and everything was cleaner and more clear.

With time came darkness, and the rain continued to fall outside and into the barroom. My friends told jokes and sang, then joined me in a toast, to a Greek immigrant everyone had called Big Nick. For a moment I wondered what he would think, seeing me now, so twisted and so far from home; that moment burned away with my next taste of whiskey, stronger than reason, stronger than love.